PRAISE FOR USA TODAY BESTSELLING AUTHOR JAN MORAN

Seabreeze Inn and *Coral Cottage* series

"A wonderful story… Will make you feel like the sea breeze is streaming through your hair." – Laura Bradbury, Bestselling Author

"A novel that gives fans of romantic sagas a compelling voice to follow." – *Booklist*

"An entertaining beach read with multi-generational context and humor." – *InD'Tale* Magazine

"Wonderful characters and a sweet story." – Kellie Coates Gilbert, Bestselling Author

"A fun read that grabs you at the start." – Tina Sloan, Author and Award-Winning Actress

"Jan Moran is the queen of the epic romance." —Rebecca Forster, *USA Today* Bestselling Author

"The women are intelligent and strong. At the core is a strong, close-knit family." — Betty's Reviews

The Chocolatier

"A delicious novel, makes you long for chocolate." – *Ciao Tutti*

"Smoothly written…full of intrigue, love, secrets, and romance." – *Lekker Lezen*

The Winemakers

"Readers will devour this page-turner as the mystery and passions spin out." – *Library Journal*

"As she did in *Scent of Triumph*, Moran weaves knowledge of wine and winemaking into this intense family drama." – *Booklist*

The Perfumer: Scent of Triumph

"Heartbreaking, evocative, and inspiring, this book is a powerful journey." – Allison Pataki, *New York Times* Bestselling Author of *The Accidental Empress*

"A sweeping saga of one woman's journey through World War II and her unwillingness to give up even when faced with the toughest challenges." — Anita Abriel, Author of *The Light After the War*

"A captivating tale of love, determination and reinvention." — Karen Marin, Givenchy Paris

"A stylish, compelling story of a family. What sets this apart is the backdrop of perfumery that suffuses the story with the delicious aromas – a remarkable feat!" — Liz Trenow, *New York Times* Bestselling Author of *The Forgotten Seamstress*

"Courageous heroine, star-crossed lovers, splendid sense of time and place capturing the unease and turmoil of the 1940s; HEA." — *Heroes and Heartbreakers*

"Jan rivals Danielle Steel at her romantic best." — Allegra Jordan, Author of *The End of Innocence*

BOOKS BY JAN MORAN

Summer Beach: Seabreeze Inn Series

Seabreeze Inn

Seabreeze Summer

Seabreeze Sunset

Seabreeze Christmas

Seabreeze Wedding

Seabreeze Book Club

Summer Beach: Coral Cottage Series

Coral Cottage

Coral Cafe

Coral Holiday

The Love, California Series

Flawless

Beauty Mark

Runway

Essence

Style

Sparkle

20th-Century Historical

Hepburn's Necklace

The Chocolatier

The Winemakers: A Novel of Wine and Secrets

The Perfumer: Scent of Triumph

Seabreeze Wedding

USA TODAY BESTSELLING AUTHOR

JAN MORAN

SEABREEZE WEDDING

SUMMER BEACH, BOOK 5

JAN MORAN

SUNNY PALMS

PRESS

Library of Congress Cataloging-in-Publication Data

Moran, Jan.

/ by Jan Moran

ISBN 978-1-64778-028-9 (epub ebook)

ISBN 978-1-64778-030-2 (hardcover)

ISBN 978-1-64778-029-6 (paperback)

ISBN 978-1-64778-032-6 (audiobook)

ISBN 978-1-64778-031-9 (large print)

Published by Sunny Palms Press. Cover design by Sleepy Fox Studios. Cover images copyright Deposit Photos.

Sunny Palms Press

9663 Santa Monica Blvd STE 1158

Beverly Hills, CA 90210 USA

www.sunnypalmspress.com

www.JanMoran.com

1

*S*ummer Beach, California

FRESH SPRING BREEZES tinged with salty ocean air swept through the old beach house. As Ivy descended the stairway, she drank in the soul-cleansing air that held the aromas of sun-warmed sand and fresh flowers. They'd had a marine layer for several days that kept the beach pinned under a blanket of gloomy gray and cool days, so this was a welcome change.

As she cleared the last step, she imagined the day ahead. On such a perfect spring day such as this, anything seemed possible. Yet with each passing day, it was one day fewer until her parents departed on their around-the-world sail. Although Ivy was happy that they were fit and healthy enough for this adventure they'd longed for, she would miss them.

At a table in the foyer, her younger sister Shelly was arranging a bouquet of yellow and white blossoms she'd clipped from the garden. "What do you think of this arrangement?"

"You've brought the sunshine indoors," Ivy said, pausing near the reception desk they'd placed near the entrance to welcome guests.

With an expert motion, Shelly stripped leaves from a creamy white rose before inserting it among a cluster of yellow roses and white daisies. "The morning sun flooded my room, so I woke up feeling this yellow-and-white theme." Sweet scents were already permeating the fresh ocean air flowing through open windows.

Shelly grew most of the flowers and herbs they used on the property, and she was happily putting her horticulture degree to work. She nodded toward Ivy's lemon-yellow sundress. "Looks like you're channeling the sunshine, too."

"I suppose I am. This is another dress Mom sent over." Ivy touched the cotton seersucker fabric, soft from frequent washings.

Their mother had given them some of the clothes she couldn't fit onto their new boat. Although Carlotta and Sterling Bay were in their seventies, they were still vibrant and adventurous. They had been planning this trip for more than a year, and their excitement was palpable.

Ivy couldn't help but worry about their safety, and now she knew how her parents must have felt when each of their children set off on adventures. While Carlotta and Sterling were experienced sailors, unexpected winds could transform a calm sea into a hungry, treacherous creature.

"I'm going to miss Mom and Dad," Shelly said, continuing to strip leaves from roses.

"We all will," Ivy said. "But we're adults, and this is probably their last chance for a long trip like this."

Seeking to change the subject, Ivy picked up a glossy fern frond and idly twirled it. "How's your new vegetable garden coming along?"

Shelly brushed back strands of chestnut hair that had escaped her messy topknot. "Thanks to the seeds I started in the hothouse, the cherry tomatoes should be ready next week, along with several types of lettuce. My big heirloom tomatoes still need a few more weeks."

"I can hardly wait for those," Ivy said.

Shelly drew her lower lip in and frowned. "I'm going to miss Mom and Dad a lot more than when I lived in New York. I've gotten used to seeing them more often now. Do you think we should be worried about them?"

"They're in better shape than I am," Ivy replied as she stuffed the fern frond into the vase. She hated to think about anything that could happen to them.

Shelly curved her lips into a knowing half-smile. "You didn't answer my question, so that's a definite *yes*."

"This journey is their dream," Ivy said, trying to sound reasonable. "They've always supported ours. And they're not leaving until after you and Mitch get married. Which we're all guessing will be pretty soon, right?" Shelly and Mitch liked spontaneity, but Ivy wished they'd decide on a firm date. They had already pushed back one date Shelly had wanted. Ivy wondered if anything had changed between them.

Shelly cast her gaze to one side and drew in her lip. "This trip is different," she said, avoiding Ivy's question. "It's such a long one. What if they—"

"Here you are," Poppy called out, bounding around the corner. With her long blond hair swinging around her shoulders, she waved a message slip in her hand. "I've been looking for you, Aunty Ivy."

Ivy turned toward her niece, an energetic young woman who worked at the inn between her marketing jobs in Los Angeles. "What's up?"

Poppy grinned. "I just spoke to a woman who wants to talk to you about having a wedding here at the inn. And I also want you to review the story I wrote for my blogger friend— the one about the Seabreeze Inn being the perfect small wedding venue. Looks like we're diving into the wedding business."

Shelly shook her head. "I know we have to fill rooms during the off-season, but we should be careful that wedding parties don't take over the inn. Remember what happened at Carol Reston's daughter's wedding? Our other guests played along only because Carol is a huge celebrity, but many won't be crazy about rowdy wedding parties."

"That one was different," Ivy said. "They're not always that rowdy."

"I worked plenty of weddings in New York." Shelly arched an eyebrow. "I don't know why we need any wedding parties in the summer anyway. We were booked solid last year."

"Weddings are scheduled year-round, and that's business we need," Ivy said firmly. "We can charge more fees for the use of the ballroom and dining room—and you can make extra money on the flowers."

"We can be selective," Poppy said, sounding conciliatory.

Ivy threw a look at her niece. They couldn't afford to be too choosy. This month marked the first anniversary of the inn, and as with any new business, it had been a challenging year.

Summer Beach was a seasonal spot for summer tourists. Ivy and Shelly had made it through the lean winter months by creating special events that Poppy promoted. They had hosted a Halloween sleepover for kids and their parents, a Christmas and New Year's week for singles, and a romantic Valentine's weekend. They'd planned spa weeks and featured cooking classes. The last event was a family Easter egg hunt on the grounds, followed by a luncheon that Mitch catered from his Java Beach kitchen.

Poppy handed Ivy the message. "Eleanor York. She made sure to intimate that she is related to the royal Yorks."

"See? I smell trouble already." Shelly clipped the end of

another sturdy rose stem with force and shot a look at Ivy. "With an attitude like that, she has to be a bridezilla."

Poppy held up a finger. "Except she's not the bride; she's the bride's mom."

"A momzilla, then," Shelly said. "They're even worse. I handled flowers at enough weddings to know to steer clear of those designer-clad monsters."

Poppy giggled. "Actually, she introduced herself as Mrs. Churchill York. The third."

Shelly grimaced. "Does that mean she's the third Mrs. Churchill? Or is Churchie the third unfortunate soul to bear that name?"

"The latter, I think." Poppy's eyes flashed with laughter as she joined in the merriment. "And who names a baby Churchill?"

"Enough, you two," Ivy said, lowering her voice. "Remember what we agreed? No talking about the guests."

"They're not guests yet," Shelly said, grinning.

Poppy blushed. "You're right, Aunt Ivy." Turning to Shelly, she added, "Eleanor loved your floral arrangements posted on our website. She said she hadn't seen anything that creative outside of the pages of *Town & Country.*"

Shelly sniffed. "What she saw in that magazine was probably my work. The staff photographer was a friend and often came to shoot events where I'd provided flowers."

Ivy seized on that. "See? You could make a lot of money from a job like this." She turned to Poppy. "Have you searched them online? Surely they can't be too hard to find."

Poppy's eyes widened. "Aunt Ivy, you told us not to look up guests."

"She's not a guest yet, is she?" When Shelly chuckled, Ivy quickly added, "This is business."

"On it," Poppy said, sliding behind the reception desk and flipping open her laptop.

Shelly rolled her eyes. "Don't say I didn't warn you." She

filled in bare spots in the arrangement with the remaining lacy fern fronds before brushing discarded leaves and stems into a paper bag.

Ivy touched Shelly's shoulder. "A big floral job could help pay for the wedding and honeymoon you and Mitch want."

Over the New Year's holidays, Shelly had drummed up the courage to propose to Mitch Kline, the proprietor of Java Beach, the town's most popular coffee shop. Although at twenty-nine, he was younger than Shelly, the two of them had grown close over the past year. They were both creative free-spirits with a strong work ethic. Ivy felt they were a good match. At thirty-eight, Shelly was eager to start a family.

As for Ivy, she and Bennett—the town's mayor—had yet to set a date for their wedding. This wasn't the first marriage for either of them, so Ivy wanted Shelly to celebrate her wedding first.

Shelly lifted her eyes to the ceiling and sighed. "We could use the money. But the wedding guests had better behave themselves. You remember what happened at the last one. Fishing drunks out of the pool isn't my idea of a great event."

"What was I supposed to do?" Ivy spread her hands. "Let a famous actor drown? That would've landed us on the celebrity graveyard tour list."

Shelly laughed. "I can just imagine how that would go."

Poppy snapped her fingers. "Hey, that might be an idea. With such an old house, I wonder if anyone famous has ever died here?" Her eyes glittered at the possibilities. "Or even better—*murdered?* What with Amelia Erickson's ghost already here, I could really promote that—"

"No," Ivy and Shelly cried in unison, holding up their hands.

Ivy shivered. "There is no ghost. No spirits, no appari-tions. Nothing. Rumors like that can chase away potential guests. Besides, we all have to sleep here."

Shelly and Poppy suppressed smiles.

"I mean it." Glaring at them, Ivy took her phone from her pocket. "Now, if you'll watch the desk, Poppy, I'll call Mrs. York. We're also expecting that group from Los Angeles any time now. They called and asked to check in early."

"All the rooms are ready," Poppy said as she peered at her laptop screen. "Wow, the Yorks look loaded. Billionaire-rich. But I wonder why they'd want to have their daughter's wedding here?"

"People have their reasons," Ivy replied, though she was curious about the couple, too. "Maybe they want an intimate setting. Just because they're wealthy doesn't mean they want an extravagant affair."

"I have to clip flowers for the guestrooms," Shelly said, disappearing through the front door with her shears and pail.

A new guest strolled in, and Ivy nodded in greeting. Mrs. Mehta was a retired schoolteacher from Seattle and still had the sweet voice and manner of the kindergarten teacher she had been for years. She and Ivy had chatted at length over breakfast. Mrs. Mehta had spoken so fondly of her young students, many of whom still kept in contact with her. She had even taught the children of former students.

Meeting interesting people was a bonus that Ivy enjoyed, and their stories often moved her.

"Could one of you help me with the coffeemaker in the dining room?" Mrs. Mehta asked. "I don't know how to use those new-fangled machines with those little cups. I'm afraid I'll break it, but I sure would like another cup of that delicious coffee."

"I'll help you," Poppy said. "Those are coffee pods. It's easy to use them once you know how."

Ivy eased behind the desk. "I'll watch the front."

Mrs. Mehta told Ivy she had traveled the length of the western coast from Seattle to see her children. She planned to go first to San Diego and then continue to Phoenix to visit another child. Although Summer Beach was just an hour north of San Diego, the older woman said she needed to rest from her drive before taking on five grandchildren.

Ivy could only imagine, but with Sunny and Misty now in their twenties, she might soon be a grandmother, too. Still, with Sunny in college and Misty determined to make a career out of acting, even marriage was on the distant horizon.

After Poppy left, Ivy put down her phone and glanced at her niece's computer screen, squinting without her reading glasses. Images of Eleanor York dressed in eveningwear filled the screen, although photos of the husband weren't clear. "Hmm, you certainly go to a lot of fancy parties. Who are you?"

She clicked on another link, and photos of an older professorial gentleman in a herringbone coat popped up. *Hardly the same one*, she thought, dismissing the image.

Ivy had attended the occasional office holiday party with Jeremy, so she had a couple of black evening dresses she rotated. As a stay-at-home mom, she hadn't needed much. She peered closer and enlarged an image. Eleanor York's jewelry was quite impressive.

As guest voices floated downstairs, Ivy felt a twinge of guilt about snooping. She closed the laptop and rested her hands on it. Her fingers were bare of rings. She stroked the faint indentation where her wedding band had rested, growing tighter over the years until she didn't bother taking it off.

She had a few other rings she wore from time to time, including a modest, ruby-and-diamond ring she'd found tucked under one of the wooden floorboards in her bedroom. It had belonged to the original owner of the house, Amelia Erickson, whose presence they all felt from time to time.

Amelia had left a trail of secrets in the old house she had christened Las Brisas Del Mar, from historic art and important jewels she'd tucked away to hidden rooms she'd built in the attic during the war.

Yet after discovering a cache of beautiful vintage

Christmas ornaments in the garage, Ivy couldn't imagine there was any other place where something could be stashed away.

Amelia and her husband Gustav had been important art collectors from Europe. During the Second World War, Amelia had rescued significant works from Europe that Ivy had promptly returned to their owners.

After Gustav's death, Amelia had been hospitalized for Alzheimer's disease in Switzerland, where she passed away decades ago. The grand old home, once a glittering summer gathering place for the intellectual, artistic, and accomplished, had gone silent—frozen with its mid-century decor. The estate had been managed for decades until such time that a long-lost heir was deemed unlikely to surface. Aside from occasional charity fundraising events, the house had seen little use in years.

Ivy turned over her hand. The old callus at the top of her palm where her wedding band had rested was nearly invisible now. After Jeremy had died, it had been months before Ivy could bring herself to remove her wedding band.

Soon, another would take its place. Her heart ached at the bittersweet thought.

Ivy's phone trilled, startling her. Carlotta Reina Bay's number floated to the screen. "Hi, Mom. What's up?"

"If you haven't had lunch yet, I'm meeting my friend Ginger Delavie at her granddaughter's beach cafe. I thought you might like to join me and see them at the same time."

"When?"

"About half an hour? I know it's last minute, but we just decided."

Through the window, Ivy could see a car pull to the curb in front of the house. Behind them, Ivy spied Bennett walking toward the inn from the village. She recalled that he'd left his SUV at the mechanic's shop, and he'd had a meeting with the Summer Beach Retailers Association at Java Beach.

"I'd love to, but I think our guests just arrived," Ivy said. "Shelly is off to the nursery, and Poppy has a client meeting."

"Can Sunny watch the inn for you?"

"She's at school today."

Ivy's daughter would soon graduate from college. If guests needed anything, Ivy would have to be available. As the weekend neared, drop-in guests often arrived, too. Although they couldn't afford to miss any opportunities, Ivy wanted to see her mother, too. "Would you like to come by later?"

Just then, laughter burst through the open door that Bennett stood holding open for a group of young women. "After you, ladies."

"What a gentleman," one woman said, smiling flirtatiously. Four twenty-something women stepped into the foyer, their arms around each other and still laughing.

Carlotta's voice floated through the phone. "Sounds like someone is having a good time there. Why don't you and Shelly come over tomorrow instead? I have more things to give you."

"I'd like that." Ivy clicked off the phone and turned to the group in front of her. "Welcome to the Seabreeze Inn."

A pale blond woman wearing a rhinestone tiara and a glittery white satin sash that read *Bride* stepped up to the desk. She gave her name, and Ivy smiled.

"Bachelorette party?"

The three women behind the bride-to-be let out a cheer. The last woman through the door was checking out Bennett, who cleared his throat behind an amused grin.

"Are you checking in, too?" the woman asked him. She wore a short, form-fitting pink dress, and her long brunette hair was slightly disheveled.

"You might say I live here," Bennett said as he winked at Ivy.

The woman twirled a strand of hair and smiled at him. "I

sure hope to see you by the pool. We're going for a dip right away."

"The mayor might have work to do this afternoon," Ivy cut in.

The woman raised an eyebrow. "I've never seen a mayor with such muscles. Very impressive. I'm Carrie, by the way." She extended her hand.

"Bennett Dylan, at your service," he said, shaking her hand as Ivy suppressed a laugh. "If you'll excuse me, ladies, I have some calls to make."

Leaning toward Ivy, Carrie asked, "Is he married? I didn't see a ring."

"Almost," Ivy said with a small smile.

"Now that's a challenge if I ever heard one."

The bride, an earnest-looking young woman with clear blue eyes, turned to Ivy. "I'm Rachel Evans. My cousin and my friends obviously started the party before I arrived. I'm the designated driver anyway." She leaned in. "I'll try to keep them quiet."

Recalling her bachelorette party from years ago, Ivy smiled, though she would keep an eye on the outgoing Carrie who had flirted with Bennett, even though she was half his age.

Taking keys from the drawer, Ivy said, "I've put you all in the Sunset Suites behind the main house so that you won't disturb anyone. We simply ask that the pool area be quiet after eleven at night so that other guests can sleep." Mrs. Mehta was the only other new guest, so Ivy was glad to have this party here.

A few long-term guests were still in residence at the inn after a fire had ravaged their homes on the ridgetop overlooking the town, such as Imani Jones, the local attorney-turned-flower-vendor, and her son, Jamir, who was studying pre-med. Their home had been rebuilt and would be ready as soon as the interior was finished.

Another guest, Gilda, wrote for magazines. She didn't seem to be in a hurry to go anywhere. She'd told Ivy that she and Pixie, her Chihuahua, liked the ease of living at the inn. And although Bennett's house had been repaired, he'd leased it to a family and decided to remain in the old chauffeur's apartment above the garages behind the house. Ivy had been glad to see him stay.

"First thing we're going to do is dive into the pool," Rachel said. "It looked gorgeous in the website photos."

"Julia Morgan designed it," Ivy explained. "She was the architect who designed Hearst Castle on the northern coast of California."

"That's so cool," Carrie said, speaking up again. "I've read about her. I'm going to be an architect, too. Starting in September." She did a little happy dance.

"We're all graduating in June," Rachel said. "I'm the only one not going on to graduate school right away. My cousin Carrie will design our homes, Belinda will clean up the ocean, and Giselle will handle our taxes. I might catch up in another year or two." She blushed slightly.

"After the baby," one of her friends said before clapping her hand over her mouth.

Rachel sighed. "I just found out. My boyfriend Topper and I were both going to law school. We hadn't planned it this way, but now we'll have to get married sooner…" Her voice trailed off, and a flush gathered in her cheeks. "Before, I was only worried about the wedding. Now, that's the least of my concerns."

"Except that her mom is such a perfectionist," Carrie interjected.

Rachel nodded. "At this point, a wedding seems almost irrelevant," she said, lowering her voice almost to a whisper. "I'm scared to death. I don't know if I'm ready to be a mother. What if I'm terrible at it?"

Ivy remembered her early, angst-filled years of motherhood. "Your love is what matters most." She smiled at the nervous young woman. "Maybe you'd like to go to the local day spa for a massage while you're here."

Rachel's eyes lit with relief. "I'd love that. The others want to go to Spirits & Vine tomorrow, but I'd rather do something else. Just the thought of smelling alcohol in a bar—even a very nice one—turns my stomach." Paling at the idea, Rachel pressed a hand against her abdomen. "I almost didn't come at all, but they insisted."

"Under the circumstances, this is a low-key version of what we'd originally planned," Carrie added. "We all sneaked out of town to do this."

Ivy withdrew a card from the desk and handed it to Rachel. "Here's the number to the spa. Let me know if you want me to call for appointments."

"Thanks," Rachel said, tucking the card into her pocket. "I'd like that."

Ivy showed the young women to their rooms. They were about Sunny's age, and Ivy couldn't help smiling at their constant chatter. And why not? They were on the brink of exciting, life-changing adventures.

Ivy remembered how exciting those years had been—when anything and everything seemed possible. Life could change in a moment—like when she'd decided to move to Boston for school or when she'd met Jeremy in a coffee shop.

As Ivy closed the door behind Rachel, she made a note to put another lined trash bin in her room near the bed. The young woman looked queasy, and Ivy thought she might be suffering from morning sickness. She'd also bring a basket of ginger ale and peppermint tea, along with plain saltine crackers, to the room.

During this past year, Ivy had learned that little touches could make guests more comfortable, and she enjoyed doing it. She'd spent her adult life taking care of her family, so this role came naturally to her. Except for her painting, she hadn't trained for much else.

At college, she'd studied art history. She might have gone to work for a museum or an auction house when she was young, but she and Jeremy had started their family right away. He preferred that she stay home with the children, and she had enjoyed having that opportunity, too. Yet, in watching her classmates' success, she had often wondered about what she might have missed.

Ivy made her way back to the main house and opened the kitchen door, which seemed to have shifted in its frame. She had to lift the knob to close the door behind her.

The upkeep on a home this large was expensive. Fortunately, her brother Flint owned a construction company and had helped her with repairs, but she couldn't depend on him forever. Besides learning how to wield a hammer and screwdriver and unclog toilets, she also had to figure out how to fill the inn year-round.

When her husband had bought the house—unbeknownst to her—and drained their retirement savings, it was still structurally sound, though dated. Jeremy had neglected upkeep. The landscape was practically gasping for water. Although Ivy had tried to sell the house that dominated the beachside village that had developed around it, its historic designation and poor condition had dissuaded buyers.

With property taxes looming and a battle brewing with Jeremy's mistress—another fact Ivy hadn't discovered until she'd arrived in Summer Beach—she had decided to rent out rooms to save the property from a tax sale.

Now, in the spacious, 1950s-era kitchen, Ivy gathered tea bags and plucked crackers from the pantry. She tucked a vintage embroidered napkin from Amelia's linen collection into a basket and arranged the items.

Ivy paused, absently rubbing her bare ring finger again with her thumb. The summer before she'd left for college on the East Coast, she had a crush on a surfer named Bennett Dylan. Yet it hadn't been long before she'd met Jeremy in Boston and succumbed to his French charm, intelligence, and relentless pursuit of her.

Thinking about her new guest, Ivy had recognized the look in Rachel's eyes, which held glimmers of excitement and determination—as well as trepidation over the unknown and unexpected.

Even in her mid-forties, Ivy knew that feeling. Through the kitchen window, she could see Bennett on the balcony of the old chauffeur's apartment above the garages. Seated on the new outdoor furniture he'd bought to feel more at home, he was speaking on the phone and making notes.

Since she had arrived in the sleepy beach community, the unexpected had certainly occurred in the form of Bennett Dylan. Despite her initial misgivings, she'd found herself growing to care for him. Her older daughter Misty approved of their dating, and even Sunny, her mercurial younger daughter, had finally come around.

This past Christmas, Bennett had asked Ivy to marry him. At the time, it seemed the most natural thing in the world to accept his proposal, though they had yet to confirm a date. He was waiting for her.

And she was waiting on Shelly.

The Bennett that Ivy knew was the man she wanted in her life. Yet after awakening this past year to Jeremy's secret duplicity, she had to wonder if there was more than one side to Bennett.

Was he too good to be true?

She didn't have time to think about that now. With resolve, Ivy tucked several bottles of ginger ale into the basket for her young guest and slid it onto her arm.

When she reached Rachel's unit, she tapped on the door. The pale young woman cracked the door, and Ivy said, "I brought you a few things you might like to have on hand.

Just in case you start feeling queasy." She held out the basket.

Rachel's eyes widened as she accepted the offering. "I wasn't sure what to do. I haven't told my mother yet." Behind her, a mobile phone played a Barry Manilow tune. Rachel made a face. "That's her favorite song." She bit her lip and wrinkled her forehead with apprehension.

"Maybe you should answer it," Ivy said gently. "Call if you need anything." Although she wondered why Rachel felt she couldn't tell her mother, that was none of her business.

After leaving her new guest, Ivy wound through the tropical garden path that Shelly had planted around the Sunset suites. Sweet white plumeria blossoms opened to the sunshine, while lacy ferns peeked from beneath larger plantings and rippled in the light ocean breeze. Ivy trailed a hand over pink ginger flowers. The myriad aromas were redolent of Hawaii and other Polynesian islands, which is what Shelly had intended.

Spying her sister in the garden, Ivy made her way past the pool area to her. Shelly held a shiny tin of fresh-cut flowers.

"Your flowers have really come in this season," Ivy said. Shelly had brought the neglected grounds back to life with trimming, fresh plantings, and a lot of care.

Shelly snipped a pale pink rose that was just unfurling from its bud. "Pink and white seem like sweet bride-to-be colors."

Ivy smiled at her comment. "Is that what you plan on having?"

"Me? Oh, no." Shelly twirled the flower she held. "I'd like to have the most exotic, fascinating arrangements this coast has ever seen." She laughed as she tucked the shears into the back pocket of her worn jeans. "Though what I'll probably do is clip flowers from the garden for our small affair. Large weddings come with a lot of headaches. Mitch and I don't need any of that. It's about the marriage, not the wedding."

"Yes, but weddings are nice to look back on." Ivy hesitated. She didn't want to cause concern for Shelly, but she needed to plan, too. "Are you and Mitch still planning on getting married before Mom and Dad leave for their trip?"

"I'd like to." Shelly handed the pink rose to Ivy. "Maybe I'm not as free-spirited as I pretend to be." She drew a breath to say something else but hesitated.

"You're exactly who you are, Shelly. Why try to be anything else? That's exhausting."

A thoughtful expression filled Shelly's face. "That's what Mitch says, too. But I'm ready for my real life to begin. I've waited years to sail into my sunrise."

Ivy knew what she meant. Shelly wanted to start a family, and her former boyfriend in New York, Ezzra, had dangled a promise of a future together for years—without specifically committing. After numerous break-ups, he'd lure her back with another promise, though the future Shelly longed for never materialized.

Now, Ivy had her suspicions, though she might be treading on sensitive nerves. "What's holding you back?"

Shelly fiddled with a long strand of chestnut hair that had escaped her messy topknot, twirling it around her finger. "Mitch might be having second thoughts."

"Or maybe he needed time to adjust to the idea of marriage," Ivy said, sliding her arm across Shelly's shoulder and drawing her close. "What did he tell you?"

Shelly's eyes glistened, and she blinked hard. "He doesn't have to say anything. I know the signs. Ezrra painted them in vivid color for me. The truth is, I can't drag a date out of Mitch. I gave him a choice of three, and one has already passed."

Ivy tried to remain upbeat. "That might not mean what you think it does."

"It's pretty clear to me." Shelly scrunched her eyebrows together. "I'm the one who proposed. Mitch got swept up with the idea, and now he's had time to reconsider. If I'm honest with myself, I should have known he wasn't ready. He's a young, good-looking surfer and still has years to play around before settling down. And he could find someone a lot younger who doesn't have a shelf-date nearing expiration."

"That last part is hardly true." Thirty-eight wasn't necessarily too old, but Shelly's age did increase her medical risk of pregnancy. Yet Mitch seemed as devoted as ever. What was Ivy missing?

Ivy brought the rose to her nose, inhaling as she thought. "Have you tried to talk about this?"

"We're both avoiding the obvious."

"You might be misinterpreting his actions," Ivy said. "From what I've seen, Mitch is completely enamored with you. Maybe he simply wants to get to know you better. Or he wants to be spontaneous."

Shelly pursed her lips. "It's been a whole year. And I don't see Bennett backing out on you. He knows what he wants. Maybe you two should get married before Mom and Dad leave."

"Speaking of Mom, she asked us to come over tomorrow to pick up another load of housewares and clothing she wants to leave with us," Ivy said, swiftly avoiding Shelly's comment. Since they had both become engaged over the holidays, Ivy had been concerned about the competition that Shelly might feel. "Ask her what she thinks about Mitch."

"Maybe I will." Shelly drew fingers across her cheeks. "After I put these flowers in the guest rooms, I'll head to Hidden Garden. Need anything?"

"Not a thing. Say hello to Leilani and Roy for me." Ivy sent the owners business whenever she could. They had been kind enough to donate a tree to them for Christmas last year. "Our new guests are going for a swim soon, so I'll put the flowers in their rooms then."

"Thanks," Shelly said. When she passed the tin of flowers,

Ivy chuckled. "Wait a minute. You have stripes on your cheeks."

Looking at her hands, Shelly grinned. "Guess I should've worn my gloves before digging in the dirt." She lifted an edge of her T-shirt and wiped her face. "Better?"

"Gorgeous." Ivy smoothed Shelly's knotted hair and tucked the loose ends into her bun.

"You always did take care of me," Shelly said. "Even now."

"You take care of yourself pretty well. Imagine, you could still be in New York with Ezzra." Ivy hugged her sister. "This will all work out."

In Shelly's favor, she hoped. If Mitch backed out of the wedding as Ezzra had, Shelly would be devastated.

2

*T*he next morning, a gusty breeze lifted Ivy's natural straw hat, sending it tumbling across the terrace and onto the beach. She cried out and started after it.

"Got it," Bennett called out, racing from behind. He scooped it up and brought it back to her. "Good morning," he said in a slightly gravelly voice. He dropped a kiss on her cheek. "Looking for this?"

"Thanks," she said, catching her breath. "I just bought this one, too."

She'd lost her last hat to the ocean when the winds had teased it from her head and tossed it to a wave, which stole it out to sea like a newly prized possession. At least the straw would break down, unlike the plastic that careless visitors left on the beach. Like many Summer Beach locals, she often carried a bag to pick up and dispose of discarded wrappers, bottles, and broken beach toys that could prove deadly to marine life.

Bennett held the hat above her head, his hazel eyes twinkling with love and laughter. His short, cropped hair was sun-streaked, and daily runs on the beach had toned his physique. Everything about him quickened her heart rate.

"And what's on your mind?" she asked, although she could just imagine—because she had the same thoughts. This was her fiancé, the man she'd promised her heart to a few months ago at Christmas. At her age, it almost seemed silly to call him that.

A smile danced on his lips. "Don't I get some sort of reward?"

Lifting onto her toes, she gave him a soft kiss that brought a smile to each of them. "Consider that a down payment."

"I'm going to hold you to that."

Ivy arched a brow. "I certainly hope so."

"When do you think that might be?" Bennett asked, threading his fingers with hers. His voice held a note of anticipation.

"Soon enough," she said, smiling. "After Shelly gets married. And then, when we can find a quiet week." With summer on the horizon and weekends the busiest time at the Seabreeze Inn, Ivy couldn't imagine leaving the inn shorthanded.

"We'll make time. Everyone will understand and cover for you." Bennett brushed her hair back and placed the hat snugly on her head. "And just to prove that they can manage without you, I have a surprise planned for you."

"What?"

Instead of answering, Bennett drew up the strings that she'd carelessly let fall down her back. "This is what these are for."

She nudged him. "As if I hadn't grown up on the beach, too." She'd meant to rearrange her hat, but she'd been in a hurry for a beach walk before the day began. Her curiosity piqued, she turned to him, wondering what he had in mind. "Aren't you going to tell me?"

"Nope."

She punched him playfully in the arm, and he only laughed.

"Later," he said as he slung his arm across her shoulders. "Where's the rest of your morning crew? I thought you'd be out for a walk by now."

Obviously, she wasn't going to get anything out of him now. "The bachelorette party that checked in last night stayed out late. Between the sun and the wine, they didn't even make it down for breakfast. I waited as long as I could for my walk because they had been enthusiastic about joining me yesterday."

Guests could walk the beach on their own, of course, but Ivy liked to lead because they often had questions about the village—the best restaurants, shops, and entertainment. She could answer all the guests' questions at once while they enjoyed a brisk walk and fresh sea air.

Most visitors came to enjoy the beach and the small-town ambiance. Aside from the local farmers market, the one-screen movie theater, and the wine shop that often featured jazz artists passing through to San Diego from Los Angeles, there wasn't much to do in Summer Beach. The community organized some events, such as the Independence Day fire-works and the holiday coastal cruise. Boat owners went all out decorating their watercraft. Last year, Ivy and Shelly and Poppy had organized an arts and crafts fair that brought in a lot of new visitors to Summer Beach. But the main attraction was still the beach.

Bennett rubbed his stubbled chin. "I missed my early run, too. Had an early morning call with a client back east. They're looking for a house in Summer Beach, but they're also considering a lot to build a custom home. I still have just enough time for a quick run before heading to City Hall."

"Don't go without breakfast," Ivy said, gently scolding him. "Surely Nan won't mind if the mayor is a little late." Bennett still had a few real estate clients—as long as they didn't conflict with his mayoral duties.

"Only if you'll join me."

"I'll meet you in the dining room." She'd already told Shelly to hold breakfast for their late-sleeping guests. "Now shoo. You're wasting time."

"Yes, ma'am." Bennett took off, kicking up sand behind him as he headed toward the surf.

Ivy strolled behind, watching him. His legs were firm and muscular, and he kept in shape. She counted herself lucky. Frankly, there wasn't anyone else who'd ever touched her heart as Bennett did—except for her late husband. But that had been a different relationship altogether.

She and Jeremy had been married more than two decades when she'd received that dreadful call that had changed the course of her life. Their marriage had been traditional, which was how her husband liked it. Jeremy worked, and she had taken care of the girls and the house. That left little time for her painting. Even after their daughters went to college, she was still washing their clothes on weekends, arranging birthdays and holidays, booking everyone's appointments, and tending to household repairs and tasks. Her lists were endless.

A future with Bennett would look different. Although just how different, she wasn't sure.

She glanced back at the grand old house that Jeremy had never intended to leave her. She couldn't have turned that house into an inn without Shelly's help. Or their brothers and nieces and nephews. Everyone had pitched in to help Ivy and Shelly get back on their feet.

Had it only been a year since she'd returned to California? So much had happened in that time, from the discovery of rare paintings and other precious objects sequestered within the old house's walls to an unexpected new relationship.

Only a year.

She'd known Jeremy for just six months before they married. Though their lives stretched before them, they had been in a hurry, confident that their love would never fade. Yet for him, it had. Maybe their familiarity with each other had killed the excitement he craved. His desire had driven him to act upon a new life without her.

Ivy blinked against the breeze and tucked her hands into her windbreaker. Though she'd worked hard to come to terms with his infidelity, the wound hadn't entirely healed.

She slowed to a stop. Bennett was a speck ahead of her on the shoreline now. She wondered, how well did she know the mayor of Summer Beach? Forever was a long time.

Just my nerves, she told herself, thrusting her shoulders back and picking up her pace. They loved each other, and they would make it work.

Remembering that she had a meeting with Mrs. York, Ivy walked briskly for ten minutes to increase her heart rate. Twenty minutes is better than nothing, she thought. She had just enough time to bathe and dress before meeting Mrs. York, who was eager to inspect the inn as a possible wedding venue for her daughter.

They had spoken briefly on the phone yesterday, and Ivy had barely had a chance to share the package prices. Costs didn't seem to concern Mrs. York. She was clearly a woman on a mission.

"ANOTHER MUFFIN?" Bennett asked, offering Ivy a cranberry orange muffin dusted with sugar on top.

"No thanks, that would only add to the muffin-top," Ivy replied, resisting. She'd already indulged this morning, but at least she had walked. She placed her napkin on the table. "Maybe I'll ask Mitch to develop a gluten-free recipe for us. A lot of guests ask for that. And maybe a skinny version. I need that."

Bennett tapped her nose. "I think you're beautiful just as you are."

Ivy never tired of hearing that. "Thank you, sweetheart. You sure know how to start a woman's day." It had taken her years to gain the confidence to graciously accept a compliment and not immediately disclaim it. Only when she'd heard her daughters doing that had she recognized the behavior in herself.

In her marriage, Jeremy had grown to be hypercritical. She'd become accustomed to his small, insidious remarks that she tried to ignore simply to keep the peace. She looked past his shortcomings because of her love for him and the power he held in their relationship as the breadwinner. In retrospect, she never should have.

And she wouldn't again.

Ivy glanced toward the entry to the dining room where the four women who'd arrived yesterday were straggling in. They were the last ones at breakfast, and from the looks of most of them, they'd just rolled out of bed. Only Rachel looked bright-eyed.

"I think this group is going to need a fresh pot of coffee," Ivy said.

"You tend to them. I have to get to the office." Bennett got up and snagged an apple on his way out.

"Good morning, ladies," he called out as he passed their table.

"Ow, you don't need to yell," Carrie said, holding her head.

"He's not," Rachel said. "That's your hangover screaming at you."

Carrie moaned. "More like a little monster hammering on my forehead to get out. Anyone have any hangover meds?"

Bennett grinned. "Hydrating will help, too."

"Even my ponytail hurts." Carrie slid an elastic band from her messy hair and wiped day-old mascara from underneath her eyes.

As Bennett disappeared around the corner, Ivy made her way to the women's table. "More coffee? I can put on a fresh pot."

"Absolutely," Rachel said. "My friends had a little too much fruit of the vine last night. Guess that's the silver lining to my condition."

"You have a lot of wonderful experiences to look forward to," Ivy said.

"Not everyone will think so." Rachel's eyes loomed large in her pretty face. "At least Topper is thrilled at the prospect of becoming a father, even if it is sooner than he'd thought."

Ivy assumed Rachel was referring to her mother again. She hoped that her daughters would never feel like they couldn't discuss such an important matter with her. "I'll bring fresh coffee shortly."

As Ivy was on her way to the kitchen, Poppy stopped her in the hallway. "There's a woman at the front desk. It's your Mrs. York."

"She's early," Ivy said, glancing at her watch.

"Do you want me to talk to her? I could show her around."

"No, I'll meet with her now. But could you make a fresh pot of coffee for the bachelorettes in the dining room? They had a late night at Spirits & Vine."

Poppy agreed, and Ivy made her way to the foyer.

Ivy greeted Mrs. York. Meticulously attired, the fortyish woman wore a pastel-blue knit suit with hose and heels. Her make-up was flawless, if a little obvious, and her hair was coiffed and sprayed stiff. She held herself in an imperious manner. Her outfit might have been perfect for a Beverly Hills luncheon, but this was Summer Beach, where sandals and sundresses were considered dressing up. Perhaps she had somewhere else to go later, Ivy allowed.

Nevertheless, Ivy sensed an iciness in the woman's demeanor that Poppy must have felt over the phone.

Mrs. York glanced around the foyer, her nose tilted as if she expected to encounter an unpleasant smell at any moment. "Your girl told me you were in the midst of renovations. When will all of this be replaced?"

"That was Poppy, my niece," Ivy said brightly. "She's our marketing expert and is quite talented. A USC graduate, in fact." She couldn't resist mentioning the prestigious private university in Los Angeles.

"Well now, that changes things," the woman said a little grudgingly. "My husband graduated from USC, too." After an awkward pause, she added, "You may call me Eleanor."

"Ivy." She shook Eleanor's limp extended hand. "As for the renovations, we just completed many repairs." The house was clean, and the entire Bay family had pitched in to paint it last spring. Aside from that, she couldn't afford much else right now.

"Our guests enjoy the casual beach house ambiance," Ivy said. "People come here to relax." She wondered if Eleanor ever did. "How did you hear of the Seabreeze Inn?"

"My sister suggested it. Lillian attended your spa week. She raved about the inn and your hospitality, though her standards are somewhat more relaxed than mine."

"I see," Ivy said, ignoring Eleanor's comment. She heard someone coming down the stairs behind them. A few moments later, Gilda, a writer and long-time resident, appeared in the foyer. She wore a casual, wrinkled cotton outfit, and she had a pen that matched her short pink hair perched behind her ear. In her arms, she clutched Pixie, her beloved Chihuahua. A low growl rumbled in the tiny dog's chest when she saw Ivy's visitor.

"Hi everyone," Gilda said.

"You're out early," Ivy said.

"Pixie has a doctor's appointment." All at once, Pixie's growl erupted into a high-pitched rampage aimed at Eleanor. "Pixie, behave," Gilda cried, bouncing the dog in an attempt to quiet her.

But Pixie refused to back down. Amid Pixie's verbal assault on Eleanor, Gilda hurried out the front door.

Ivy turned back to Eleanor. "Sorry about that. Pixie is usually quite good with guests." She didn't mention Pixie's little problem. The dog had a tendency to nab other people's belongings and drag them to her room for hiding. Ivy tried to watch Pixie whenever she escaped Gilda's room, snatching the dog's purloined treasures from her before she could scurry away.

"Those are evil little dogs," Eleanor muttered. "I expect she will be locked up during the wedding."

"Why don't I show you the ballroom?" Ivy was uninterested in delving into the root of this woman's family or pet dynamics. Seldom had she—or Pixie, for that matter—developed such an instant dislike of a person.

When they entered the ballroom, Eleanor's gaze immediately traveled from the intricate wooden parquet floor up to the chandeliers before resting on the carved marble fireplace. "Well, well, this might do after all. How surprising." She nodded with satisfaction. "The dates I mentioned are still available?"

"At the moment, yes. However, we'd had many inquiries, so it's first come, first served."

Eleanor glanced out the tall windows to the ocean. "This will photograph well enough, as long as we can persuade a decent photographer to make the trek here."

"We have a good wedding photographer in town."

Eleanor gave her a withering look. She turned away and sauntered toward the fireplace. "This is the spot. Yes, it will do." She framed the area with her hands as if she were a director. "Thank goodness the dress still fits her."

"Excuse me?"

Eleanor whipped around. "I don't believe I said anything to you."

Ivy swallowed a retort. This was business, and they needed

the income for maintenance and taxes. She didn't have to like every guest or client of the inn. Ivy arranged a smile on her face. "Does the groom's family live nearby?"

"Dear heavens, no."

That's it, Ivy thought. She looked at Eleanor and arched an eyebrow. "I beg your pardon?"

Eleanor responded with an elaborate shrug. "I suppose Summer Beach is nice enough as an out-of-the-way sort of place. We had another venue reserved in Bel Air, but now we're forced to move up the wedding. Through no fault of mine, I might add. Goodness knows I have done my part as a mother. Unfortunately, the Hotel Bel-Air can't accommodate a schedule change. Churchill and I must also cancel our trip to Europe." She lifted her gaze to the ceiling. "These young people are so impetuous." Eleanor stretched her lips into what Ivy took to be a smile, however uncomfortable it looked. She opened her purse and withdrew a check. "This is for the deposit."

Ivy accepted the check. The amount was what she had quoted for their most expensive deluxe wedding package. Although she had reservations about Eleanor, this was good pay for a weekend. She couldn't turn it down, despite what Shelly might think.

"We look forward to welcoming you to the Seabreeze Inn," Ivy said.

Eleanor merely sighed.

The Seabreeze Inn was a long way from a posh Bel Air hotel. Still, this home had once been a showcase, no matter how shabby around the edges it was now. Ivy slipped the check into her pocket.

Ivy went on. "The grounds are also lovely for weddings. Before we go outside onto the terraces, we can look at the formal dining room, which you may use for the rehearsal dinner. Right this way, please."

Eleanor's high heels clicked sharply on the wooden floors

behind Ivy. She stopped at the entry to the dining room and turned to Eleanor. "After breakfast, this room can be rearranged to accommodate a reception or private dinner."

When Eleanor stepped inside the room, her mouth dropped open. "Rachel, what in heaven's name are you doing here—and why haven't you been answering my calls?"

The young guest whirled around. "Mom?"

"And Carrie," Eleanor said accusingly. "You haven't been returning my calls either."

"I'm sorry, Aunt Eleanor." Carrie slunk in her seat. "We've been so busy planning this bachelorette party."

"Rachel doesn't need a reward for her behavior," Eleanor snapped.

Ivy quickly pieced together the situation. This is the mother Rachel had been avoiding. And the reason for moving up the wedding would soon be apparent. Standing behind Eleanor, Ivy gave Rachel a sympathetic smile.

"How did you find me here?" Rachel asked.

"I've been looking for an appropriate replacement venue for you. Somewhere out of the way, but still close enough for your grandparents to attend. Three hours in a limousine won't kill them." She folded her arms. "It seems we've both been talking to your Aunt Lillian. And she told me *everything*."

A look of horror filled Rachel's face, and she gripped the arms of the chair.

"Don't worry. Your mother is handling this—as I always do." Eleanor snapped her fingers. "Everyone out while my daughter and I have a tête-à-tête."

Ivy looked on in awe as Carrie and the two friends scurried from their chairs. Eleanor clearly had a fierce reputation.

"Is that coffee ready yet?" Carrie asked in a pleading voice as she brushed past Ivy.

"Follow me," Ivy said. "Poppy is brewing a fresh pot. You can wait in the kitchen with her." That mother-daughter conversation would probably take a while.

Ivy led the way and swung open the kitchen door. "Poppy, our guests would like to wait in here." She showed them to the large table in the kitchen where family and friends usually gathered. "I'll be in the library if you need anything." That was close enough to the dining room, and she could still answer a few emails until Eleanor and Rachel finished.

"Okay, the coffee is almost ready." Poppy threw a quizzical glance at Ivy, but to her credit, she turned a broad smile toward the three young women, welcoming them. "Would you like anything to eat?"

Carrie groaned again, and Ivy chuckled. Poppy was only a few years older than they were. She would understand.

Ivy hurried to the library. She could hear the rise and fall of voices from the dining room. She felt sorry for Rachel, who seemed like a sweet girl saddled with a self-centered, self-indulgent woman for a mother. Just when Rachel needed her the most, Eleanor was acting angry and inconvenienced. But that was none of Ivy's business.

She sat down at the computer and brought out the check that Eleanor had given her.

Just then, an alert from her bank popped onto the screen. She slid on a new pair of leopard-print reading glasses that she kept in the library. The alert was a notice she'd set for a low balance in the inn's checking account. *Just in time.* Ivy rested her chin on her hand. *Where does it all go?* She'd have to go to the bank today to make a deposit.

A few minutes later, Poppy came into the library. "What in the world happened in the dining room? I couldn't help but overhear part of what Carrie and her friends were saying in the kitchen."

Ivy quickly summarized the situation for her.

"What a disaster of a family," Poppy said. "It's a good thing we can choose our customers, right?"

Ivy peered over her reading glasses. "What do you mean by that?"

"If you don't like Eleanor York, you can tell her the dates she wants are already reserved on our calendar. I'll tell her if you want me to. I don't think any of us want to work with someone like that. Shelly was right. Eleanor is a total Momzilla. The wedding is bound to be a fiasco."

"If you and Shelly are against this, I suppose I could do that," Ivy said slowly. She glanced at the check on the desk. Maybe she could wait another couple of days until the bachelorette party settled their bill.

Then she remembered the anguished look in Rachel's eyes when she saw her mother. That young woman deserved a happy wedding. Ivy would want that for her daughters, just as she did for Shelly. A woman's wedding day was the one day in her life she should enjoy. However, Rachel probably wouldn't get that from her mother.

But Ivy could make a difference. Isn't that why she loved welcoming guests to the inn? In the year since she'd arrived, Ivy had discovered that being an innkeeper was more than renting rooms; it was caring for guests and attending to their needs.

Right now, Rachel needed someone on her side to help make her wedding special. Every woman deserved that.

"Actually, the wedding is on. Rachel needs us. And I'll handle Eleanor York."

As Poppy stared at her, Ivy had the uncomfortable feeling she might regret her decision.

*I*vy crouched in front of the vintage refrigerator she called Gertie, wiping out the interior with a cleaning rag. She had put a pot of hot water inside to speed the defrosting of the upper freezer, which had grown thick with ice. She rocked back on her heels and drew her hand across her forehead.

"Hi, Ivy. Can you talk?"

Ivy looked up at Rachel, her young guest from the bachelorette party, and stretched out her hand. "As long as you give me a hand up." She'd been in that position so long that her legs were aching.

"What are you doing?" Rachel asked.

"Defrosting the freezer."

"I didn't know you had to do that," Rachel said, biting her lip. "Guess I have a lot to learn about taking care of a house —and a baby and a husband. Not that my mother is any sort of a role model. All she does is order the staff around. Topper and I won't be able to afford help—and we don't want it anyway. I want it to be just the three of us in our home. Mom tells me that's ridiculous."

"Don't worry. Defrosting freezers isn't done much

anymore—unless you have refrigerators older than I am, which you probably won't. We're just lucky that way." Ivy wasn't sure she was doing the defrosting right either. "I was just about to take a break and make a cup of tea. If you like, we can talk over tea."

"Thanks," Rachel said. "We're checking out today, but I'll be back for the wedding."

Ivy gestured for her to sit on a stool at the long counter in the kitchen. She hadn't been planning to take a break, but Rachel's voice sounded so plaintive. The young woman had been scarce after speaking to her mother. Since Eleanor had paid to reserve space for the wedding, Ivy was committed. She only hoped it wouldn't be a fiasco.

While Ivy put the kettle on, Rachel said, "I guess you overheard everything. I had confided in my Aunt Lillian—my mom's sister. She was concerned, so she told my mother. Mom went ballistic, and now she's rushing around moving up the wedding for us."

Ivy measured fragrant tea leaves into a mesh ball and hung it on the side of a teapot. "Is that what you want?"

"Topper and I want to get married—even more now—but our original wedding date is now the baby's due date. So we have to do something. We'd thought about getting married at City Hall. I always wanted a small ceremony, but Mom planned her extravagant dream wedding. That's needlessly extravagant, especially now."

Ivy listened while Rachel went on. "After the divorce, Mom and I lived on a modest income until she remarried. My father is a musician. He's a rock-and-roller at heart, but he makes his living as a studio musician. He's the kindest person you've ever met, but Mom was always angry because he didn't get the huge break she'd thought he would. She dreamed of being a famous rock-and-roller's wife, touring the world, and living in Malibu. She says Dad let her down."

Rachel picked at a hangnail. "Mom finally got what she

wanted, except for the rock-and-roll wife part. She usually does."

As Rachel's words hung in the air, Ivy studied the young woman's face. What a shame it was that Rachel couldn't celebrate what should be one of the happiest moments of her life because of a domineering mother. Ivy tried to imagine Eleanor as a rock-and-roll wife, but she couldn't. It sounded like Eleanor derived her identity from whomever she was with, rather than having the confidence to create her own.

Ivy could understand that. It was easy to get swept up in someone else's dream when you were young, especially if they were good-looking, adored you—and spoke with a swoony French accent. But she was past that now.

Gently, Ivy asked, "Do you have a good relationship with your father?"

"I do, but Mom is jealous of that." Rachel fidgeted with her fingernail. "I want both my father and stepfather to walk me down the aisle. Churchill is a good guy, even though he's a lot older than Mom. He's been really nice to me." She shook her head. "I don't know how Mom attracts such nice guys when she's such a tyrant. It's her looks, I guess. She really puts herself out there."

Eleanor was attractive, Ivy allowed, but in a highly polished, trophy-wife sort of way. She couldn't picture Eleanor with a musician. Watching Rachel fidget, Ivy opened what she and Shelly called their kitchen junk drawer, a collection of lost buttons, hair clips, coupons, and pencils. She extracted a nail file and handed it to Rachel.

At this simple action, the young woman's face brightened. "You always seem to know what I need."

Ivy almost said, *I'm a mom*, but she immediately thought better of it. She refilled Rachel's tea instead. "So, what do you want?"

Rachel grew thoughtful as she filed the edge of her rough nail. "Instead of a costly wedding, I'd feel better about giving that money to a good cause. My closest friends are here with me, but my mom was pushing for a dozen bridesmaids because her best friend's daughter had ten. She has to outdo everyone. It's such a waste of money. Churchill will do whatever Mom wants, and I guess he can afford it because he inherited a lot, but that's not the point."

Rachel paused. "I won that round only by telling her that Topper and I didn't want casual acquaintances in our wedding. Mom wants the best of everything now. She says since she had so little growing up, she has to make up for lost time." Rachel blushed. "She would die if she knew I was talking about her. Still, I have ideas. Or, I'd like to."

The teakettle whistled, and Ivy turned off the flame. "Sounds like a smaller wedding is more along the lines of what you wanted anyway." She poured hot water into the teapot. While the tea was steeping, she brought out scones and raspberry jam.

"My mother will still find a way to make it grander than it needs to be," Rachel said. "At least it will be over quickly." She slid the emery board across the counter.

"It's your day to enjoy," Ivy said as she put out the scones and poured the tea. "Tell her what you want."

"She doesn't listen. At this point, I'm just showing up. My mom thinks I have a style deficit—her words—so she appointed herself my wedding coordinator. At least I got to choose my dress. Aunt Lillian made sure of that."

It seemed to Ivy that Eleanor was trying to solve problems with money, but that's not what her daughter wanted.

"Shelly agreed to handle the flowers," Ivy said. "She'll create whatever sort of arrangements and bouquet you want. Why don't you talk with her before you leave? She's in the garden now."

"I guess I could do that." Rachel brightened a little. "I hardly even know. With Mom around, I don't get to make many decisions on my own."

"You'll soon be on your own with your husband," Ivy said. "You'll be making decisions every day."

"I can hardly wait." Rachel sipped the tea and picked at the scone. "It's not that I'm not excited about getting married —I am, but having a baby overshadows having a big wedding."

"I would agree with that," Ivy said. "Having a child will be a highlight of your life."

Rachel slid a hand over her abdomen and smiled shyly. "Topper is truly excited about the baby. Thankfully, that makes up for Mom being mortified over my pregnancy. Besides the moral implications, which she's in no position to lecture me about, she told me she's too young to be a grandmother."

"She'll probably come around." Listening to Rachel speak, Ivy was even more thankful for her mother. Carlotta had listened to Ivy and her siblings, offered advice when asked, and let them make decisions—and occasional mistakes. Ivy didn't realize how fortunate she was until she was older. "I bet she'll spoil her grandchild."

"That's what I'm afraid of." Rachel sipped her tea. "I wish I had someone to talk to. Someone like you."

"You can call on me anytime," Ivy said, and she meant it. Rachel reminded Ivy of her daughters. She also remembered what it was like to be young and pregnant and living thousands of miles away from her mother. "Do you have a good relationship with your aunt?"

"I do, but she lives in Florida. Aunt Lillian is Carrie's mom. We wanted to go to college together, which is why Carrie lives here. Aunt Lillian is younger than Mom. As the baby of the family, she probably got a lot of attention, so there's that jealousy, too."

Ivy had never felt that way about Shelly, so she couldn't relate. But she remembered Lillian, who was as different as she could be from Eleanor.

Lillian had visited the inn with a group of friends during the spa week. Shelly had taught yoga and water aerobics, and Ivy led walks and watercolor classes. They brought in massage therapists and hired Marina Moore, Ivy's old friend who was now opening a beach cafe, to make healthy meals. Although Lillian favored Eleanor in appearance, Lillian was friendly and relaxed. People gravitated toward her. Ivy understood why Rachel had a better relationship with her aunt than her mother.

Rachel stared at her tea. "Since my mom and dad are divorced, I know my mother is going to make my dad uncomfortable. She didn't want him to come to the wedding, but I insisted. At least my stepdad is cool with it. He's nice, but he's more like a grandpa to me. My mom must amuse him in some weird way. She's always been self-centered; I just didn't realize it until I grew up."

Ivy's heart went out to the young woman. "So that's why your last name is different. If I had recognized your mother's name, I could have warned you."

"Well, it's done now." Rachel gave her a shy smile. "I never thanked you for bringing that basket of goodies to my room."

"I hope it helped."

"It did. I felt so queasy, but the crackers and tea settled my stomach. Could I ask you a few more questions?"

The block of ice in the refrigerator was dripping slowly, so Ivy would have to wait for it anyway. "I'm happy to help if I can," Ivy said, refilling Rachel's tea.

The younger woman went on, asking questions about how long morning sickness lasted and how long Ivy had been in labor, among other things. Rachel should have been comfortable asking her mother these questions, but Ivy was happy to help put her at ease.

Finally, Rachel rose. "I'd better see Shelly before I leave. But I'll be back in a few weeks for the wedding." She smiled.

"Thanks for the tea and the talk. I'm happy the wedding will be here, and I know Topper will like it, too. I guess I should thank Mom for that, even though it was really Aunt Lillian."

"I'm sure your mother has your best interest at heart." Ivy couldn't imagine otherwise.

Rachel paused in the doorway. "Maybe. Way, way down in her heart somewhere—I hope."

"I look forward to meeting Topper soon, too."

"You'll love him," Rachel said, her face glowing. "Everyone does."

Ivy watched Rachel go, thinking about how young she was to be making such important decisions in her life.

And yet, regardless of age, marriage was always a leap of faith.

"TURN the wheels a little more to the right." Ivy stood at the rear of her parents' garage, guiding Shelly as she backed the old Jeep inside.

Their mother had asked them to bring the larger vehicle today because she wanted to send special items home with them for storage. Ivy's parents had already leased their house for the duration of their round-the-world sail. The new tenant would be moving in soon.

Ivy held up her hands. "That's it. Stop."

Shelly stepped out of the car and slid the keys into the pocket of her faded jeans. "I still can't believe you booked that wedding."

"Aren't you glad to have the business?"

"I know we need the money, but I'm only going to deal with you and Rachel. Don't subject me to Momzilla. Eleanor is all yours."

Ivy opened the door to the airy breezeway between the garage and the Spanish Revival-style house where they'd grown up. "Rachel deserves the wedding she wants. Did she tell you what kind of flowers she wants?"

"Not exactly," Shelly said, following her. "She asked me what I like, so I showed her photos of some of my favorite arrangements on my phone. She said that was fine."

"Then I'll tell Eleanor that's what Rachel decided on."

"She'd better not find fault with it—it's my best work," Shelly said. "I wish I could afford that for my wedding." As they approached the house, she added, "I wonder what Mom has for us?"

"She mentioned old family photos," Ivy replied. "She doesn't trust putting cherished mementos into storage. A friend of hers had put everything they owned into one of those units while they were relocating, and the entire storage facility burned to the ground."

Shelly made a face. "I'm not sure the inn isn't a fire hazard, too."

"Don't even say that," Ivy said, holding up a finger in warning. "Especially after what we spent on fire alarms, carbon monoxide sensors, and electrical upgrades."

After a near fiasco last Christmas with actor Rowan Zachary, who had torched a wreath in the ballroom during an event, Ivy spent quite a lot to ensure guest safety.

"Maybe we ought to ban Rowan Zachary from the property," Shelly said. "He almost drowned last summer, and then he nearly set the place on fire."

Ivy grimaced as she opened the door to the kitchen. "It's his martinis we should ban. Every time he visits, we need emergency services standing by."

Stepping inside, Shelly said, "I wonder how many times he's cheated death."

Their mother turned from a box she was packing in the colorful, Mexican Talavera-tiled kitchen, where the aroma of roasting Anaheim chiles suggested she had been prepping for *chile rellenos* tonight. A bowl of avocado and lemons from the orchard sat on the counter.

"Who's cheating death, *mija*?" Carlotta asked. "I hope you're not talking about your father and this trip."

Ivy hugged her mother. "Not at all. We were talking about Rowan Zachary."

Carlotta shook her head. "According to Carol Reston, too many times to count." She paused to tuck dark wisps of hair into a clasp. A few strands of silver glinted in the sunlight from tall windows. "I hope you don't think our voyage is too dangerous."

Ivy and Shelly exchanged a glance before Shelly draped an arm around their petite mother. "We're always concerned about you."

Carlotta waved off the comment with a flick of her hand, her silver-and-turquoise bracelets clinking. "Your father has never been more prepared. We've been sailing since before you were born. So, I hope you're not alluding to our age again."

"Not me," Ivy said. "I hear seventy is the new forty. And you two are in better shape than we are."

"Speak for yourself," Shelly said, bumping Ivy's shoulder. "Come to my yoga class more often."

"Someone has to set up breakfast," Ivy said.

She'd accepted long ago that she'd never have Shelly's lanky, bendable frame. Petite like her mother and a bit plump around the middle was Ivy's mid-life look, and she accepted that. Her doctor told her she was perimenopausal. Thankfully, Bennett loved her as she was, and she'd never felt better with daily beach walks and fresh ocean air.

"I thought Poppy was handling breakfast," Shelly said.

"We take turns. I'm surprised you didn't know that. And she's not always here."

Carlotta threw her arms around her daughters and pulled

each of them to one side. "Girls, girls. Still bickering after all these years."

Shelly twisted her lips to one side with a sheepish look. "She usually starts it."

Ivy's mouth dropped open, but she immediately thought better of defending herself. They were here to help their mother, not argue like kids.

"We just like to poke fun at each other. Right, Shells?" Ivy inclined her head toward their mother.

Shelly caught her meaning and grinned. "Right, Ives." She gestured toward the packing box that rested on the tile counter. "What's in there?"

"Family photos." Carlotta picked up a hammered silver frame with a photo of her young Bay family brood acting silly on the beach. "Even though we're renting the house furnished, we have to make room for them. They don't need our trinkets and family photos on every surface."

Ivy took the old photo from her mother. "I've always liked this one."

"Keep it or pack it," Carlotta said. "We can't take much on the boat. You might as well enjoy these things while we're gone. Your brothers and their wives like that minimalist beach look."

Ivy gazed around the large kitchen and family room. Carlotta had cleared the photos Ivy and her siblings had given their parents over the years, along with those that Carlotta and Sterling had taken of their growing family.

Ivy loved this home. Her parents favored vivid colors and layered designs. The décor was eclectic with artwork from Lima's bohemian Barranco district, antique Japanese furniture with carved dragons, and handmade Italian pottery. Every piece held a story and reflected their world travels.

"I'd like a few photos," Shelly said. A smile brightened her face. "For my new home."

Shelly planned to move into the beach house that Mitch

had bought after Java Beach proved popular. Bennett had once told them how he'd encouraged Mitch to invest the money he was making in a house. With only one bedroom, it was the quintessential surf cottage. The lot had room to expand the house, and the village location was convenient.

Carlotta kissed Shelly's cheek. "I'm so happy for you." She took Ivy's hand. "For both of my lovely daughters. And soon, we'll welcome two new sons-in-law to the Bay family."

Shelly's cheeks flushed, and Ivy couldn't be happier for her.

"Even though we're packing, I still have time to help with your wedding plans," Carlotta said. "Three weeks isn't very far away."

Shelly chewed her lip. "Is that all it is?"

"I've made a wedding list for her," Ivy said.

Expelling a breath, Shelly said, "I don't know where I'd be without the queen of organization here, though we only plan to invite family. Very casual, lots of flowers, toes in the sand. I want everyone to be comfortable. I worked far too many stuffy weddings in New York."

"I think that's perfect for you and Mitch," Carlotta said. "Have you decided what you're going to wear?"

Shelly touched a finger to her chin. "I'm thinking about a white swimsuit with a long white cover-up and flowers in my hair."

Carlotta's smile froze. Her gaze darted across photos of various siblings' weddings on the counter before them. "Oh, darling, are you sure? You could have a casual, flowing white dress. I'd love to take you shopping, and I know just the shop."

When Shelly shrugged, Ivy added, "I'm working on her, Mom. She should wear something pretty for the photographs." She watched Shelly's expression. Her usually ebullient sister seemed troubled, and Ivy wondered what was bothering her.

"Well, it's Shelly's wedding, and she should do as she wishes," Carlotta said, although Ivy could tell her mother was disappointed. She recalled how her mother had helped her choose her wedding dress for her marriage to Jeremy. That seemed so long ago now, and here she was, engaged again.

"The marriage is what's important," Carlotta said. "Will you invite any of your friends from New York?"

As Shelly picked up a frame to wrap, she shook her head. "None of them can understand why I left New York for Summer Beach. Their lives move at lightning speed—like mine once did. Anyway, my closest friend there is married to Ezzra's best friend, and she doesn't want to travel without him, so that's awkward."

"Mitch has a lot of friends in Summer Beach." Carlotta plucked another family photo from the wall.

"Too many to invite to the wedding," Shelly replied. "We decided on family only, except for Bennett and Darla."

Carlotta frowned. "Isn't that the neighbor who sued Ivy?"

"Darla can be cranky sometimes, but we've become friends." Since Ivy persuaded Darla to drop the lawsuit, she had made every effort to be friendly. Ivy baked for her, Shelly trimmed her trees and planted flowers, and they always included Darla in holiday celebrations. She was just lonely. Mitch had become her surrogate son and a replacement for her young son, who had died.

Shelly laughed. "Quite the mother-in-law, right? Maybe we'll throw a party at Java Beach for people in town afterward. That would be easy."

Ivy caught a wistful note in Shelly's voice that she hadn't heard before, and it made her wonder. Surely Mitch had already organized a party, or was he leaving it to Shelly? Her sister hadn't wanted much help in planning. Other than making a list for her, Ivy hadn't interfered. She would ask Shelly again later, she decided.

Ivy and Shelly helped Carlotta pack the remaining pictures and tape the box.

"I have suitcases and a few boxes in the bedroom," Carlotta said, starting toward the other end of the house. "Some things I hate to put in storage. With a closed storage unit, the summer heat can do a lot of damage to delicate clothes."

They entered her parents' bedroom, an all-white setting filled with vivid artwork and pottery from their travels around the world. Double French-paned doors stood open to a wide deck where her parents often enjoyed coffee and the morning newspaper. The house sat on a hillside promontory point, and the land fell away to the ocean beyond.

Ivy had always felt safe in this room. She trailed her fingers across the polished cherrywood of her mother's mirrored vanity. Breathing in, she recognized the familiar lily of the valley perfume her mother favored. *Diorissimo.*

Turning toward the large bed, she recalled her parents reading to her and her siblings on a similar fluffy white duvet that smelled of sunshine and sea breezes, fresh from the clothesline.

At the windows, sheer white curtains billowed, and a whimsical wind chime made of antique silver cutlery tinkled in wispy ocean winds. Her mother had always loved her bright whites in the bedroom, calling the neutral palette restful and the perfect background for their artwork.

Inspired, Ivy had followed the same scheme in her bedroom at the inn.

Carlotta motioned toward two open suitcases perched on a bench at the foot of the bed. "I've put aside some clothes that you might like to use while we're gone. My perfumes certainly wouldn't survive the summer heat in storage. And why would I want to pack away my jewelry when you girls could be enjoying it?"

One entire suitcase was devoted to jewelry that Carlotta had collected from the artisans they'd worked with around the world. Bright strands of turquoise and coral, iridescent pearls and shells, hand-carved bracelets, and sparkling earrings brimmed to the top of the suitcase, each encased in a sheer organza pouch.

For years, Carlotta and Sterling had traveled the world seeking out talented artisans and artists to supply their crafts to department and specialty stores. The couple had developed keen eyes for talent and enjoyed showing the work of people who often became cherished friends.

In the last year, they had scaled back their representation, although they still provided introductions for a few artisans. Their father was determined to spend more time sailing and traveling while they were still in good health.

Shelly cooed over the assortment. "May I pick out something to wear for my wedding?"

"I hope you do," Carlotta said, waving her hand over the glittering array. "Anything you like." She picked up a small leather-covered case. "And here is my best jewelry, along with pieces from my mother and grandmother. You girls might like to borrow the pearls. Take what you'd like to use, and I'll put the rest in a safety deposit box at the bank and leave the key with you. It's all going to be yours someday anyway."

Shelly's eyes gleamed. "This is like every birthday and holiday rolled into one."

Ivy didn't like to think about her parents not being around, though she knew that was eventually inevitable. Though not until far, far in the future, she hoped. Ivy was concerned about their safety on this trip. While Carlotta and Sterling were expert sailors, a big storm could quickly capsize a boat. Ivy tucked her hair behind her ears and tried to banish the thought.

Carlotta untied a vintage satin pouch and lifted a strand of pearls to the light. "My mother wore these for her wedding. Pearls should be worn a few times a year to maintain their sheen." She held the strand up to Ivy's neck. "You could wear these on your wedding day."

Ivy touched the smooth pearls with reverence. She'd worn them when she married Jeremy. "These would be better on Shelly. They would be delightfully unexpected with that white swimsuit." Besides, she had planned to wear the necklace that Bennett had given her for Christmas.

Shelly beamed at her. "I like that idea." She bent her neck while her mother fastened the necklace on her.

Clasping her hands, Carlotta stepped back to admire her youngest daughter. "They light your face beautifully, *mija*."

Shelly ran her fingers over the lustrous pearls. "Thanks, Mom. I'd love to wear these."

Carlotta took Ivy's hand. "If you move your date up, you and Shelly could have a double wedding. That way, we could see both of you down the aisle before we leave."

Shelly's smile froze on her face while Ivy shook her head. "It's Shelly's day first." Bennett understood, too.

"We'll just have to fly back for yours," Carlotta said.

"There's no rush," Ivy said, though Bennett might disagree with that.

With excitement flicking in her dark eyes, Carlotta put an arm around her. "It's easy to fly from Mazatlan or Puerta Vallarta. The airports aren't too far from the marinas. Or from Costa Rica. We're meeting friends at Marina Pez Vela in Quepos. Once we sail for French Polynesia, following the trade winds, we'll be at sea for a while."

"Dad said it should take a couple of months," Shelly interjected.

"It's not necessary for you to return for our wedding," Ivy said. "I'd rather you and Dad enjoy your journey."

"Or you could meet us somewhere along the way," Carlotta said. "On a Polynesian island, or when we visit friends who have a vineyard in South Africa. That would be a beautiful setting."

"That's tempting," Ivy said, though she didn't know if Bennett would want to be away from his family.

Carlotta secured the pearls in a satin jewelry roll. "I'll put these in a safety deposit box until you're ready for them. You'll want to install a safe at the inn. Not that I don't trust your guests, but one never knows."

"That's probably a good idea," Ivy agreed. She'd contact Forrest and ask him about having a safe built in. "As open as we are in welcoming guests, I know we can't trust everyone."

As her mother tucked the jewelry into her purse, Ivy thought about Bennett. She trusted what she knew of him. Yet, she'd learned that time was a critical factor in a relationship.

She'd trusted Jeremy, too.

Anyone could pretend or cover up for a few months, Ivy thought. However, the longer you knew someone, the more likely they would slip if they were hiding something.

Not that Ivy thought Bennett had any nefarious intentions. Still, there might be a lot about Bennett she didn't know, and she didn't have much longer to find out everything she could.

4

*I*n the marina, water lapped lazily against the hull of Bennett's boat, and seagulls squawked overhead. The day before, he'd stripped the old varnish from teakwood sections of the boat, and today he was sealing the wood.

Working on the boat was therapeutic for him. This morning, he'd put on jazz and mixed a pitcher of freshly squeezed grapefruit juice, courtesy of an old tree on the grounds of the Seabreeze Inn. He helped pick the fruit from the tops of trees no one else could reach. He'd brought his juicer from his house when he leased it and enjoyed squeezing fresh juice for Ivy.

"Hey, old man," Mitch called out. "Need a helper?"

"Could have used you yesterday for the stripping and sanding. This is the easy part."

"Why do you think I waited until today?" Mitch climbed aboard.

"Smart guy. What's going on?"

"I spent the morning training another part-timer at Java Beach to help with the summer traffic. That will give me more time off, too."

"Good move. You're going to need that as a married man. Can't be a total workaholic." He squinted against the sun.

"Shelly works pretty hard, too," Mitch said. "Caring for the grounds, helping Ivy with guests, and filming videos for her gardening and lifestyle online channel—she's always busy."

Bennett squinted against the sun. "That's good. She's just as industrious as you are. But things will change when the baby comes along."

"How would you—" Mitch caught himself and flushed. "Hey, I'm sorry about that. Sometimes I still make an idiot of myself."

"That's okay. It's been so long that most folks have forgotten or never knew that I was looking forward to being a father."

"That must've been a pretty tough time for you."

Bennett put down the sponge applicator he'd been using to spread sealer on the teakwood. "Worst thing I have ever been through. I wouldn't wish that on anyone."

Suddenly Mitch looked stricken. "How often do women have medical issues with pregnancy? I'd never want anything to happen to Shelly. I mean, if having a baby is that risky, I don't know if I want to take the chance on kids, even though Shelly wants a family." He hesitated. "I have enough reservations, anyway."

Bennett detected a strained note in Mitch's voice. The kid was probably just worried. "Pregnancy complications like Jackie had are extremely rare. Don't worry too much about it. Chances are you and Shelly will have smooth sailing through delivery."

"Yeah, about that..." He ran a hand through his short spiky hair.

Bennett looked at him. "Want to talk about it?"

"It's not my favorite subject." Mitch picked up the sponge applicator that Bennett had put down and dipped it into the sealant. As he spread it across the teakwood in long strokes, he began to talk. "See, my old man—my ma, too—were pretty tough on me when I was a kid."

Bennett listened, letting Mitch take over his job. His friend had never spoken about his family—other than to say his parents had died in an accident. Bennett hadn't pushed him to talk about his family or his childhood, although he'd often wondered how Mitch had grown up. He always figured that when Mitch was ready to unburden himself, he would be there for him.

Slowly, Mitch continued. "I overhear a lot of conversations at Java Beach, and someone said that if folks were hard on their kids, then when those kids grow up, chances are they'll do the same when they have kids. So I searched online about that, and it turns out that it can be true. That scares me."

Bennett pondered Mitch's words. "When you say 'hard on their kids,' I'm not sure I follow. Do you mean that they demanded a lot from you, or do you mean they were abusive?"

Mitch heaved a sigh. "Pa wasn't a big guy, but when he was mad, I knew to clear out. I wasn't a match for him until I was older. And that only seemed to anger him more."

"And your mother?"

"She never beat me like my pop did, but she sure had a mouth on her. Ma thought that since she'd never hit me, she was better than Pa. But she could make you wish she'd just belt you and get it over with."

"I'm sorry you had to suffer abuse like that," Bennett said. *Physically and verbally.* He rested a hand on Mitch's shoulder. That explained a lot about the poor decisions Mitch had made early in life and how he came to serve a short prison sentence for theft.

Mitch shrugged. "Doesn't matter anymore. I don't like to talk about it. But what happens when Shelly and I have kids?"

"You know how to treat people now." Bennett hesitated, but he had to ask. "Do you and Shelly ever have the kind of arguments your parents did?"

"Not at all. I couldn't imagine treating her badly." Mitch frowned. "Now that I've told you this about my folks, I hope you don't think I'll do that to Shelly."

"I don't see you doing that. You're one of the most easy-going guys I know." The relaxed beach vibe seemed deep in Mitch's soul. Bennett sensed his friend had been striving for inner calm for a long time, but he'd never known why.

Mitch looked out toward the horizon. "I took up surfing because I wanted to conquer something bigger than my pa, bigger than myself. Out there, I could be free. I could forget my anger, overcome monster waves, and not hurt anyone."

Bennett realized Mitch had been waging an internal battle. "Surfing can be very therapeutic."

Mitch paused with the applicator in mid-air. "So, there's this generational angle. Experts say that kids who were beaten…" He stopped, unable to go on.

"Might be apt to repeat it?" Bennett offered gently.

"Yeah," Mitch replied, letting out a whoosh of breath. "I'd never want to hurt my kids, but people say you have to have a lot of patience with them."

"That's true." Bennett had seen that with Logan, his ten-year-old nephew, and Logan was a pretty good kid. Many young children had melt-downs.

Mitch curled a fist into his stomach. "What if this meanness is inside of me, and I don't even know it? What if it comes out when Shelly has a baby, or the kid gets older? If that's what's going to happen, then I'm not fit to be a father. I don't think I should risk it."

Bennett could hear the anguish in Mitch's voice. "Has this been keeping you up at night?"

"You have no idea. And what's worse is that I can't talk to

Shelly about this. I'm afraid it would scare her away to think that I could turn into some kind of monster."

"You have to talk to her. I think she'll understand."

Mitch finished the application of the sealant and put down the sponge. "Not if I tell her I can't risk having children. I know how much she wants a baby. And I can't stand to break her heart."

Bennett nodded. This explained why Mitch had been acting odd and shying away from setting a date for the wedding. "You need to resolve these feelings before you and Shelly tie the knot. Speaking as your friend, I don't see any signs of abusive behavior in you. But I'm no expert in that field. I think you're right to be concerned and brave to face it. That's half the battle. You're a good man, Mitch. Never forget that."

Mitch's frown eased a little. "Thanks for saying that."

"It's true," Bennett said. "Still, if you can't come to terms with having children before you get married, you're going to leave Shelly with a tough choice."

Mitch drew his hands over his face. "That would be a nightmare for both of us. I still have a lot of years ahead of me if I decide to have kids later, but Shelly doesn't. That doesn't matter though, because I wouldn't want to have children with anyone else. I just don't know what to say to her. Maybe the words will come to me."

Bennett looked at his friend with compassion. "You shouldn't wait until after you get married and then decide you don't want to have children. That would be deceitful of you, even though I know you wouldn't mean to be."

"You're right." Mitch pressed his hand against his chest. "I've never met anyone like Shelly. She makes me feel like anything is possible, and I feel like the best version of me when I'm with her. Do you know what I mean?"

"That's called love, my friend." Bennett was proud of

Mitch for having the courage to talk about his feelings. A lot of men he knew didn't like to talk about that.

"Shelly is the best thing in my life. I don't want to blow this or let her down. Her parents are so great that I'm afraid she can't understand what I went through with mine. On top of that, Sterling and Carlotta are leaving soon, and I know Shelly wants to get married before they leave. But I've got this hard knot in my stomach. I'm not sure what to do."

"You could delay the wedding, but you should tell Shelly why." Bennett understood what Mitch was going through, and he wasn't going to minimize his feelings. He hoped Mitch would take his advice the right way.

"After Jackie died," Bennett began, "I couldn't keep my feelings bottled up. I felt like I'd implode if I did. That's when I started running marathons, pounding out my anger over the injustice of having her and our baby taken away from me. I never thought I could care as deeply for another woman as I had for her. Now I do, but it took ten long years before Ivy came along."

"So running helped you?"

Bennett picked up the applicator to clean it. "That was part of it, much like your surfing. I kept my pain and anger bottled up for a long time, trying to be stoic about it. My father encouraged me to talk about it, a little at a time. Finally, on his urging, I went to see a professional counselor. It helped to talk to someone who wasn't involved in my life. I could open up to them without any judgment, and I learned a lot about myself in the process." He looked at Mitch earnestly. "You might find it helpful, too."

For a few minutes, Mitch seemed at a loss of what to say. He stood watching waves slap against the hull. Finally, he said, "I've never told anyone but you about this. I don't know if I could talk to a stranger."

"Can't hurt to try," Bennett said. "It could put your mind

at ease. They might have some insights you haven't thought about."

Mitch nodded slowly. "But I don't even know how to find someone like that. I'd feel weird about calling a shrink."

"I'll ask my old therapist for referrals for you." Bennett understood Mitch's reluctance. "He's moved, but maybe he can recommend others. Referrals are a good way to find the right people for you."

That seemed to put Mitch's mind at ease. "Sounds good, thanks."

While Bennett finished cleaning and storing his supplies, he and Mitch talked, though Bennett was careful not to bring up wedding plans. Mitch was under a lot of stress right now, and that would only add to it.

Bennett would call his former therapist as soon as Mitch left. With Shelly's heart set on getting married before her parents set sail on their voyage, there was no time to lose.

5

"*I* smell rain," Ivy said as Shelly pulled the Jeep into the car court behind the main house. The wind kicked up white caps on the ocean and rustled palm fronds overhead. "There's a heavy cloud coming this way."

"Let's get these bags and boxes inside." Shelly opened the rear hatch and slid out a pair of boxes.

Ivy hefted the heavy carton of photos while her sister picked up a box of mementos. "Oof, memories sure are heavy." Ivy shifted the carton up with her knee.

"That sounds philosophical," Shelly said.

"Sometimes they're hard to leave behind, too." Ivy caught Shelly's eye.

"The problem is, there are good memories mixed in with the bad." Shelly nodded toward the garage. "Here comes your hero."

"My what?" She turned around.

Bennett jogged toward them. "I'll get that for you." He relieved Ivy of her box and dropped a kiss on her cheek. "Put that other one on top," he said to Shelly.

"Sure, if you insist," Shelly said, gladly handing him her load.

"Thanks, honey," Ivy said, the term of endearment rolling effortlessly from her lips.

Bennett smiled at that. "Is everything in the Jeep coming inside, sweetheart?"

Ivy felt her cheeks warm while Shelly chuckled. "Mom is leaving some things with us. If you'll take everything up to my room, we'll sort it out there."

Bennett started ahead of them.

"You mean fight over it," Shelly said.

"We should save some things for Honey, too." Their eldest sister lived in Sydney, Australia, although she and her husband often visited their daughter Elena, a jewelry designer in Los Angeles. "And Mom is giving us the use of all this only while she's gone, remember?"

"Possession is nine-tenths of the law," Shelly shot back.

"It is not." Ivy poked her sister. "What, you're an attorney now?"

Ahead of them, Bennett laughed. "Come on, you two. Show me where to put these."

"In my closet," Ivy called out. She and Shelly divided the hanging clothes between them and hurried after him.

Bennett stacked the cartons in the closet and hung the clothing for them. As he glanced around the closet and bedroom, Ivy couldn't help but wonder if he was mentally placing himself there. What would it be like after they married?

"Are you rearranging the furniture?" Ivy asked.

Sheepishly, Bennett ran a hand over his hair. "Caught me. Guess we'll have to figure out where we're going to live. I gave my tenants a two-year lease on my house."

"Your room or mine, I suppose." Ivy smoothed her hand over his shoulder.

"Doesn't matter, as long as we're together." Bennett met her gaze and brought her hand to his lips. "I'll get the rest of your things from the Jeep, and then I have a community meeting to attend."

He nodded toward Shelly, who had already torn into the first box. "Mitch called and said he's just returned from his boat with a big fresh catch. Red snapper, rockfish, and bluefin tuna. If you ladies are up for supper on the beach, we'll barbecue on the patio. Sunny and Poppy, too, of course."

Shelly's eyes lit. "I sure love a man who can cook."

"We'll make a side salad and vegetable kabobs," Ivy said. "Sunny has plans with friends tonight, but I'll mention it to Poppy." She appreciated that Bennett automatically included her daughter and niece in supper and other activities.

"That's a plan then." Bennett left to bring in another load of boxes. As she watched him walk down the hallway that she had filled with beach watercolor scenes she'd painted, a guestroom door swung open.

Gilda came out of her room clutching Pixie. The high-strung Chihuahua was seeing a doggie therapist for treatment for anxiety and kleptomania.

Bennett bent down to scratch Pixie behind the ears, and she eagerly yapped her approval. She loved Bennett. "Out for your walk with Pixie?"

"Every day if I can manage it." Gilda's short spiky hair was a brighter shade of pink today. "Pixie's therapist says it's good for socialization. I have my umbrella if it starts raining."

After the Ridgetop fire that had swallowed Gilda's home like a fiery beast, Pixie had lost her world, too, even though Gilda hadn't had her very long before that occurred. The inn was fairly quiet, but occasionally guests were loud or up late. Dogs heard more than humans, and Ivy imagined that activity might be unsettling for Pixie.

Bennett grinned. "You two sure take care of each other. Are you writing any new articles this week?"

"An editor called yesterday with a new story. I'm working on an article about dating after the death of a spouse."

"Tough subject," Bennett said quietly. "If anyone can do it justice, I'm sure you can."

"Would you mind if I asked you a few questions later?"

Bennett barely hesitated. "Of course. Happy to share anything that might help others."

Leaning against the doorjamb, Ivy observed the exchange with interest. It was the little things Bennett did that meant so much to her. He was easy-going, active, and spontaneous, but most of all, he truly cared about people. Even the crabby ones such as Darla next door. He treated everyone he met with dignity and respect regardless of their station in life—or whether their behavior had earned it.

Looking back, Ivy had often found herself cringing at Jeremy's mistreatment of restaurant servers and hotel staff. Over the last few months, she had been watching Bennett for any potential red flags: too much alcohol, signs of gambling, flirting, or watching other women when Ivy was with him.

She hadn't seen any signs yet. Still, she was cautious. As her father had once said when she started dating, *a little due diligence doesn't hurt.*

When Bennett disappeared down the stairs, Ivy turned away. She often wondered why he hadn't remarried after his wife died. He told her he simply hadn't found anyone. Yet it had been ten years, and Ivy knew the statistics. According to studies she'd read after Jeremy died, most men remarried within two to three years on average after their spouse died. Women took a little longer, if they remarried at all.

So why hadn't Bennett been motivated to marry again, especially in the prime of his life when he could have started another family?

Ivy joined Shelly in the large closet. It was more than a closet; it was also a dressing room. At the far end was a large trifold mirror with a round, raised fitting platform in front of it that had probably served for alterations. On either side, rows of mirrored closets and cedar shelves lined the perimeter. A chandelier sparkled overhead, casting a pretty glow over the room. Two vintage wingback chairs that Ivy had updated with marine-blue slipcovers sat to one side.

Shelly was admiring her mother's silk scarves. "I remember Mom wearing every one of these. Around her hair or neck, sometimes tied to her purse or worn as a halter top or skirt." She held a beautifully printed Italian silk scarf to her face. "I can still detect her perfume." Shelly looked up. "I hope nothing happens to them on this trip."

"I think they'll be fine." Though Ivy was trying to ease Shelly's worries, she was concerned. "They've traveled the world. We shouldn't worry. Besides, they seem so happy and excited," she added, which was true. "They're doing what they've always loved."

Shelly sighed. "I guess we should be glad they can still can."

"That's right," Ivy said. "Now, about all this." She waved her hand. "I have plenty of open drawers and shelves in here for Mom's things. Take what you want, or help yourself any time."

"I'll leave most of it in here. My closet is a little crowded. So is Mitch's."

Shelly knelt and began to fill the empty drawers. She shared her room with Poppy—and sometimes with Sunny when they needed another guest room, or Poppy was in Los Angeles visiting her marketing clients. Sunny stayed in one of the Sunset suites when she could.

Ivy was glad that Sunny had become flexible about that.

When Ivy had moved from Boston, she hadn't brought many clothes because they were all wrong for Summer Beach. Sweaters and woolen skirts and slacks were too heavy for the mild climate. She gave away all but a few lightweight sweaters to a shelter before she moved.

Since she'd arrived in Summer Beach, she sometimes shopped at a local thrift store, and her mother had given her a few sundresses. Fortunately, she didn't need much for beach living, as any extra money was earmarked for improvements at the inn.

After Bennett brought the rest of the suitcases and boxes upstairs and deposited them in the dressing room, he turned to Ivy. "See you at supper tonight." He dropped another kiss on her cheek and left.

Ivy stepped to the window and pressed her fingers against the old, wavy glass panes. She watched him race to his SUV as raindrops dotted his shoulders. She really loved this man.

Just then, a raincloud passed over the sun, darkening the room. Ivy turned on the overhead chandelier and joined her sister.

Shelly rocked back on her heels. "We got lucky with these guys, didn't we?"

"They're the lucky ones." Ivy nudged her sister, and they both laughed.

Ivy unzipped one of the suitcases and lifted out another stack of her mother's silk scarves. She tucked them into an open drawer and ran her hand over the brilliant rainbow of colors. Shades of turquoise, coral, yellow, emerald, and sapphire gleamed under light cast through the chandelier's sparkling crystal prisms. As she gazed at the silken colors, she realized she'd inherited her mother's appreciation for color— now evident in her painting.

"Shoes on the shelves?" Shelly asked.

"That's right," Ivy replied. "And I'll put the empty suit-cases in the last closet."

Shelly zipped a suitcase. "This one is ready to go."

"I'll get that." Ivy stood and carried the empty suitcase to the farthest closet. Like the rest, this one was cedar lined. Even today, the faint aroma of sweet cedarwood wafted into the air whenever she opened a closet door.

Ivy lifted the case into the closet and pushed it toward the back wall.

"Here's another one," Shelly said, hefting an old tapestry bag.

"I'll put it on top of the other one to save room." While she still had space, Sunny had already filled another closet. Ivy took the case and shoved it on top of the first one. As she did, she suddenly lost her balance and stumbled against the luggage.

"Oh, geez!" Flailing, Ivy kept falling. At once, the closet's rear wall gave way, and she crashed down onto the suitcases.

"Are you okay?" Shelly reached out to her. "Take my hand."

Ivy was sprawled across the suitcases, which had tumbled through a cracked edge in the wall. "Something else to repair," she muttered. "Can you get your phone and shine some light here? Some old nails must have popped out."

Dust floated through the opening, and Ivy sneezed.

"Here you go," Shelly said. She held up her phone to shine the built-in flashlight across the damaged wall. "Maybe we can fix it. Or get the guys to help."

Blinking through the dusty air, Ivy peered ahead. "Wait a minute. Bring that light closer."

"What is it?"

"I don't know, but I feel a draft."

Shelly steadied the light. "Can you see anything?"

"Not much." Ivy reached a hand into the space. "Can you give me the light?"

Shelly passed the phone to her, and Ivy shone it into the darkness. "Oh, wow." She scrambled to her feet and turned around. "There's another room back there. I saw a rack of clothes."

Shelly's eyes widened. "Let's go. Maybe that's where Amelia hid the gold."

"What gold?"

Her sister sighed. "Isn't there always hidden treasure in the old mystery shows? Surely Amelia kept a nest egg stashed away. She hid everything else. I'm expecting to find stacks of gold bars or baskets of coins any day now."

"You're too funny." Ivy pushed the suitcases aside. "Why didn't we see this on the plans?"

"I have no idea," Shelly replied. "I was looking for a space labeled Secret Room, but I didn't see it. Maybe this was built later."

Ivy drew a breath and glanced at her sister. "Ready?"

Shelly grinned. "Here we go again."

Ivy shone the light ahead, and they stepped inside a small, windowless room so quiet that even their footsteps seemed muffled in the heavy, decades-old silence.

As Shelly swept the light across the darkness, Ivy gasped. As if suspended in mid-air, a form of a woman seemed to float before them.

*a*n ivory dress from a bygone era shimmered in the shaft of light. Ivy stepped toward it. On closer inspection, the long vintage gown skimmed a dressmaker's form. This is what had appeared suspended in air.

Ivy expelled a breath of relief.

"For a moment there, I thought we'd found our ghost," Shelly said. She swung the back panel of the closet wider.

"Shh," Ivy said, rubbing her arms. She got chills whenever someone mentioned spirits. Whatever she'd seen in her room that day—now months ago—she refused to call it a ghost.

Shelly chuckled. "Afraid Amelia will hear us?"

"I've warned you before about that." Ivy shook her head and stepped around the dress. A row of tiny, silk-covered buttons lined the back of the dress, from the neckline to below the waist.

She swung the light across the room. Next to the dressmaker's form was a wood-framed loveseat and a side table with a lantern and a rattan sewing basket. Beside the basket sat a silver thimble and a spool of ivory thread with a needle jabbed through the wound thread. A small skein of silky thread lay next to that, along with a small, ornate pair of scissors.

The nostalgic tableau was evocative of a time long past, yet it also suggested someone had just left the room, intending to return.

Why hadn't they? Ivy wondered.

Shelly brushed dust from the shoulders of the dress. "Looks like an evening gown. Very old, but gorgeous."

Ivy sized up the intricate design. Slim fit, draped silk, delicate lace. "This style looks like it might have been from the first part of the last century. Probably Edwardian, because skirt lengths rose in the 1920s. Someone must have been working on this dress."

She swept the light to another hanger that held lengths of folded lace. Several garments hung beside that. "Let's move these clothes into the light so we can get a better look."

Working together, they brought the old garments, the dressmaker's form, and the sewing basket and lantern into Ivy's room.

Ivy pushed the drapes aside, trying to let more light into the room to examine their discovery. Raindrops were pelting the window, but the sun was already trying to peek through the clouds. Spring showers were often intermittent on the coastline.

"This dress is beautifully constructed," Ivy said, settling onto the bench in front of the bed. "Ivory silk charmeuse, beaded lace trim with real pearls, fully finished interior seams. You hardly ever see this type of artistry now, except on very expensive clothes."

The gown was cinched at the waist, with a skirt that flowed into a bell shape. Luxurious and feminine. Ivy could just imagine a woman wearing this.

"Wow, look at this," Shelly said, holding up a full-length lace coat. "It probably goes with it."

"That's striking." Ivy ran her fingers along the garment.

"Just look at this standing corded collar. Imagine how it would frame the face." She inspected the scalloped lace and tiny silk-covered buttons.

Shelly seemed equally enthralled. "You could wear this today and still be right in style."

Ivy turned to the delicate embroidered lace folded over an old wooden coat hanger. "I bet this was for a bridal veil. I've seen old photos of wedding gowns, and this one looks similar, although much nicer."

Shelly's lips parted. "Are you thinking what I'm thinking?"

"What?"

"You should wear this gown for your wedding," Shelly said. "We could have worn Mom's if it hadn't gone missing."

Carlotta's wedding dress had been lost years ago. She had loaned it to a friend for her marriage, and afterward, the suitcase had disappeared at the airport.

Ivy shook her head. "Look at the waist on that dress. I don't think I could've worn it even when I was young and slim. What about you?"

"Sadly, it's too short for me," Shelly said with a sigh. "That would have been better than a swimsuit and coverup."

"I'll say."

The two women stared longingly at the dress and the accompanying lace coat and lace fabric.

"What a shame," Ivy finally said. "It would have been such a nice tribute to Amelia."

Shelly ran her hand along the smooth silk. "Sure wish I could wear this. But I do want a long dress, even if it is a beach cover-up. Maybe this dress will fit Poppy or one of our other nieces someday."

"That's an idea. I'll have it cleaned."

Wistfully, Shelly touched the lace collar. "Ask them to be extra careful."

They continued going through the clothes. The menswear looked dapper yet dated, though Ivy thought a few of the women's styles could be worn today. One was a drop-waisted flapper style, and another was a trim navy suit. Still, they looked more like costumes.

Later that day, Ivy shared their findings with Poppy, who was also amazed at the discovery. After the rain ceased and sunny skies again prevailed, they checked in another guest, bade Mrs. Mehta farewell on her journey to see her grandchildren, and made reservations for massages for the bachelorette party.

"Ready for a break?" Ivy asked Poppy. "I hear Shelly in the kitchen."

When they opened the door, Shelly looked over her shoulder at the sink where she was rinsing fresh mint. Sliced oranges sat to one side. "I'm going to whip up a virgin Sea Breeze cocktail. Want one?"

"Sounds refreshing," Poppy said. "I need extra energy to finish that marketing campaign for my new client. We're meeting later."

"One of you can grab the pink grapefruit and cranberry juices in Gertie," Shelly said, patting the mint dry.

Ivy opened one of the twin turquoise refrigerators they'd nicknamed Gert and Gertie and brought out the juices. "Here you go."

After Shelly poured the juice coolers, she slid onto a stool at the center prep island. "So why do you think that little room was concealed?"

"I'll bet it had something to do with the secret attic rooms," Ivy replied. "The closet next to the one we broke open has the trap door to the attic. It would make sense to have a place where people could quickly dash into hiding." She had inspected the rear panel, which was actually a hinged door. A strip of fabric could be used to pull the panel shut, and clothes on the rack in front would conceal it.

"They probably needed a place to dress after they bathed," Poppy said, leaning her chin on her hand. "If it were me, I'd store extra stuff in there for them. Bet that's why there were a lot of old clothes. Imagine having to start over with nothing and hide like that."

"It takes a lot of faith, resilience, and perseverance." Ivy sighed. She spoke from experience.

Poppy took in her words and said softly, "It must have been hard for you after Jeremy died, Aunt Ivy."

"It was." To get through that period, Ivy had tried to put her situation in perspective. "I often thought about how, in comparison, so many others have suffered far worse. Remember the story that Nick shared with us?"

At Christmas, Ivy had discovered that one of their guest's grandparents had fled the war in Europe. Nick Snow had sought out the inn to visit the home his grandparents had once talked about. He shared how Amelia Erickson had sheltered them until they could find work and obtain work permits. Amelia had provided a second chance for many European artists caught in the literal crossfire of the Second World War.

According to Amelia's writings that Ivy had discovered, the news story of a refugee ship from Europe turned back from American shores devastated the former owner. The passengers had been so close to freedom in a vast country, yet they had been denied entry and returned to Europe. Subsequently, many of those passengers died in the war.

Upon learning their fate, Amelia had vowed to help as many World War II refugees as she could begin new lives in a new country. Nick's grandparents owed their lives to Amelia. In turn, they had built a farm for their family, employed others, and produced Nick, whose ingenuity had contributed to a valuable medical breakthrough.

"I wonder how many people Amelia looked after here," Shelly said.

Ivy had often wondered, too. "I don't know if we'll ever know that. However, we can continue to do what we can, just as Amelia might have."

"Except we don't have her gazillions," Shelly said pointedly.

"A hand up is often more valuable than a handout," Poppy said.

Shelly raised her brow. "That's deep. Where'd you learn that?"

"One of my professors taught conscientious marketing," Poppy replied. "And the cost, if any, is usually less. Certainly in the long term."

Ivy was impressed. Poppy was young, but Ivy had always thought their niece was destined for great work.

"That's part of a conscientious marketing plan I'm working on for my new client." Poppy went on with enthusiasm. "I'm suggesting that for every specialty food item they sell, they donate a percentage to a farmers co-op in a lower socio-economic region, here or abroad. They can buy seed or upgrade their farming equipment to produce more food for their community."

"I think people are often willing to pay more for a healthy product that gives back," Shelly said thoughtfully. "I know I am. It makes me feel better about what I buy, especially if it's something I might not need."

Ivy stole a glance at Shelly. She rarely heard her sister admit to such profound thinking, even though she knew Shelly had a soft heart for those in need. Shelly was volunteering at the local high school and mentoring kids who were interested in gardening. Most of them didn't know the options that were available in the field.

"See the psychology at work?" Poppy's eyes sparkled with excitement. "My client can spend less on advertising, and we'll run a publicity campaign to spread the news. It's a win for everyone."

Ivy listened to Shelly and Poppy chat. Her sister had changed since she'd moved to Summer Beach. Maybe part of that was due to Mitch, who was often the first to offer help to those in need, just as Bennett had helped him when he'd arrived in Summer Beach.

Mitch had been a surf bum who'd just served time in prison for theft, sleeping wherever he could. But Bennett had seen his potential and helped him find his way, encouraging him to think beyond his station and helping him secure a small business loan to open Java Beach. And that was one of the many reasons Ivy admired her new fiancé.

Poppy said, "Most of all, my clients are the kind of people who want to make a difference in the world. This can be their way. If I present it right, I think they'll like it."

"And recommend you to others." Ivy smiled at her niece, thinking about how mature and responsible Poppy had become.

Ivy hoped that some of Poppy's ideas would continue to rub off on Sunny. Her daughter had become more grounded since moving here, too. Although Sunny was in her last year of school, she still didn't have a strong direction.

"So what can we do with these old clothes we found?" Ivy asked. "They're so out of date I can't imagine they'd be much use to anyone."

Shelly held up a finger, and her lips formed a circle. "Maybe our new Summer Beach theater group could use them. Kai tells me that Axe aims to be ready with a new show in a few months." She took a sip of her drink. "But maybe we'll keep the wedding dress ensemble. It's so exquisite."

"That's a great idea." Ivy winked at Poppy. She would have the dress carefully cleaned and stored.

Their new friend Kai was Marina Moore's younger sister. Recently, they had both returned to their grandmother's beach house, which everyone called the Coral Cottage. Ivy knew Marina from years ago when they were teenagers spending a summer on the beach.

A local contractor, Axel Woodson—Axe to all who knew him—had also performed in summer stock. A few years ago, he'd bought a piece of land with the dream of turning it into an amphitheater to stage outdoor productions.

"Do you think Kai will stay in Summer Beach and help run the new theater?" Poppy asked.

"I can see your mind whirring," Ivy said, chuckling. "Axe could probably use your help to market the kick-off event."

"Kai told me she doubts she'll go back on tour with the theater group." Shelly folded her arms and leaned forward. "And she said that Carol Reston made a substantial donation to fund the new facility that Axe is building on his land. He started a nonprofit organization to run it."

Poppy bounced a little on her stool. "Do you think Kai and Axe might get married?"

"I think it's too soon to start that rumor," Ivy said, wagging a finger at Poppy. "This town is too small for such talk."

"Hey, Mom, I'm back," Sunny called out as the back door banged. "Hey, Aunt Shelly, Poppy."

"How was school?" Ivy asked automatically. Sunny wore a sky-blue top and faded jeans with flip-flops. With help from her cousin Poppy and Imani's son Jamir, Sunny had made the transition from Boston to Summer Beach and the university in nearby San Diego.

Sunny dropped her backpack by the door. "Pretty good. I have to start studying for final exams soon."

"Let me know if you need any help studying," Poppy said. She slid off her stool and gathered the empty glasses. "Break time is over for me. I need to finish this marketing plan."

"And I want to pick up my gardening boots and see Mitch," Shelly said, stretching her arms overhead.

"Could you bring back some supplies for me from Nailed It?" Ivy asked. The hardware store was next to Java Beach. "Washers and screws, some sort of drain de-clogger, and a couple of other things." Although solidly built, the old house was still a constant work-in-progress.

Shelly pushed back from the counter. "Sure, just tell me what you need."

"I'll have to make a list," Ivy said.

Sunny placed her hands on her mother's shoulders. "I have some time before I'm going out tonight. If you want to go with Aunt Shelly, I can watch the front desk and set up for tonight's wine-and-tea event."

Ivy swung around, surprised and pleased at Sunny's offer. "Why, I'd appreciate that. That would be a huge help."

Sunny grinned shyly. "I'm part of this team, too. I mean, as long as I'm here, right?"

"Yes, you are," Ivy replied, hugging her. No longer spoiled and belligerent, Sunny had overcome the attitude of privilege that her father had instilled in her by lavishing money, cars, and gifts on her. Shelly and Poppy grinned and gave Sunny high-fives.

"You're on," Shelly said. "Let's go, Ives. We can take the old Jeep. But I want to change first. That yellow sundress Mom gave us is calling my name."

Ivy smiled. "Mitch will like that."

As she watched Shelly race up the back stairs, Ivy thought about how much she would miss Shelly. After moving in with Mitch, Shelly would still come to work, but knowing her sister was sleeping at the other end of the hallway had given Ivy a feeling of comfort over the past year. Together, they had made it through a difficult period—Ivy with Jeremy's death and Shelly with the end of her long relationship with Ezzra.

And now, here they were, together at the beginning of new chapters in their lives. Mitch and Bennett were essentially good men. Yet Ivy still sensed warning signs simmering just beneath the surface. Were they really the men that Ivy and Shelly thought they were?

And how could they ever be sure?

7

"*I*'ll meet you back at the Jeep," Ivy said as Shelly pulled into a parking space on Main Street. While they could have walked to the village, carrying the vintage wedding dress would have been cumbersome.

"Sounds good. Then we can go to Java Beach and the hardware store." After Shelly parked, she hurried to the shoe repair shop to pick up her gardening boots. The old soles had come loose.

While her sister did that, Ivy carried the dingy wedding dress, lace coat, and extra lace into the Laundry Basket, a dry cleaner and alterations shop. Everything needed to be freshened.

When she stepped inside, the fresh aroma of lavender and laundry detergent reminded her of her mother's linen closet. A capable looking woman with steel-gray hair stood behind the counter.

"Welcome to the Laundry Basket. Laundry or dry cleaning for you today?"

"I'm not sure. Do you handle vintage clothes?" Ivy asked.

"Everything is vintage around here, including me. I'm Louise, and this is my shop. I'll do my best for you."

"I'm Ivy. I run the Seabreeze Inn with my sister." She placed her bundle on the counter next to the woman's coffee cup, noticing that it was from Java Beach. She probably knew Mitch, like most people in town.

"Oh, everyone knows who you girls are," Louise said lightly.

"I suppose new folks stand out."

Louise chuckled. "Ones like you sure do."

Ivy wasn't sure what the woman meant or how to respond to that, so she let the comment go. "We just found these stored in the house, and they're pretty dusty. Also very old. Possibly Edwardian."

Louise inspected the garments. "You're probably close. This style is from the 1920s at the latest. A hundred years old, but very well made." She turned back a seam to show Ivy. "You don't see this level of hand-finishing much anymore. I'll take extra care by hand with these. They'll be ready in a few days." A smile crossed her face. "This could be a beautiful wedding outfit. Maybe for you or Shelly soon?"

The comment caught Ivy off guard. She hadn't mentioned Shelly's name. Still, this was typical for Summer Beach. Once Bennett had shared their engagement with Nan at City Hall and Mitch had told Darla, their neighbor, news of their engagements had circulated through the town like a beach boomerang.

Quickly, Ivy recovered and smiled. "It's too small for me and too short for Shelly."

"Shelly is a lot taller than you," Louise agreed. "With those long legs, her skirts are awfully short."

That's an odd thing to say, Ivy thought, especially in a beach town where visitors wore the skimpiest of bikinis on the beach. She didn't think there was anything wrong with how Shelly dressed, but Louise was very direct.

Again, Ivy ignored the comment and went on. "This might fit one of our nieces."

"It's quite a lovely set," Louise said, nodding. Lowering her voice, she added, "I want you to know I'm on your side. I wish you all the luck with our mayor. He's quite the catch."

Ivy inclined her head. "Excuse me, but what do you mean by on *my side?*"

The woman's ruddy forehead creased. "I'm not one to gossip, but you know how small towns are. Everyone has an opinion about things that are none of their business. They don't mean any harm, though."

"No, of course not," Ivy said slowly. But words could have an impact.

Louise went on as she inspected the garments. "Many folks are pleased with the work you've done on the old Las Brisas del Mar estate. And that art show you put on brought in a lot of new visitors to the community. Summer Beach is lucky to have you; that's what I always tell them, despite what they might say."

"And we're happy to be part of Summer Beach," Ivy ventured. A strange feeling prickled her neck, and she couldn't help but wonder what had been said about them.

Louise patted the clothes. "Don't worry yourself about it. I'm sure everything will work out between Mitch and your sister, too. Yes, ma'am, I'm on both your sides."

"I sure appreciate that," Ivy said, somewhat awkwardly. What else could she say? If she seemed interested, that would only fuel more gossip.

As Ivy walked back to the Jeep, she tried to shake off Louise's comments. She certainly wouldn't worry Shelly with such trivial matters.

"Hey, Ivy." Her sister waved at her from across the street. A breeze lifted the fluttery skirt of Shelly's sundress, and she tugged it down. "Can you help me with these plants?"

Maybe a little short, Ivy conceded, but that was only because their mother was shorter. Besides, Shelly had great legs. It wasn't as if her sister was trying to be sexy. Shelly had a natural outdoors look and energy, and she seldom wore any makeup other than lip gloss and a touch of blush. Shelly would rather be working in the garden than primping in front of a mirror.

Ivy attributed the woman's comment to idle gossip and hurried across the street where Shelly stood with two sickly potted palms. A few thin fronds stuck out at awkward angles.

"The cobbler was throwing these out, so I offered to take them home," Shelly said. "They've almost been killed with kindness. Too much water, too much sun. I stripped off the dead stuff, and I'm pretty sure I can nurse them back to health." She pointed to a front window flooded with direct sunlight. "They got burned in that spot. This type of palm likes filtered light."

"I'll get this one," Ivy said, lifting a pot.

Shelly tucked her gardening boots under one arm and hoisted a pot. "I'll return them when they're healthy—if he agrees to follow my instructions."

"You're getting quite the reputation as a plant doctor."

Shelly shifted the palm and laughed. "That's all Nan's doing. Ever since I rescued a couple of ailing plants at City Hall. You just have to figure out what each plant likes."

They crossed the street and secured the pots in the back of the Jeep.

"Last stop for me is Java Beach," Shelly said, brushing dirt from her hands.

"I'll go in with you," Ivy said. "I could use a cup of Mitch's coffee before I dive into the nuts and bolts at Nailed It." She patted her pocket. "I brought the gizmos I need replaced. Jen and George always seem to know what to do." Jen was about her age, and she'd inherited the hardware shop from her father. Ivy always enjoyed seeing her.

They left the Jeep and walked the short way to Java Beach, nodding at familiar faces and visitors they passed. As the days grew warmer, tourists were trickling in, opening their beach houses and preparing for the summer ahead.

"It's hard to believe it's been a year since we arrived," Shelly said as they strolled past shops with open doors. "Although I loved New York when I lived there, that vibe seems a million miles away."

"Our lives are different now," Ivy said. "No more surprise spring snowstorms."

"I don't miss those," Shelly said. "It's funny, but I never thought Summer Beach would feel so much like home. And Mitch knows almost everyone. It's like one big family."

"And all the characters that come with that," Ivy said, thinking about what the dry cleaner had said.

"Oh, it's not so bad anymore. Especially since you tamed dragon-lady Darla." Shelly chuckled. "I've been giving her some of our garden harvests, but I think she's growing hard of hearing. I've called out to her a couple of times over the back fence, but she seemed like she didn't hear me and went inside. I just leave the veggies on her doorstep." She shrugged. "Maybe Mitch can suggest she have her hearing checked."

Ivy's neck prickled again, and she slid a hand across it. She couldn't help but wonder which team Darla was on. Ivy decided she would bake some banana nut bread and take it to their neighbor. Mitch had said that was one of her favorite treats.

Shelly opened the door to Java Beach. "After you, big sister."

Ivy stepped inside the coffee shop, which was fairly full this afternoon. Chatter rippled across the room, and beach reggae music played in the background. Old fishing nets hung from the ceiling, vintage Polynesian travels posters covered the walls, and the smell of roasted coffee and pastries filled the air.

"...two big-city girls, that's all they are."

Ivy hesitated. Snippets of a conversation floated from the other side of a thin bamboo screen in the entry.

"Swooped in to dazzle and steal our two most desirable bachelors."

Sucking in a breath, Ivy froze.

"That young one is always showing off her long legs. Can't blame Mitch for looking. But did you know she's a lot older than him? A cougar, that's what she is."

"So I've heard. Mitch is young, but our mayor should know better. He needs to be with a younger woman who'll give him another chance at having children. That's all I'm saying."

Shelly gave her a little push from behind. "Why are you waiting? Go in."

As the women talked, rage surged through Ivy, elevating her blood pressure. It wouldn't do Shelly any good to hear this kind of talk.

Ivy swung around and pressed a hand against Shelly's shoulder. "Why don't we go around back to the kitchen to see Mitch?" Her sister didn't need to hear that conversation.

"You're sure acting strange." Shelly stepped past her and strode toward the counter, short strappy sundress and all.

"Wait a minute," Ivy called, but Shelly marched on. Ivy winced and heaved a sigh. If her sister heard this, she'd be all over those women in a New York millisecond. It wouldn't be pretty.

She peeked through a spot on the screen to see who was talking. She recognized three women from the village, but she didn't know them.

Squinting, Ivy caught sight of a fourth woman. Her heart sank. Royal-blue hair, rhinestone visor.

Darla.

Their neighbor's raspy voice rang out. "I told Mitch to keep looking for someone his age. That Shelly is just too big-city for him—all short skirts and yoga-schmoga. He's just blinded by her faux worldliness. You know how men are."

Shelly stopped. She whirled around and stalked toward the table.

"Here we go," Ivy muttered, bracing herself emotionally.

Darla's raspy voice croaked out again. "I'll see to it that Mitch comes to his senses soon enough because—"

Shelly jabbed her hands on her hips and glared at the women. "Because of *what*?"

An uncomfortable hush spread across the room, and all heads swiveled toward Shelly.

Ivy raced around the bamboo screen and grabbed Shelly's arm. "They're not worth your time."

Turning to Darla, Ivy spat out, "You should be ashamed of yourself. I heard everything you said." She glared at the older women hunched over the table. "All of you."

Suddenly petulant, Darla folded her arms and leaned back against her chair. "Don't look at me. I'm not the one taking bets on if the weddings will take place." She jerked a thumb across the room. "That would be old Charlie back there."

"Hey, leave me out of it," Charlie shouted across the room.

Mitch appeared from the kitchen wearing a tie-dyed Grateful Dead T-shirt. His spiky bleached hair looked like he'd simply shaken it after surfing. "What's going on out here?"

Ivy shook her finger at Darla and her friends before answering Mitch. "It seems people in this town have divided into teams for and against us. And they're betting on us. Maybe you should be more careful about who you serve here."

She tugged Shelly's arm. "Let's go."

Shelly jerked away. "I will not. And I don't care what these old biddies are saying about me. I came to see Mitch." She whirled around and hurried to him.

Mitch slid a protective arm around Shelly and raised a finger to the room. "I don't know what's going on, but if any of you have a problem with Shelly or me, you can leave right now."

Darla jerked to her feet. "I won't stand to be treated this way." She brushed against Ivy's shoulder on her way out, and it was all Ivy could do to control herself.

The other women averted their gazes like naughty school-children, ashamed at being caught gossiping.

Ivy scanned the tables. Nan's husband Arthur was sitting with Charlie. She'd have a serious talk with him later.

"I hope you're better than this," Ivy said, fixing her gaze on Darla's friends and Charlie before sweeping across other familiar faces. "What have we ever done to any of you—except invite you into our home and provide lodging for your friends and families?"

A few people at other tables mumbled apologies and sheepishly turned back to their friends and conversations.

Since Mitch had swept Shelly into the kitchen, Ivy followed them.

As Shelly explained to Mitch what had happened, her face grew crimson with anger.

Mitch listened, his eyes narrowed. "They're just a bunch of small-town busybodies. Try not to let it bother you."

"Well, it does," Shelly cried. "That kind of talk can affect our reputation and our business." She drew her hands into fists. "Let me finish with them. They'll never show their cranky faces around here again."

"Hey, hey, I've got this," Mitch said, though he was clearly upset, too. "I'll talk to Darla and set her straight. I love you, babe. I've got your back." He took Shelly into his arms and rocked her on her feet.

Reluctantly, Shelly rested her head on his shoulder.

Ivy placed her hand on her sister's back. "Forget what they said. It's not important. I'll meet you at Nailed It."

She no longer needed that pick-me-up coffee; she was wide-awake now.

Still seething, Ivy ducked out the rear door and headed toward the hardware store. She thought they had been accepted in Summer Beach, but maybe they'd always be outsiders here. However, that wouldn't stop her or Shelly from marrying the men they loved.

She slowed her step. But what about Bennett and Mitch? Would what people said make them question their commitments? Maybe this was behind Mitch's hesitation.

8

"*V*egetable kabobs are ready," Bennett called out. He stood beside the wide barbecue grill on the terrace and readied the fresh fish he'd brought home from Mitch.

Looking up, he saw Ivy walking toward him, and a warm feeling suffused his chest. Even in a simple sundress, she looked beautiful. Bennett knew he was a lucky man. It was hard to believe that his life had changed so much in just a year.

With the ocean in the background and jazz on the outdoor speakers he'd rigged up at the inn, he couldn't think of any place he'd rather be. Not even his old house up on the ridgetop. Even though he'd had more space there, he'd grown lonely. While he'd tried to alleviate that feeling by filling his hours with work, he missed having a partner in his life.

He hadn't wanted to settle for just anyone. He'd held out for the perfect woman for him, and that was Ivy.

"I'll cover them with foil until the fish is ready," Ivy said, her eyes glittering like rare emeralds in the firelight. She held up a large platter.

"Thanks for making these," Bennett said as he plucked the charbroiled skewers from the grill. Portobello mushrooms, cherry tomatoes, and zucchini were spaced between garlic cloves and sweet Maui onion slices. Ivy had drizzled the vegetables with olive oil and seasoned them with rosemary and oregano from Shelly's garden.

"It was easy," Ivy said, leaning into him. "I love making supper like this."

"So do I." Bennett loved everything about tonight, but most of all, he loved Ivy. Ever since she'd come back into his life—their teenage crush hardly mattered now—she'd occupied his mind and heart every day. If someone had told him a year ago that he would be marrying the widow of his worst nightmare client, he never would have believed it.

"How long will the fish take?" Ivy asked.

"Just a few minutes for the tuna." Bennett picked up a plate of thickly sliced bluefin tuna brushed with olive oil. "I'm searing these a couple of minutes on each side. They cook fast on a hot grill."

Standing beside him and managing the other half of the broad grill was Mitch. He looked up. "The red snapper and rockfish are almost ready." Mitch had taken great care to prepare the whole snapper for the grill. Rockfish fillets filled a long-handled wire basket positioned over another part of the barbecue. "This grill was a great investment."

"Makes the place seem more like home," Bennett said. "We can use it for guests, too."

"The barbecue was a complete surprise." Ivy smiled up at Bennett. "I appreciate it so much. I didn't know you were such a good cook."

"Everyone has to eat," Bennett said, modestly deflecting her praise, though he enjoyed hearing it.

He'd been making a few additions to make the inn more comfortable for them. The new barbecue grill where he could cook for Ivy and her family, as well as patio furniture for his balcony so he and Ivy could share a glass of wine in private at the end of the day—these touches brought them together.

Bennett assumed he and Ivy would live at the inn for now, since Shelly would move out and Sunny was still living here. They hadn't figured out if they would share Ivy's master bedroom in the main house or his apartment above the garage. He didn't know if she'd want to be closer to guests or if she'd prefer some distance.

Ivy kissed his cheek. "I'll check on that salad Shelly is making in the kitchen."

As soon as Ivy was out of earshot, Mitch cleared his throat. "Thanks for making that call for me. I appreciate the referrals."

"Did you follow up with any of the therapists?"

"I've got an appointment tomorrow."

Bennett nodded, impressed with Mitch's actions. "Good man. Go with an open mind. Have you said anything to Shelly?"

"Not yet." He nodded toward the kitchen. "But I'm doing this for her."

"And for you," Bennett added. "I think you're long over-due." He adjusted the flame on the gas grill. "How is the heat on your side?"

"Just fine," Mitch replied, shifting the basket of rockfish filets to a cooler part of the grill. "Did you hear about what happened between Darla and Ivy and Shelly today?"

"No. Better fill me in."

Mitch tested the snapper with a fork before taking a half step back. "I was in the kitchen this afternoon when I heard a commotion in the dining area. I came out to find Shelly and Darla going at each other, and then Ivy jumped in to defend Shelly."

"As sisters do," Bennett said, grinning. He liked the fact that Ivy and Shelly—the entire Bay family, actually—looked after each other.

"This isn't funny," Mitch shot back. "Darla has been

talking a lot of smack about Shelly—Ivy, too—and she's got people taking sides."

"Talking *smack?*"

"Yeah, smack means being critical behind someone's back. Sorry, I forgot you're an old man."

Bennett punched Mitch in the arm. "I know what it means, and I'm not that old." He looked at Mitch as a younger brother. "Maybe Darla feels threatened by the attention you've been giving Shelly. She might think she's going to lose you. Have you talked to her about this?"

"I don't know why she'd think that," Mitch said. "But maybe I haven't said much. I mean, I talk about Shelly all the time..."

"There's your reason." Bennett flipped the tuna steaks.

"This whole thing has gotten out of hand," Mitch said. "Some folks in town have divided into Team Shelly and Team Ivy, and they're pushing back against those betting that the weddings won't take place. I overheard them arguing earlier."

Bennett paused, holding his long-handled spatula in mid-air. "Old Charlie isn't taking bets again, is he?"

"Afraid so."

"So that explains why they've been a little quiet today." Bennett watched Ivy and Shelly through the kitchen windows. The two women looked like they were having a deep discussion.

Mitch checked the red snapper again before scooping the fish from the grill. "Ivy didn't mention it?"

"She was with a guest who wasn't feeling well when I came home."

"Home, huh?"

"That's right—home." Bennett enjoyed saying the word. "The inn feels more like home than the house I've had for years. Since Jackie died, that is. Home is more than a place; home is feeling you belong."

"I like that," Mitch said.

"Thanks for filling me in," Bennett said. "I guess the gossip wheel hasn't rolled around to me yet, though I'm sure Nan knows about this."

"She probably didn't want to say anything."

Bennett chuckled. "That would be a first for Nan, bless her heart. And I mean that in a good way." Nan didn't mean to harm anyone, but he couldn't say the same about Darla. Still, he'd have a talk with Nan about spreading rumors.

The kitchen door slammed, and Shelly walked out with a large salad bowl. Ivy followed with the silverware and napkins. She had a bottle of wine tucked under her arm.

"The big-city girls are here," Shelly announced. "Ready to steal men with the most amazing salad you've ever tasted."

Mitch nudged Bennett. "Those were some of the insults thrown around. Darla's upset because she thinks Shelly and Ivy stole us from the locals with some kind of spell. As if we didn't have free will in this."

After placing the salad on the table, Shelly flounced toward them and stopped beside Mitch. "And with our short skirts, of course. You should have been there, Mr. Mayor. I almost decked Darla."

"First time I've had to break up a fight at Java Beach," Mitch said.

"It wasn't only Darla," Ivy said as she finished setting the table. Her demeanor quickly shifted. "I don't know the women she was sitting with, but they all jumped on that hate-train with her."

"I already told them to zip it, or they wouldn't be welcome at my place," Mitch added.

As Bennett lifted the last of the seared tuna onto a plate, he shook his head, stalling to choose his words with care. "They probably didn't mean any harm if they were only talking among themselves."

"I disagree," Ivy said, her eyes flashing with anger. "Words *are* harmful. They were in a public place, and plenty of others were privy to their conversation. And for Pete's sake, Charlie is taking bets on whether any of us get married. That's simply cruel. Wagering on whether someone's heart gets broken? Horrible. Darla was talking about my sister. And *us*," she said, motioning between them. "All of us here."

Ivy put her fists on her hips. "I know you're trying to be magnanimous and see all sides of an issue like you do at City Hall. But Darla has broadcast her opinion and turned a lot of people against us."

"Yeah," Shelly added, jumping in. "We have people hating on us who don't even know us."

"Or worse," Ivy continued, her voice escalating. "Charlie and his wife were here at Christmas. And I can't count the number of times Darla has enjoyed our hospitality, from taking my painting classes to attending our wine evenings and joining us for walks on the beach."

Trying to diffuse the situation, Bennett said, "Maybe it seemed worse than it was."

Glaring at him, Ivy gestured toward the shoreline. "If you think Summer Beach is one big happy family, then you have your head stuck in that sand out there."

"Okay, I get it. I misspoke." Bennett took a step back. He'd never seen Ivy explode like that, even when she was angry at Jeremy and his mistress, Paisley. This time, she was protecting Shelly and her sister's relationship with Mitch. "I see your point. Sounds like we have an instigator stirring up discord."

"Also known as the proverbial bad apple that spoils the bunch," Shelly said.

Ivy shivered. "Even worse, Darla is about to be your *de facto* mother-in-law."

"Not if she can help it," Shelly said. "I'm being sabotaged from the inside."

"No, you're not." Mitch took Shelly in her arms. "I hate that they hurt you. I'll make it very clear to Darla that Team

Mitch and Shelly are a package deal. She won't see me without you. She'll come around." He tilted her chin. "Will that work?"

Shelly thought for a moment before nodding. "Thanks for stepping in to defend me."

Bennett put his arm around Ivy. "Mitch will take care of this situation. Java Beach is gossip headquarters. It probably started there—so, he can end it there. He'll look after Shelly, and I'll look after you."

"That's right," Mitch said. "No one talks smack about my girlfriend—or her sister—and gets away with it. Although you two took pretty good care of yourselves without us."

Bennett kissed Ivy's cheek. "You can be quite formidable. But let your guys help you this time. Mitch and I know the people in Summer Beach pretty well. In fact, it took folks a while to accept Mitch."

"And that was only because of you," Mitch added. "I was just some lone surfer dude to them."

Bennett shook his head. "You're an entrepreneur who serves up a lot more than coffee and pastries. You make people feel good, lighter and happier. That's a gift, my friend."

Ivy gazed up at Bennett. "You don't have to rescue us."

"I'm aware of that," Bennett said. "But in a partnership, we share the load, right?"

"In that case, I appreciate it." Ivy seemed quick to understand. They were working their way toward the ultimate partnership—that's how he looked at marriage.

Bennett brushed a stray strand of hair caught in the wind from her face. Every day, he felt like more of a partner to Ivy. She was smart and highly capable, though he suspected she might still harbor vestiges of self-doubt—likely sown for years by the overbearing Jeremy. Yet Ivy had certainly proven herself here in Summer Beach. And for that reason, he was even more disturbed by what villagers were saying about her. He'd talk to Nan tomorrow.

Mitch grinned and gestured toward the red snapper and rockfish resting on a platter. "Enough of that. Who's hungry?"

Shelly managed a smile and nodded.

Ivy looked at the seared tuna. "Smells delicious."

They brought the food to a table on the terrace that had an expansive view of the ocean. The tide was going out, and the ocean was calm tonight. Eager to shift the mood and enjoy the meal they'd prepared, Bennett drew in a deep breath of feel-good ions that surrounded the sea. Gazing out, he saw shorebirds skittering along the water's edge, pecking the sand as the waves swept out to reveal what lay beneath.

Bennett paused to watch the waves guided by gravitational pull, considering that as the social tides in Summer Beach shifted, so too were problems uncovered. As a leader in the community, he would have to address these issues. Left to fester, a rotting core could damage that same proverbial apple.

Turning from the beach and his troubling thoughts, Bennett scooped an assortment of fish onto his plate, along with Mitch's condiments. "Looks like a new salsa tonight."

"I've been experimenting," Mitch said as he opened and poured the wine. He had made a spicy Cajun sauce and tropical fruit salsa for the fish.

Bennett was often amazed at Mitch's creativity with food. The younger man had plenty of skills that came so naturally, he didn't think they were special. And he was still young. Mitch had already done well, and an even brighter future loomed.

"Here's to happy times ahead," Bennett said, lifting his glass and touching it to others.

As everyone ate, Bennett shifted the conversation to more pleasant topics surrounding upcoming summer events. He asked Ivy if she and Shelly planned to host another art show this summer, and they chatted about their plans. The conversation veered to Independence Day, and Mitch wanted everyone to come on his boat for the annual coastal cruise.

Ivy glanced at Bennett. "This seared tuna is delicious. You added just the right amount of lime and sesame seeds." She turned to Mitch. "And the salsa is amazing. Papaya, pineapple, and mango with a spicy kick to it. It's fabulous on the snapper."

"Might be good to serve at a wedding," Bennett said to Ivy with a wink. He savored the last bite of his seared tuna. If he ate any more, he'd have to do a much longer run in the morning.

Ivy caught his gaze and smiled. "Maybe it would be."

"When are your parents leaving on their voyage?" Bennett asked, hoping he sounded nonchalant. The lack of firm plans for their wedding was troubling, though he tried his best to exercise patience. He understood waiting for Shelly, but he still wanted to know where he stood with Ivy.

"In a few weeks," Ivy said vaguely.

Bennett nodded at that and pressed on. "So, is there anything we want to plan before they leave?"

Ivy grinned and looked at Mitch and Shelly. "I don't know. Is there?"

Raising his head, Mitch looked surprised, but he didn't say anything. Shelly seemed to be waiting.

Ivy sliced into a portobello mushroom and paused, looking at Mitch. "Our parents offered to fly back from any port. Unless you want to make plans before they go."

Bennett knew that was the plan, but Mitch had to come to terms with his feelings about having children before he married Shelly. Since Bennett had met Mitch, the younger man had always lived in the present, seldom planning ahead even to the weekend unless someone wanted to charter his boat.

People who lived at the beach were often like that— enjoying every day as it came. Bennett understood that. He'd once been a surfer living only for great waves. But Mitch's problems ran deeper.

"Hey, I have an idea," Shelly said. "Why don't we all go get our marriage licenses together? There's a county office nearby, and we could have lunch afterward to celebrate."

Bennett glanced at Mitch out of the corner of his eye. "We still have time for that."

"What if there is a run on marriage licenses?" Shelly asked. "I checked online, and they're good for ninety days. Come on, you guys. This will be fun."

"Sure," Mitch said with only a slight hesitation.

Shelly's face lit with happiness.

Bennett squeezed Ivy's hand under the table. "I think we're up for that, right?"

Ivy hesitated a moment, then smiled at Shelly. "You're right. It sounds like fun."

Shelly pushed on. "How's tomorrow morning for everyone?"

"Don't we have to get blood tests in California?" Ivy asked.

"Not anymore," Shelly replied. "Mitch, do you have someone to cover the coffee run for you?"

"Let's make it around ten," Mitch said. "My new part-timer is working out pretty well. That will give me two on the floor even when I'm gone."

"You're on," Shelly said, raising her glass.

They all clinked to the plan. Bennett watched Mitch, who had probably agreed just to keep Shelly happy. He hoped that Mitch could come to grips with his issues soon. If not, Shelly would be devastated. And knowing Ivy, she would want to push back their wedding, too. She wouldn't want to celebrate too soon after Shelly's misfortune. If it came to that.

Later that evening, after they'd all pitched in to wash dishes, Ivy joined Bennett on the balcony. They eased onto the rattan sofa. Navy and white cushions looked crisp and inviting.

"This is so cozy up here," Ivy said, lifting her cup of tea to her lips. "Except for the argument about Darla and her friends, this was a magical evening."

"I'll work on that issue," Bennett said.

Thoughtfully, Ivy stared out to sea. "People have no right to ruin Shelly and Mitch's wedding."

"I don't think that will happen," he said. "I've always had faith that right will prevail."

Ivy looked up at him. "How can you be so sure?"

"If I felt otherwise, the pessimism would destroy me. I'm an optimist at heart, but that also means being willing to work hard toward what's right."

Ivy seemed to consider his words. After a few moments, she turned to him, her eyes shimmering with earnestness. "Do you think what Darla and others have said might have affected Mitch?"

"What makes you think that?"

"Mitch hasn't set a date with Shelly. Don't you think that's odd?"

"We haven't either," he pointed out as gently as he could. He couldn't share what Mitch had confided in him.

"But we're waiting on them. I appreciate your being so understanding about that. I don't want to steal Shelly's spotlight."

"You're a thoughtful sister." Bennett put his arm around her. "This crazy business with Darla will soon pass. And marriage licenses are good for ninety days. Mitch will probably come to a decision by then."

"Then you don't think he has?"

Bennett gazed at Ivy. She caught that quickly. "Maybe Mitch made his decision a long time ago. Perhaps he wants to appear spontaneous because it's in keeping with the personality he's cultivated among people. If you're known for being spontaneous, people don't ask or expect too much of you. All he wants to do is serve up great coffee, enjoy his life, and be good to Shelly. They seem very much in love."

That seemed to put Ivy more at ease, and she sipped her tea contentedly.

Bennett grazed the top of her head with his chin. That would give him and Ivy ninety days as well before they'd have to apply for another license. They were growing closer, but he wondered if that would be enough time for her.

9

*W*ith her heart full of love for Bennett, Ivy signed the bottom of the marriage license as the young county clerk with the jaunty plaid bow-tie had instructed. Efficiently, the clerk checked the completed application.

Ivy put down the pen and leaned over to kiss Bennett on the cheek.

"It's almost officially approved," Bennett said, hugging her. "Are you happy?"

"More than I've been in such a long time." Ivy was excited, yet her insides were as fluttery as a leaf. This was an enormous step for her. *A lifetime commitment.* She let out the breath she realized she'd been holding.

Standing beside them, Shelly and Mitch finished signing their marriage license.

Ivy and Shelly had decided to make a special event of the day, so they had dressed up in floral sundresses and kitten-heeled sandals. They had gone through their mother's jewelry to coordinate their outfits with earrings and bracelets.

Bennett and Mitch had also dressed in pressed shirts and trousers. Ivy rarely saw Mitch in anything but T-shirts and board shorts or sweats and windbreakers in the winter. He looked nice, if a little uncomfortable.

Ivy wanted to remember this special day, so they'd all posed for photos outside of the license bureau.

The clerk perused the applications. "These all look fine. Now, I need to see everyone's driver's license, passport, or other form of official identification."

"Of course." Ivy snapped open her purse and brought out her driver's license. She handed it to the man behind the counter.

He looked up at her. "You're from Massachusetts?"

"I returned to California last year."

Straightening his bow-tie, he said, "You're supposed to apply for a California driver's license as soon as you become a resident."

"I've been swamped." Ivy bit her lip. Surely her current license would be acceptable.

"And too busy to get your license renewed, I see." The man handed her license back to her. "It expired last year on your birthday. And the name is different from what you wrote on your application. We need your legal name. Is it Bay or Marin?"

Ivy felt flustered. "It was Bay, and then I married, so it became Marin. But then my husband died, and I decided to go back to my maiden name."

"But you didn't legally change it?"

"No. Is that a problem?"

"It sure is. You'll have to change that on the application. Do you have another form of identification? Something with your photo on it?"

Embarrassed, Ivy dug through her wallet. "You probably won't take my Costco card, will you?"

The man sighed and shook his head.

Ivy grimaced. "You've probably heard that line before."

"You have no idea." He glanced at the clock and rattled

off the list he had memorized. "A valid California identification, driver's license, or passport. Or a certified birth certificate or baptismal record with a photo identification or an
alien resident card. And you must be over eighteen years of
age."

"Well, I've got that last bit down times two, at least," Ivy
said sheepishly. Between trying to save the house from the tax
foreclosure, renovating it and opening for business, and
worrying about her daughters, getting her driver's license
renewed had been low on her list of life-changing priorities.
She hadn't even thought to check the date on it. Still, she
had mailed in an application to have her name changed on
her social security card, although she hadn't heard back
on it.

Bennett slid his arm around her. "Do you have a
passport?"

"That expired a couple of years ago," Ivy replied with a
sinking feeling. "Guess I have to apply for a new license." She
turned back to the clerk. "How long does it take to get a
driver's license?"

"Last I heard, about six weeks, give or take. Or, you could
use your certified birth certificate and a California identification card."

Bennett looked hopeful, but Ivy shook her head. "I'll have
to order a birth certificate." She recalled having to do that
before, and she hadn't ordered any extra copies.

"That could take a few weeks, too," the clerk said. "I'm
sorry, folks. You two seem like you're eager to get married, but
you've got your whole life ahead of you."

Ivy felt terrible. She knew she'd ruined the planned celebration by not being prepared. She blinked back sudden tears.

Bennett wrapped his arms around her. "It's all right,
sweetheart. What's a few more weeks or months?"

Shelly rested her hand on Ivy's shoulder. "If you need me
to cover for you so you can take care of this, you can count on

me. I took care of my license a few months ago. It doesn't take too long."

Next, the clerk accepted proof of identification from Shelly and Mitch, ticked off a box on the form, and said, "Congratulations. Your marriage license is approved."

"Woo-hoo," Shelly cried out, throwing her arms around Mitch. "The clock is ticking on us now, babe."

Mitch looked slightly stunned. His smile froze on his face.

"I've never been so happy," Shelly said. "I can't wait to move all my things into your house."

"My place is pretty small," Mitch said nervously, creasing his brow.

Shelly laughed. "I moved from New York with a couple of suitcases and a few boxes. I didn't have much room in the city either. But I have big plans for the house and garden. Your yard is large enough to add on another bedroom when we need to. And that time might not be too far away."

Mitch blinked and opened his mouth, but no words came out.

Ivy suspected that he was in a mild state of shock. Shelly had proposed to him, and maybe he'd been caught up in the novelty of the moment. Ivy had always thought that Mitch was a good match for Shelly. But now, he looked as jittery as a rabbit. Ivy hoped he wasn't having second thoughts.

Bennett clamped his hand onto Mitch's shoulder. "Congratulations," he said with a good-natured laugh. "Let's get out of here and have some lunch."

At that, Mitch's emotions thawed. They walked out into the bright sunshine, and Mitch lifted Shelly, her feet dangling above the sidewalk. "Can I get that woo-hoo again?"

Shelly called out, and then the two of them burst into laughter.

Ivy was relieved. She laughed along with them, though she still felt awful that she and Bennett hadn't been able to get their marriage license because of her negligence.

She clutched Bennett's hand, and he squeezed hers. As she walked beside him toward the cafe, she felt her cares dissipate, lifting into the air like the sparrows around them. With each passing day, Ivy became more confident that Bennett was all that she could ask for in a husband and life partner. He was respectful, patient, considerate, fun—plus, he was easy on the eyes. A man like that could have had his choice of any woman, but he loved her.

And she loved him.

The thought suffused her with an inner warmth that she'd never thought she'd feel again. Still, her chest quivered as she considered the enormity of the decision represented by her signature on a piece of paper.

Maybe not today, but soon.

Bennett tucked her arm through his, and they strolled through the town until they came to a pier. With the sun on her shoulders and the cool breeze off the water, Ivy relaxed. Everyone seemed to be enjoying the day now.

Around them, couples and young families strolled with pets and took selfies against the water. A few retired people fished from the pier. Surfers paddled among the swells, waiting for the right sets on waves.

At the end of the pier stood a cafe with blue umbrellas shading round tables. Red-checked tablecloths anchored with potted succulents fluttered in the breeze. Soon, the four of them gathered around a table.

After ordering shrimp cocktails, salads, and crab legs with drawn butter, Ivy and Bennett toasted to Shelly and Mitch.

"It's our turn next time," Ivy said, taking Bennett's hand.

As the designated driver, Bennett sipped sparkling water. "I half expected you to come to your senses and race out of there like a runaway fiancée."

Ivy laughed. "I wouldn't have done that."

Bennett turned a thoughtful gaze on her. "I think about

our future a great deal and how fortunate we are to have found each other. What we have doesn't happen often in life."

At his words, a warm feeling gathered in her chest. "I couldn't agree more."

"I hope you don't feel that I've been rushing you," he said, holding her hand. "It's just that when it's right, you know it."

"There's a lot we're still learning about each other," Ivy said slowly, watching the expression on Bennett's face. "Maybe a little extra time isn't such a bad thing."

He squeezed her hand. "I'm not going anywhere."

Ivy couldn't help wondering if events worked out as they were meant. If so, maybe her expired driver's license was the universe's way of telling her she needed to slow down.

Or that she needed to pay more attention to life's details.

10

The next day, Ivy ordered her birth certificate and tried to sort through the process to change other identification cards and documents.

"Evidence of a legal name change…" Ivy stared at the computer in the library, her mind glazing over at the tangle of instructions, forms, and fees. She peered through her leopard glasses and shook her head.

Shelly strolled in. "Are you making any headway there?"

"Not yet. I submitted forms for a legal name change a couple of months ago, but I haven't received anything back. I need that before I can renew my driver's license or passport, or I'll have to do it all over again. Maybe it will be processed this week—or next month—who knows? But I already applied to change my name on the social security card, and it looks like I'll need that for the driver's license, but first I need the legal name change documents." She sank her chin onto her palm. "This is so confusing. I think I might have messed up and reversed the order of this process."

"Sounds complicated," Shelly said. "I'm sure you'll figure it out, though."

"I only wanted Bay back. I thought it would be easy."

"Probably would have been if you weren't planning on getting married again. Then what will you do?"

"I have no idea." Ivy laughed. "But Bennett Bay has a nice ring to it, don't you think?"

Shelly twisted her lips to one side. "Sounds like a men's clothing line."

"See?" Ivy smiled. "Another potential opportunity I'm bringing him."

"You're a wonder," Shelly said, grinning.

Since arriving in Summer Beach, Ivy had been using her original family name of Bay to distance herself from the lawsuit Jeremy had filed against the city of Summer Beach to build his intended mega-resort. Given Jeremy's infidelity and plan to exclude her from his life, she no longer wanted to carry his surname of Marin, even though that was fine for their children. She had struggled to forgive him, and she didn't need to be reminded of him every day.

She enjoyed being Ivy Bay again. At this stage of her life and after all she'd been through, reclaiming her individuality appealed to her. While she cherished the good times she and Jeremy had, the hard truth was that he had fallen out of love with her. She no longer owed him the courtesy in death of retaining his surname.

Frowning at the computer screen, Ivy tried to sort out the process again. Finally, she removed her glasses and drew her hands over her face. "This is such a pain." And she hadn't even started on the exhaustive list of medical records, credit cards, bank accounts, utilities, and every other detail of life.

Shelly perched on the arm of a chair and swung her leg. "You need a break."

"I sure do." In addition to this mind-numbing task, she'd also spent the morning answering Eleanor's emails and handling wedding details for her and Rachel.

On the one hand, maybe Shelly had been right about not wanting to book this wedding. Instead of just providing the venue, Ivy was turning into a wedding coordinator. Many of Eleanor's vendors didn't want to drive the distance to Summer Beach, so Ivy was arranging myriad details.

However, this gave Ivy another idea. They could advertise the inn as a venue with add-on wedding services. This wedding was essentially a test run to determine what people might need. Besides, Ivy wanted to be there for Rachel.

Ivy stood and shook tension from her hands. "If you've got some time, there's something else I'd like to do."

"Like what?" Shelly asked.

"I want to check that little room we found again."

Although they'd brought all the clothes out of the dark nook, she still had an odd feeling whenever she thought about it. Most people were creatures of habit. Including, she imagined, Amelia Erickson.

Since the older woman had hidden some items in the house, then she might have concealed other things. Maybe not Shelly's imagined gold bars and coins, but other items of value to Amelia.

Ivy had been thinking about where she might stash things if she were Amelia. While part of Amelia's unusual behavior could be attributed to her progressive Alzheimer's disease, if the woman had been in the habit of hiding things, perhaps that's why she continued.

Furthermore, what did Amelia consider important? Ivy wished she could find Amelia's journals. She had found some letters and journal pages, but these only told part of the woman's story.

Shelly peered at her. "You're obsessed with Amelia Erickson, aren't you?"

"Not obsessed, just curious." Ivy felt drawn to learn as much as she could about the house's former owner. They were both the mistress of this grand old house, but Ivy sensed there was something more that bound them over time. From the first day she'd seen this house, she felt a duty to protect it.

Maybe because Jeremy had intended to tear it down, or perhaps because she'd sensed its historic value.

Although she could never have imagined the secrets—large and small—that this home held.

Were there more?

"Okay, I'm in," Shelly said on her way out of the library. "It's pitch dark in that room. I'll get flashlights."

After asking Poppy to watch the front desk, Ivy climbed the stairs. As she went, she took note of details that needed attention. A loose tile on a riser between steps, a flickering lightbulb in a sconce in the hallway, scuff marks that needed cleaning. Her to-do list seemed endless.

She'd learned that there weren't enough hours in the day for perfection. Usually good enough was good enough—or she'd never have time for herself. Still, the lightbulb and the tile needed attention. Scuff marks could wait.

Ivy made her way into the spacious closet and removed the luggage they had stored in the last mirrored clothes cabinet. She pressed on the rear wall, and the hidden door swung open under her touch.

"Here's a flashlight," Shelly said as she entered the dressing area behind her.

Ivy turned on the light and stepped inside a small, dark room.

Shelly followed her. "This would make a great darkroom for photography."

"Someday, we'll add that to our list of offerings at the Seabreeze Inn," Ivy said with a chuckle.

Shelly flicked on a larger light and placed it on the side table. It illuminated the entire room. "I got this from Jen at Nailed It. Comes in handy when I'm working in the greenhouse in the evening. Now, where should we start? There isn't much here."

Ivy glanced around. "Look through that side table."

"I did that last time," Shelly said.

"Look again." Ivy was trying to think as Amelia might have thought. "There could be a false bottom to the drawer or something stuck to the bottom of it."

Ivy ran her hands over the wallboard, tapping as she went. "Nothing unusual here," she said with some dismay.

She had already been through the sewing basket, which was filled with vintage supplies, including thread, lace, and needles. She'd found a pair of intricately designed scissors, probably used for embroidery and hand sewing. Even then, sewing machines had existed, but they were not the modern marvels of today.

Ivy had put the dressmaker's form in a corner of her room. After removing the ivory dress and dusting off the wire frame, she'd draped her favorite floral-painted, white jean jacket over it. She looped a few brightly colored scarves and necklaces around the neck and topped it with a couple of straw beach hats. It was the picture of spring and brought a smile to her face.

There wasn't much else in the room except for the loveseat. It was an old-fashioned one with a wood frame and tapestry cushions. Ivy lifted them, but found nothing.

"Look underneath it," Shelly suggested.

Ivy bent over. "Well, I'll be. I see something." She slid off the loveseat and crouched before it. With her flashlight, she inspected the underside. Fabric covered the bottom, but there was another piece stretched across it that formed a sort of pocket. It bulged slightly. Ivy ran her hand across it. "There's something here."

"What is it?" Shelly asked

Ivy bit her lip with trepidation. "I don't want to stick my hand in there. Could be spiders."

"I don't see how," Shelly said. "There's nothing for them to live on."

"Maybe they call out for delivery. I should've brought gloves."

"I can't believe you're such a scaredy-cat."

"Then you reach in there."

Shelly stepped through the opening in the wardrobe and returned a moment later with a pair of knitted red gloves. She handed them to Ivy. "Here, these will slow down the critters."

Ivy tugged on the gloves their grandmother had knitted for their mother years ago. She held out her hands. "Here goes." She shoved her hand into the flap and felt around.

Her fingers closed on something. "Got it." She slid out the object.

In her hands lay a small book, not much larger than her hand. Ivy caught her breath. "Amelia's journal?"

She and Shelly eased onto the loveseat and bent their heads toward the slim volume, which was covered in soft ivory leather stamped with a gold pattern around the perimeter and stained with time.

Ivy opened it.

On the first page were words written in feathery ink. *Le trousseau d'Amelia.* Ivy smiled. "It's French. *Amelia's Trousseau.*"

"I thought she spoke German."

"She might have been studying French."

"What's a trousseau?" Shelly asked.

"It's a term that encompasses the items a woman brings into her marriage. Could be clothing, housewares, or jewelry. Anything, really. Mom said she had collected items in an old cedar chest that had belonged to her mother."

"Hmm. Did you have one of these trousseaus?"

Ivy shook her head. "Like you, I was busy planning for college."

Shelly rubbed her hands together. "So, is this little book going to tell us where the diamonds and gold are?"

Ivy laughed. "Maybe a hundred years ago." She turned a brittle page.

Stitched to the page was a square of red-and-navy woolen fabric in a herringbone design. Beside it was a sketch of a cape. On the other side was the same feathery script. Ivy ran her fingers over the fabric with reverence. "This must have been a beautiful garment."

Shelly furrowed her forehead. "Can you make out what that says?"

"*Capelet.* A short cape. The rest of it is in German. It might be a description of the cape and what she planned to wear with it. Or maybe where she planned on wearing it."

"Or with whom, right?"

Ivy nodded. "She probably made this before her wedding to Gustav."

Shelly scanned the page. "I don't see his name."

"Maybe she started this before she knew who she was going to marry."

"That seems like a waste of time."

"For some, it probably was. More than a hundred years ago—likely when Amelia was a young woman, families might have arranged marriages by introducing young people within their social strata. Not many women pursued higher education. They were brought up to marry and make a home, so they began planning for that when they were teens. Fortunately, there were outliers, the women who pursued their dreams and became doctors and scientists and writers—and continue to inspire us today. Look at what Amelia achieved and the impact she made."

Ivy turned the page to reveal a sketch of a slim-fitting jacket with full sleeves and a long skirt. A swatch of navy wool accompanied it. A sketch of a hat was angled in the corner, where a peacock feather had been stitched to the page. A few lines had been jotted beside it.

"This is probably part of the same outfit," Ivy said. "It must have been quite elegant."

She turned another page. This one did not have a sketch, but it did have several lines of writing and swatches of woven cotton and damask fabrics, marked *damassé.*

Ivy rubbed the fabric between her fingers. "These might have been for bed linens or furnishings." She imagined how that might have looked.

The little volume was a window into another time, another way of living—half a world and a century away. Yet Ivy felt a kinship with Amelia. These pages provided a glimpse of a stylish young woman with her life ahead of her. Her attention to detail, her artistic eye, her passion for recording every item. Years later, these skills would serve her in her marriage to Gustav as they collected art around the world—and later, when she sheltered art and artifacts for future generations.

Every page filled Ivy with a sense of awe.

On one page was a sketch of a day dress with a clipping of a silky cotton voile in lavender with tiny sprigs of pink flowers. Another page held the image of an antique brooch with the notation, *améthyste de Oma.*

Smiling at Amelia's mixture of French and German, Ivy recognized the words. "That was her grandmother's amethyst brooch," she said. Tiny pearls surrounded the large oval stone. "It must have been beautiful. Amethyst was quite a rare stone back then, before additional quantities were discovered. And very valuable."

Yet another page held a yellowed clipping from a newspaper with the drawing of a tea service—silver, most likely. *Silber.* Ivy imagined all these treasures tucked away, perhaps in a trunk or a chest, or whatever the custom was in Amelia's family.

The entries continued, each representing a cherished memory, the chronicle of a young woman's dreams and aspirations before embarking on a journey into a life of her own, separate from her parents. Snippets of lace, fabric, and trimmings were carefully stitched to the pages.

Ivy wondered how Amelia might have felt as she compiled this list of treasures. Perhaps she was elated, or maybe she approached this new chapter of her life with trepidation. Ivy turned the page.

There before them was a rendering of the ivory gown and lace coat they had discovered, along with the accompanying swatches of silk and lace.

And on the opposite page was a shadowy sepia photograph of the bride in the same silk charmeuse gown wearing the beaded lace coat with ropes of pearls. In her hands, she held a bouquet of calla lilies.

"She looks so young," Shelly said.

Ivy waited as her sister stared transfixed at the old photo for a long time. "Perhaps we can have these entries translated," Ivy said.

She scanned the pages. The last entry had several squares of black cloth stitched to the page, along with another entry she couldn't read.

Ivy shook her head. "I don't see anything about Gustav, but maybe she had a pet nickname for him."

"Did they do that back then?"

"Probably. I doubt we invented nicknames."

"Maybe Aristotle was just Ari to his buddies." Shelly grinned and turned the page. As she did, a photo slipped out onto the floor.

Ivy picked it up. Amelia and her husband posed in this one, both of them staring unflinchingly into the camera. "I wonder what year this was?" She turned the photo over. On the back was an inscription. "Amelia and Josef."

Shelly inclined her head. "Not Gustav?"

"No. Josef." Ivy considered this discovery. "It looks like Amelia was married before Gustav."

"I wonder what happened," Shelly said.

A cool sensation swept through Ivy, and she shivered slightly. "Megan needs to see this."

Megan Calloway was the documentary filmmaker working on Amelia's story. Megan and her husband had moved to

Summer Beach during the past year. She was recreating Amelia's life from the old film Ivy and Shelly had found in the lower level of the house. Nan and Arthur had contributed history they had gleaned from newspaper clippings for a book they wrote about Summer Beach and its residents for the historical society.

But what Ivy and Shelly held in their hands predated any of what Megan had discovered in her research. As she stared at the old photograph, Ivy felt compelled to find out who Josef was and what had happened to him. And yet, as with so many of the mysteries they'd discovered in the house, she had a feeling they would find only partial answers. Someday, perhaps, the pieces of Amelia's fascinating life would coalesce.

11

*B*ennett deposited his surfing gear on a dune. Sure enough, Mitch had beat him there. His friend rose early every morning before sunrise to surf before he opened Java Beach for breakfast. In the afternoon, Mitch still took sightseeing and fishing charters on his boat a few times a week. The kid had designed quite a nice life for himself. Bennett was proud of him for that.

Bennett was warming up, stretching his torso from side to side. "How are you doing with Darla?"

Mitch shrugged. "She hasn't been back to Java Beach since the blow-up with Shelly and Ivy. But she'll get over it. She always does."

"You should reach out to her," Bennett said. "She's probably embarrassed, especially about Charlie taking bets. I talked to him, and he said that Darla suggested that, though I don't know if that's true."

He sank into a runner's stretch to warm up his legs. With a marine layer on the beach, the weather was cool. The sun was rising, and thin rays illuminated the waves rolling onto the shore. By late morning, the sun would warm the coastline and beachgoers would emerge. But for now, the beach was bathed in solitude.

Mitch was pulling on his wetsuit, and Bennett was glad his friend had brought one for him, too. The Pacific Ocean waters were cool. Mitch had brought an extra surfboard for Bennett as he had lost his surfing gear in the fire. If he kept this up, he'd reinvest in a board and wetsuit.

The last time Mitch had dared him to go surfing, it had been years since Bennett had been on a surfboard. Since the waves hadn't beat him up too badly, he'd figured he'd do it again. As Ivy's father once said, *If not now, when?*

Sterling was referring to their planned voyage around the world, but that applied to many things in life. Still, Bennett had to balance his bias for action with patience, especially where Sterling's middle daughter was concerned.

Mitch zipped up his wetsuit. "Don't you want to know the lines?"

Bennett rolled his eyes. Mitch was referring to the betting spread on whether or not he and Shelly married—as well as Bennett and Ivy. "Absolutely not."

"You and Ivy have far better odds than we do," Mitch said.

"Experience is good for something," Bennett said. "But don't let that influence you. It's just people's opinion—and there are only two opinions that count." Bennett stripped down to the European-style swimsuit he wore and eased into the neoprene wetsuit Mitch had loaned to him. Holding the edges together, he zipped it over his chest.

Mitch watched him. "Whoa, is that wetsuit a little tight there?"

Bennett socked him in the arm. "It's my bulging muscles."

"If you say so, dude," Mitch said, grinning.

As the two men finished suiting up, Bennett said, "You're in a good mood this morning." He wondered if Mitch had followed up on his referral for counseling.

Mitch scanned the waves. "Why not? We've got offshore winds grooming easy-riding waves for us. The marine layer will probably burn off by noon, and I've got a sweet corporate sightseeing charter this afternoon to cruise the coast for sunset. They're paying a lot for the pleasure. It's some sort of morale-boosting excursion for the overworked office staff. Poor souls. Instead, they could have all this," he added, spreading his arms to the sea.

"You've set yourself up pretty well."

"Not bad for an ex-con beach bum, huh?"

"For anyone," Bennett said. "But especially at your age. Give yourself credit; you worked hard for this."

Mitch grew thoughtful. "I told my new therapist about my past. I wanted to get that right out front to see if it changed how he thought of me. I've been a few times now. I thought I'd jump onto the accelerated program."

"And?"

"I discovered I'm a deep kind of guy," Mitch replied. "This guy says that childhood trauma can take a while to work through." He picked up his surfboard. "I want to be in a good place for Shelly and be honest with her. She deserves that. And this is an important step in my life. I don't want to mess it up."

"I'm glad you're getting some advice," Bennett said.

Running his hand over his board, Mitch frowned. "Maybe Charlie's odds for Shelly and me are true."

"You know that's just idle gossip." Bennett thought Mitch had taken a big step in getting the marriage license, but maybe it was premature. He couldn't push Mitch; he could only support him. Still, if Mitch decided not to go through with the wedding, Bennett would feel bad for Shelly. Hearts would be broken.

"Plenty of time to think about that," Bennett said, not wanting Mitch to feel rushed. "Let's catch some waves." Bennett picked up his surfboard.

Once in the water, the two of them paddled out on their boards. Mitch glanced at Bennett and grinned. "It is a good life we've got here."

And a couple of wonderful women, Bennett thought, although he didn't want to sound pushy. It was important that Mitch work through his issues at this stage, and Bennett hoped he could. If he felt that Mitch had the capacity for abuse, he would have been the first to talk to him about it. From what Bennett had observed about Mitch over the years, he thought his friend would make an excellent father. But Mitch had to be confident in that decision.

Once Bennett and Mitch were a fair way out from shore, they floated on their surfboards, waiting for the right sets of waves. The ocean swelled, lifting them gently as they bobbed and waited. The cool water was a brisk wake-up, but Bennett loved it. He swirled his hands in the waves.

Finally, a powerful wave arched toward them, and Mitch called out. The wind whipped his words away, but Bennett knew a good wave when he saw one. He pushed himself to a standing position and gripped the board with the soles of his feet to gain his balance. With the wind in his hair and the wave rising to carry him, Bennett felt the thrill of being one with nature. He loved surfing for the sheer adrenaline.

"Oh, yeah," Mitch yelled after the wave carried them in. "Let's do that again."

Over and over, they rode the waves until the marine layer began to part, and the morning sun peeked through.

Feeling fully alive and invigorated, Bennett rode the last wave into the shore. And there on the beach sat Ivy, perched on a flat rock, watching and smiling.

At that moment, with his heart pounding from the adrenaline ride, he felt it beat even more furiously for her. Waving back at Mitch, he trotted toward her.

"Good morning," he said, panting from the exertion.

"You looked pretty good out there," she said, smiling up at

him. "A little like a tasty seal, but I didn't see any hungry sharks."

Bennett laughed. "We've never seen sharks that close in Summer Beach." He stretched his legs. "It felt great to be out on the water. Maybe I'm not as creaky as I thought."

Ivy inclined her head. "I'd say you're a long way from creaky."

"I'll take that as a compliment." He eased down beside her on the wide, flat rock and gave her a wet kiss on the cheek just to hear her sweet laughter.

Bennett had been feeling more at ease with her, and he could tell that she was feeling that way, too. He saw her love for him growing in the natural way she brushed against him or leaned into him while they spoke. The light in her eyes shone brighter when she saw him.

Mitch trotted across the sand with his surfboard. "Time to start the coffee," he called out as he headed toward the private beach showers before going to Java Beach. "Keep the board and the wetsuit until you get your own."

"Thanks, will do," Bennett said. Would he go out again? Sure, he thought. He liked the idea of alternating surfing with running.

After he'd caught his breath, Bennett slid off the rock and held out his hand to Ivy. "Shall we walk back to the inn together?"

"Sure," she replied, taking his hand.

Holding her hand and tucking the surfboard under his other arm, he started toward the inn. The sun was warm on his face, and gulls glided lazily over the water. Right now, he felt like the happiest man in the world with Ivy beside him.

As they walked, they talked about the usual things—new guests at the inn, news about town, their plans for the day. Bennett avoided talking about Darla or the bets placed against them. They existed—for a little while—in a world of their own.

Bennett squeezed her hand. "Can you get away this weekend?" he asked.

"Is this the surprise you've been planning?" Ivy looked up and smiled coyly.

"You remembered," he said, surprised. He shouldn't have been, though. Where he was concerned, he'd found that Ivy remembered even the little things: how he liked his coffee, his favorite wine glass, or where he'd left his sunglasses in the house.

"Well, it's one of the surprises," he said as he stepped onto the rear terrace of the inn. Near the stairs to his garage apartment, he paused. "Could you spend a day with me this weekend?"

"Saturday is better," she said, shading her eyes with her hand. "I'll ask Shelly or Poppy to cover for me. Just tell me what to wear."

He tapped the tip of her nose. "A sundress and sandals would be perfect."

As Bennett climbed the stairs, he couldn't resist looking back at her. This was the woman he wanted to spend the rest of his life with. But first, he had to make sure she felt as strongly as he did.

Even though they were engaged, he could still feel a slight hesitation on her part. He respected that. Ivy was a smart woman, and it had only been two years since her husband died. Long enough for some people, but not for others. And in matters of the heart, Ivy was a cautious woman.

No doubt about it, Ivy would challenge him. And he liked that about her.

ON SATURDAY MORNING, the sun streamed through Bennett's windows. He rolled out of bed, thankful that it wasn't raining. He showered quickly and met Ivy in the dining room for breakfast.

Ivy wore a green linen sundress with a wrist full of silver bracelets and the necklace that Bennett had given her at Christmas. The V-neckline perfectly framed the antique emerald cabochon on its platinum chain. "How is this?" she asked.

"Perfect," he said, smiling when he saw her necklace. "I'm glad you like that." He'd found it at Antique Times. It matched her eyes and brought out the color even more.

"I love it." She threaded her arm through his. "So, where are we going?"

"You'll see," he said, teasing her.

"Shall we take the convertible or your SUV?"

"If you don't mind, the old Chevy would be great. I can drive for you."

Ivy smiled at him. "I would like that."

After breakfast, Bennett opened the door to the cherry-red Chevrolet Deluxe. He'd lowered the convertible top and dusted the car so that it shone in the sunshine. Last year, he'd restored the vintage 1950s car that had been stored in the stables-turned-garage for decades for Ivy, and he was proud of how the car had turned out. She loved driving it around Summer Beach.

"Your carriage awaits," he said, holding out his hand to her.

She slid onto the refurbished red leather seat and stretched out her legs. Her flat silver sandals sparkled in the sunlight. She pulled out a pair of white cats-eye sunglasses and slid them on. "Let's go."

"Those are fun," he said, chuckling.

"I'm thinking about painting them," she said, looking at them in the rearview mirror. "How about a confetti splatter or polka dots and paisley?"

"I like your style, Ivy Bay. We're going to have fun today."

After leaving the inn, Bennett set an easterly course for the mountains that rose behind Summer Beach, cradling the village against desert winds.

En route, Ivy tried to wheedle the location out of him, but he wouldn't budge from his determination to surprise her.

Finally, he turned onto a narrow lane that led to a rugged, higher elevation. A wooden sign inset into wrought iron gates that stood open read *Chateau Boivin*. Low white fences lined the perimeter, and groomed vineyards stretched out beyond them.

Old rose bushes rambled along the fence in a profusion of pink, yellow, and orange flowers. At the end of rows on various blocks they passed, hand-lettered signs that identified the vines. *Tempranillo, Syrah, Ruby Cabernet, Barbera.* Fresh spring vines sprouting from stubby, craggy trunks were meticulously wound over a lattice of horizontal supports, outstretched like arms to the sunshine.

Ivy's eyes widened. "Oh, how lovely this is."

"Surprise," he said, pleased to see her delighted. He wound through the property and parked in front of a large home built of smooth stones and wood. Attached was a broad outdoor terrace.

A casually dressed couple about their age appeared on the steps and waved.

"These are my friends," Bennett said. "Tristan and Emilie Boivin. We met several years ago at a fundraising gala to support the arts in Summer Beach schools. It was at Carol Reston's home on the ridgetop—she's always a generous contributor. She was serving their wine, and they were there to auction off cases. We've kept in touch ever since. I think you'll like them."

"Welcome," Emilie said with a slight French accent. Her dark brown hair was swept from her face, revealing high cheekbones and a long, elegant neck. Intricate wire earrings graced either side of her delicate face. She wore a simple chambray dress belted at the waist. "We're delighted to meet you."

Bennett introduced them. "Tristan and Emilie supply wine to some of the restaurants in town."

"We're so happy to have you here today," Emilie said as she pressed her cheeks to Ivy's in a traditional French greeting. "Bennett has told us so much about you."

Ivy clasped Bennett's hand. "This is such a beautiful setting. And quite a surprise."

"We have everything ready for your private wine tasting," Tristan said. He wore soft jeans and a denim jacket, and his longish dark hair brushed the collar. "After that, we'll make lunch. You might wish to stroll through the vineyards, too. Although it's too early in the season to taste the berries, it's still a tranquil walk."

The two couples chatted while Tristan led them around the side of the house and through an open doorway flanked with old wine barrels. "Watch your head," he said, descending a stone staircase.

"The wine cellar," Bennett said, turning to Ivy. "After you."

Ivy followed Tristan. Her eyes were wide, and she was taking in everything. Bennett wondered if she was cataloging details for her painting. The red-bricked ceiling arched over the room, and pastoral murals of rolling vineyards graced the walls. Racks of slightly dusty wine bottles surrounded them.

"This is our tasting room," Tristan said. A selection of wine bottles and an assortment of glasses sat on a hand-hewn table in the center of the room.

"Few people find us here at the Chateau," Emilie said as she entered the room. "It's just us, except for our field workers, so we don't have an open tasting room as larger vintners might." She raised a shoulder and let it fall. "Occasionally someone wanders by and knocks on our door. And we're always happy to share our wine."

"Most of our business is wholesale or private clients," Tristan said. "Still, we love to host parties and groups here."

Emilie led the tasting while Tristan poured wine, beginning with a honey-colored wine. Bennett took small sips, reveling in the exquisite flavor. Keeping in mind that he would have to drive back, he discretely took advantage of the spit bowls placed beside them.

"This is a Viognier, not as well known in California as Chardonnay, but we like it because it's less acidic and more complex," Emilie said. "This varietal is grown in France's Rhône Valley and teetered on the edge of extinction in the 1980s. Its skin is thin, so it prefers our altitude and ages well in the French barrels we import. You'll detect notes of rose, peach, and herbs, such as fennel." She swirled a splash of wine in a glass and lifted it to her nose.

"This wine is quite remarkable," Ivy said, tipping her glass to inhale the bouquet before tasting.

They sampled each wine, from the lightest to the most robust, talking and laughing, and breaking off pieces of a baguette to cleanse their palates between wines.

"Tristan and Emilie are too modest to mention how many awards they've won," Bennett said. "They've served presidents and royalty around the world. They produce wine in small batches for the most discriminating of collectors."

Tristan inclined his head, quietly accepting the compliment. "This is such a small, geographically constrained region that it doesn't have a high profile like Napa and Sonoma to the north or Temecula to the east. We hide away on this secluded mountain perch that exposes our vines to the most arduous conditions."

"The more environmental strain on the berries—or grapes —the smaller and more compact they are," Emilie said, removing the glasses they'd used. She poured red wine into a larger glass and swirled it. "The flavor and personality are in the skin, which grows thicker at higher, cooler elevations. Thus, we gain a richer extraction during soaking and fermentation. For table grapes, it's the opposite—juicy plump grapes are more desirable."

After they'd finished the wine tasting, they returned to the terrace overlooking the vineyards, where a table for two was set for them.

"This is such a romantic view," Emilie said. "We never tire of it."

"Do you mind if I take photos?" Ivy asked. "I'd love to paint this."

"Not at all," Emilie replied. While she pointed out the best views for Ivy, the two women chatted about their shared interest in photography and painting.

A little later, Bennett and Ivy sat down, and Tristan brought out a bottle of the wine they had all enjoyed. Emilie served tomato bisque soup, along with a braised duck salad with pomegranate seeds and a walnut vinaigrette.

"We grow most of the produce we use here," Tristan said. "The romaine and red leaf lettuce, cucumbers, tomatoes—everything in the salad." He gestured toward a group of condiments on a small plate. "This is the balsamic vinegar, olive oil, and rose petal jam that we make here."

After Tristan left them alone, Bennett reached across the table, threading his fingers with Ivy's. "Happy?"

"This is a perfect day," she said, her eyes shimmering. "Thank you for planning this."

He brought her fingers to his lips. "To many more days just like this—for the rest of our lives."

"Of course," Ivy said, blinking tears from her eyes. Looking slightly embarrassed, she dabbed her eyes. "I'm sorry, I don't know why I'm crying. I'm really having a wonderful time." She squeezed his hand.

Bennett tilted his head. *Maybe it was just the wine.*

12

*A*fter enjoying the delicious meal that Tristan and Emilie prepared, Ivy strolled through the vineyards with Bennett. She'd needed this break from the inn and the gossip swirling around Summer Beach.

Here, breathing in the scent of sun-warmed earth and vines, she felt grounded. The wine made her relaxed. She'd been watching Bennett throughout their visit and was glad to see that he hadn't imbibed too much since he had to drive back to Summer Beach this afternoon. That was one of the red flags she'd been watching for.

While this day had been enjoyable, Ivy still had something on her mind.

As she and Bennett strolled through a block of Syrah vines, she broached a concern. "I love Summer Beach, but I find it odd—no, astonishing—that people have the gall to wager on the odds of our wedding. Is that normal?"

Bennett drew a hand over his chin. "Not from what I can recall. I think that's mostly Charlie's doing, even though he tried to pass that off on Darla. They're pointing the finger at each other, not that it matters. They're both at fault. Charlie usually sticks to sports, but he's been known to capitalize on other opportunities."

"The town had seemed so welcoming before," Ivy said.

"Have the people you know changed their attitude or how they're treating you?"

Ivy thought about this. "No, I can't think of anyone other than Darla."

He clasped her hand as they strolled. "Small towns are wonderful places to live when residents are supportive, but sometimes a few characters can change opinions. I haven't seen it happen often, but I won't say it doesn't. Overall, Summer Beach is a pretty good place to live."

Ivy was glad to hear that. "I can manage the gossip, though it is annoying. But I'm concerned about Shelly and Mitch. Since Darla is behind it, she's driving this divisiveness even more. Do you know why she has taken such a sudden dislike to Shelly?"

"It all has to do with how she feels about Mitch," Bennett replied. "She's like a protective mother hen. She only wants what's best for him."

"So, she doesn't think Shelly is?"

Bennett paused at the end of a row. "Okay, I see your point. I could talk to her if you want."

Ivy considered this offer. "I appreciate that, but it's not your place. Mitch ought to be the one to talk to her and stick up for Shelly."

"He probably will. He's just working through some things right now."

Ivy's ears pricked up at that. "Like what?"

Bennett ran a hand over his face. "Sorry, I shouldn't have said anything. That's really between Mitch and—"

"And who?" Ivy turned to face him.

Bennett blew out a breath. "I can't betray the trust that Mitch has placed in me. This is something personal for Mitch. Forget what I said."

Alarms went off in Ivy's mind. "Now I can't forget it. If my sister's happiness depends on what Mitch is working through, then she ought to know." What was Bennett keeping from her? And what was Mitch concealing from Shelly?

Bennett blinked several times, clearly at a loss as to what to say. "I don't want to ruin this beautiful day by having an argument about Mitch and Shelly."

"I wouldn't call this an argument," Ivy said. "Unless you continue keeping whatever secret could hurt Shelly."

"Trust me," Bennett said. "They will work out what they need to without our intervention. I know you're protective of Shelly. I feel the same way about Mitch, and I assure you, I want what's best for both of them. I know how much is at stake for them and their future. Mitch will tell her, but that will be between them unless they want to share it. Please trust me on this."

Reluctantly, Ivy agreed. She wondered if she should tell Shelly what Bennett said—or if that would worry her sister even more. She would have to think about this later.

"It's just that the time for our parents' planned departure is drawing closer," Ivy said, trying a different approach. "If there is anything I can do to move this wedding along…"

"There isn't," Bennett said sharply before softening his tone. "Let's focus on us today. I brought you here so that we could talk about our future and what we want."

"And we have been talking about that," she said. "Your renewed interest in surfing, my children and my painting, the inn." She paused. She didn't mean to sound defensive, but she desperately wanted Shelly to be happy. Her sister had waited so long for her turn. What had she said? *To sail into her sunrise.*

"After we get married, where would you like to live?" Bennett asked, turning onto another row of vines marked *Tempranillo.*

"We have plenty of rooms at the inn," she said, attempting

to inject some levity into their conversation. She'd hardly thought about his question.

Bennett smiled at that. "Which room—yours or mine? Or did you have another idea? Once the tenants in my home move out, we can relocate there. You can redecorate any way you want."

Ivy thought about this. As appealing as it should be, she didn't want to move. Now or in the future. "I rather like being at the inn. Sunny is still there, and it's a place for Misty to come home to as well. Not that she is, but it's available if she needs it. And I love having the space for entertaining my family."

"None of that would change if we lived in my home. You'd still have the inn. Or another house of your choosing. I could get a good price for my place if I were to sell it."

"No, don't do that. The inn just feels like home to me."

He put his arm around her. "To me, too."

Ivy leaned into him, enjoying the warmth of their bodies together and the sun on their shoulders. The climate was a little cooler at this higher altitude.

Ivy recalled when she'd sold her flat in Back Bay and rented the extra room in the professor's home. With a place of her own, she'd felt unmoored, adrift in life. Everything in her life had once been ordered and assumed. Suddenly, Jeremy's death had ripped her secure platform from beneath her feet. She'd felt like she'd been in free fall until arriving in Summer Beach. Strangely, she had Jeremy to thank for her new life, although he had never intended it.

Not that she couldn't have recovered on her own, she thought quickly. She might have sold some paintings, landed a show at an art gallery, or licensed her artwork. She might have done very well for herself.

Yet, she'd chosen to try to save Jeremy's investment of their retirement funds in Summer Beach. It hadn't been easy, but she'd done it. And in the process, the old house had become her home.

"Okay," Bennett said slowly. "So we're back to the original question. After we're married, do you want to live in your room or mine?"

Ivy honestly didn't know. She'd hardly thought about it. Was that a sign in itself? "I don't know. Why don't we wait to figure that out?"

"Mine has the kitchen, but yours has the large bath and dressing area." When she didn't say anything, he patted her hand. "We can always try one room, and if we don't like it, we can move right back into the other one. How's that?"

"That sounds perfect," she said quickly. And it was. Bennett was so understanding. On the plus side, that was another reason she loved him.

But love wasn't like accounting, with assets in one column and liabilities in another. Ivy couldn't simply tally up the scores to find the answer. In the final accounting for love, they had to be all in or all out.

Ivy fell into step with Bennett as they continued strolling through the vineyards, taking in the scenery and chatting about nothing in particular.

As pastoral as their surroundings were, beneath it all, Ivy was still bristling from their conversation and Bennett withholding information about Mitch. Maybe it wasn't any of her business, but Shelly was her sister. Family ties went deeper than friendships, and this bothered her. She tried to brush away this thought and enjoy the day, yet it was still there in the back of her mind, taunting her.

Or maybe the wine was clouding her judgment. She'd think about that tomorrow.

13

The next day, Ivy rang the silver bell on the counter at the Laundry Basket. Louise poked her head from behind a mechanized rack of clothing.

"Be right there," she called out.

Ivy waited, and a few moments later, Louise bustled to the counter. She smoothed her short, steel-gray hair from her forehead. "It's good to see you. Hey, I'm sorry about what happened with Darla at Java Beach."

"I guess you heard all about it," Ivy said.

"Word of that fiasco got around the town pretty quickly. Folks say you stuck up for yourselves pretty well." Louise grinned and tapped on the counter. "I knew I picked the right team."

Ivy had hoped that incident would die down. "Unfortunately, it's not my first run-in with Darla. But this time, it's Shelly that she's after. I wish we could get along."

Louise shook her head. "I've known Darla for a long time, and she has always been this way. People are saying that Shelly stole her boyfriend."

Ivy opened her mouth in astonishment at the intimation.

"You can't be serious. I don't think Mitch would do anything of the sort."

"Now, now," Louise said, holding up her palms. "I don't mean that literally. Darla fancies Mitch a sort of son; she wants the best for him. And to Darla's way of thinking, that would be someone just like her. But I'm still on the Bay team."

"This isn't a sporting event," Ivy said, more sharply than she'd intended. She clenched her teeth to contain further comments she might regret.

Embarrassed, Louise drew a hand over her jaw. "We don't mean anything by that. Well, I don't, but I can't speak for other people. They're just bored. You have to understand; you big-city ladies came breezing into town and then opened that old haunted house—"

"It's not haunted," Ivy said quickly. "That was just a rumor."

"Maybe so, but that was the biggest thing that had happened here in a while. Except for when Jeremy Marin sued the city. That sure got everyone's attention, and so did his girl—"

"About the clothes I dropped off," Ivy said, interrupting. "Are they ready?"

"Oh, sure." Louise's face flushed. "Look at me, standing here yammering as if I were a gossip hound, which I'm not. No, ma'am. I'm on—"

"My team," Ivy said. *Thank goodness for small favors*, she thought. There were few secrets in Summer Beach—and even fewer who could keep them, it seemed. Yet, if that were the only downside to living here, Ivy could manage that.

Louise disappeared. A few moments later, she emerged from the long clothing rack with Ivy's order draped over her arm. She hung it on a clothes rack by the cash register and beamed. "Since these are old and delicate, I steamed and spot cleaned them by hand. I think I did some of my finest work. I hope you're happy with it."

Ivy lifted the plastic covering and was impressed. Louise had taken special care of the delicate fabric. "You did a beautiful job. Why, these pieces almost look new." The silk shimmered, and the lace looked fresh.

"It's a shame that this won't fit you or Shelly. Are you sure your sister wouldn't wear a mid-calf length?"

"Shelly has her heart set on a long dress." Ivy touched the length of lace that Louise had folded over the hanger. It was a shame that neither she nor Shelly could wear this.

Ivy stared at the dress, trying to envision a restyling of some sort. "Say, I have an idea." She picked up a pencil on the counter and sketched an idea on a notepad imprinted with a laundry basket and a swimsuit.

"Do you think you could do something like this?" Ivy asked.

Louise studied the drawing and nodded. "That would be pretty. I'll see what I can do. Of course, I'll need measurements."

"I'll call you with them later," Ivy said.

She walked out of the Laundry Basket, smiling at what she had in mind. Checking her watch, she saw she still had a little time before meeting Megan at the Starfish Café. Ivy had brought Amelia Erickson's trousseau log with her to share.

Strolling along Main Street to her car, Ivy passed several local shops. A few owners were outside chatting, and Ivy noticed that some conversations paused as she passed. Were others dividing up between Team Darla and Team Ivy and Shelly? She wondered.

As Ivy neared Antique Times, the shop that Nan and her husband Arthur ran, she saw a sign on the front door saying they would be back in ten minutes.

Like many of the Summer Beach shopkeepers, when Arthur and Nan stepped away from the store, they simply hung out a sign that invited shoppers to come back later.

During the day, Nan served as the receptionist at City Hall. She joined Arthur in the late afternoon and on weekends.

Ivy was wondering if she should wait or go when she saw Arthur ambling along the sidewalk. His Hawaiian print shirt was right on brand for Summer Beach. She lifted her hand in greeting.

"What brings you out today?" Arthur asked, his English accent evident. "With such beautiful weather, I should think the inn would be quite busy by now. Can you be spared?"

"Our reservations have picked up," Ivy said. "But Shelly and Poppy are watching the inn." She hesitated. "Do you have time for a question?"

"Of course. Please come in."

She followed Arthur into the quaint shop. "I've been hearing talk about Team Darla versus Team Ivy and Shelly. Do you know anything about this?"

Surprised, Arthur coughed into his hand. "Don't let that bother you. It's nothing but people having too much time on their hands."

"I'm concerned about the effect it might have on Shelly and Mitch." Although Ivy didn't like the gossip about her and Bennett, she was more concerned about her sister. Mitch still hadn't committed to a date—even after they'd received their marriage license. Although Ivy was hopeful, with each passing day, Mitch seemed to become more nervous.

Darla's actions certainly weren't helping matters.

Ivy spoke directly. "What can I do to bring Darla to our team? After all, once Shelly and Mitch are married, Darla will practically be an in-law. You know how close she and Mitch are."

"That is a problem," Arthur said, taking off his glasses to clean them. "Have you thought of involving her in the wedding festivities?"

"Shelly has been reaching out to share herbs and vegetables she is growing, but Darla ignores her. Shelly leaves produce on Darla's doorstep."

"If Darla takes Shelly's offerings inside, then there's hope. If Shelly involved Darla in the wedding plans, it might help."

Ivy wondered about that. That could work, but then again, it might turn into a disaster.

When Ivy returned to her car, she lowered the convertible top on the old red-and-white 1950s Chevy. She loved driving it on mild sunny days. By the time she arrived at the Starfish Café to meet Megan, the crisp sea breeze had cleared her mind and lifted her spirits. As Shelly often said, there was nothing like a good dose of negative ions from the ocean to soothe the soul.

She parked the car in the shade of the old 1930s house that had been converted to a restaurant, although most of the seating was outside. Ivy saw Megan seated mid-way down the cantilevered hillside with decks facing the sea. Ivy started on the path that crisscrossed the slope. Old-fashioned rose bushes rambled along the path, perfuming the air with their sweet scents. Spotting Megan's short, wavy blond hair, Ivy made her way toward the young filmmaker.

Megan greeted her with a kiss on each cheek. "I can hardly wait to see what you've found."

"I've been dying to show it to you," Ivy said.

After they ordered the homemade carrot ginger soup and wilted spinach and bacon salads, Ivy brought out the book. She slid it out of a protective fabric case she'd put it in and opened the cover.

Megan's eyes grew wide when she saw the swatches stitched to the pages. "I've never seen anything like this. Where did you find it?"

Ivy told her the story about the discovery. "But there's more, and I thought you might like to see this." She slid out the old photo of Amelia and Josef. "It looks like Amelia might have had another marriage before Gustav."

Megan studied the photo. "This adds a new perspective on Amelia Erickson. Would you mind if I snapped a few photos of this photo and the book? I'm still conducting research, and I'll be happy to have this text translated for you."

"That would be wonderful. I'd love to know what Amelia's notes say." Ivy was curious to read the writings of Amelia as a teen or young woman.

As they ate, Ivy thought about Amelia and this latest discovery. While the wedding ensemble and the trousseau journal weren't as spectacular as their initial finds in the house, they were more personal. Other discoveries reflected Amelia's exterior life and the important work she had done in her life, but this little book might help Ivy understand what motived Amelia. Even then, she might never know the woman's whole story or what motivated her to act as she did.

After lunch, Megan promised to call when she received the translations, and Ivy wished her well and returned to her car.

THE NEXT DAY after all the guests were served at breakfast, Ivy and Shelly gathered on the veranda with Poppy to coordinate the York wedding. Shelly had installed a bell at the front desk that would ring in the kitchen and outside. They would hear if anyone came in, although they weren't expecting any new guests until the afternoon.

"We need room to stage everything for Rachel's wedding," Ivy said. "I thought about the lower level, but we'd have to carry everything up and down the stairs. We'll outgrow the kitchen and butler's pantry pretty fast. On the day of the event, we'll work in the ballroom, but I'd like to keep the area nice for guests until then. Any ideas?"

Shelly thought for a moment. "If I move the morning yoga classes poolside, I'll have room and the light I need on the enclosed porch to work with the flowers and decorative accessories. The mornings have grown warmer these last couple of weeks, so I think guests will like being outdoors."

"Good," Ivy said. "I can also put away my paints and set up another table if you need room to work on accessories."

Poppy was making notes. "We haven't much time. Is Eleanor expecting us to provide the guest book, place cards, and menus at each place setting?"

"I'll ask, but the answer is probably yes," Ivy said. "I've arranged for the cake—Shelly, she wants flowers on that, too —and I've asked Marina to cater the dinner." Her friend ran the Coral Cafe on the beach, and Ivy was glad to give her the business. Having lived in San Francisco until recently, Marina was familiar with the upscale food Eleanor wanted for the formal dinner following the ceremony.

"And the photographer?" Poppy asked.

"Check," Shelly said. "A friend from New York who used to be a wedding photographer is working in Hollywood now. She agreed to shoot the wedding as long as I didn't tell anyone she was still doing weddings. It's all about appearances. She photographed a lot of my floral creations for magazines."

"This is all thanks to Eleanor's generous budget," Ivy said. "Speaking of finances, I have some good news. I spoke with Eleanor this morning, and she recognizes how much work we've been putting into the wedding. I told her this amount of work wasn't part of the original agreement. So she agreed to what I asked—and I went high. Although I think we'll earn every penny."

"That's great," Shelly said. "I knew you could do it. And if you didn't, I would have. In New York, I learned that you couldn't be shy about what you're worth."

Ivy shook her head. "I don't know why asking for what we deserve should be such a scary proposition."

"You just aren't used to doing it," Shelly said. "But when you work for yourself, you have to. It gets easier. And depositing the check always feels good."

"It sure does," Ivy said.

"As to flowers, what do you think of this arrangement?" Shelly asked, bringing up photos on her laptop. "This is a job I did for a spring wedding in New York."

"You sure have an eye for color," Ivy replied, peering through her reading glasses. Each design was so artistic. "Is this what Rachel wants?"

Shelly pulled up another image. "Rachel doesn't know what she wants, so she left it up to me. So I'm creating exactly what I would want if I had the budget. I'll live vicariously through her. And I guarantee that Rachel and Eleanor will love it."

Ivy listened with mixed feelings. Neither of them mentioned that they might have been planning their weddings right now. Shelly was nervous about Mitch, and Ivy didn't want to think about her wedding until after Shelly's. So they said little, but Ivy could tell that Shelly was thinking about it. Her thoughts drifted to the talk she'd had with Bennett at the vineyard. They'd had a beautiful day there, marred only by their conversation about Mitch and Shelly.

"Beach meets traditional—that's the theme," Shelly said, her gaze drawn toward the ocean. "Roses and lilies and tuberose, of course, along with peonies, ranunculus, and anemones. Voluptuous hydrangeas spilling from ginger jars with trailing vines of jasmine and ivy," she added, sketching the scene in her mind's eye with her hands. "Weathered beach accents like driftwood, beach glass, and seashells. I'm also having an arch built, and I plan to drape blankets of flowers over that and along the length of the tables in place of center-pieces. The entire ballroom will be a floral fantasy."

Poppy scribbled a note. "What color palette are you using, Shelly?"

Shelly spread her hands toward the beach. "With the ocean as a backdrop, instead of the more common white or marine-blue theme, I'm going for contrast against the blue water and sandy beach with vivid coral, pink, and mauve, finishing with dusky red. I'll use an ombré technique of fading colors from light to dark that will be spectacular. Rachel's bouquet will be gorgeous."

"And it will blend with the bridesmaid dresses," Ivy said, recalling the photos Eleanor had shared with her.

"I'll coordinate the other items we'll need," Poppy said.

Fortunately, Amelia Erickson had entertained on a grand scale, and they'd found crates of dishes and silver on the lower level, besides what they had found in the butler's pantry.

"I'm going to the wholesale flower market with Imani," Shelly said. "I need a lot more than she can provide through her shop, although she is ordering a lot for me. Since she knows all the best places for the trimmings and flowers, she offered to introduce me to her suppliers for special items I need. I'm enlisting her help, and we'll have a lot of fun."

"Is there anything else you need for decorations?" Ivy asked

Shelly twirled her pencil in thought. "I would like some unusual pieces. Hey, remember the old baskets and beach cruisers we found on the lower level? I could do something with those. I can just see an old bike by the front door, flowers spilling out of its wicker basket on the front."

"Sounds pretty," Ivy said. "That would make such a charming painting."

"I'll create it; you paint it," Shelly said, giving her a high five.

As they were finishing, the front bell rang.

"I'll get that," Poppy said.

After Poppy left, Ivy reached across the table and touched Shelly's hand. She wondered if she should tell her sister what Bennett had said. "Shelly, I've been thinking…"

"If it's about Mitch, I don't want to talk about it. It's obvious we're not getting married before Mom and Dad leave.

He's still being evasive." Shelly sank her face into her hands. "I've been through this before, haven't I?"

"He's not Ezzra," Ivy said. "I can't imagine what's going on in his mind, but it's clear that he loves you very much. Don't give up on him just yet."

Shelly sighed. "I don't know if I could give him up if I tried. Maybe I ought to, though."

Ivy's heart broke for her sister. She clutched Shelly's hand. "Try to keep the faith. A delay isn't a cancellation."

And then, a thought struck her. Could she say the same to Bennett?

14

*I*vy had just returned from the front desk after checking in a weekend guest when she saw Mitch carrying a wooden baluster up the stairs from the lower level. "Do you need help?"

"Thanks, but I've got this," Mitch replied.

"Looks like Shelly found a lot of things she can use down there. Here, I can dust that off for you. Put it on the kitchen counter."

Mitch slid the short pillar carefully onto the tile. The lathe-turned column had been one of many that might have held up a balustrade, perhaps for a staircase or a railing.

Ivy brought out a cleaning rag with a special wood-cleaning formula and smoothed it over the old piece. "This restores old wood. Look how beautiful it is now."

After the paintings Ivy and Shelly had discovered in the lower level had been removed and they'd brought up all the furniture they could use in the main house, they hadn't given much more thought to the space. The maintenance in the guest rooms, bathrooms, and main floor was enough to cover without added expense. Still, she wondered what they could do on that level that might bring in more income.

Shelly followed Mitch up the stairs. In her arms were vintage wicker baskets. Some were open, while others had lids and leather straps for hinges and fasteners.

"These baskets will be gorgeous," Shelly said. "I'll fill them with flowers. These are so much prettier than those that have been distressed to look old. Rachel and her mother will love these." She plopped them onto the counter and brushed dust from her hands.

"What are your plans for the balusters?" Ivy asked.

"I'll crown each one with a bouquet and twirl vines around the columns. Since we have several, I can use these to flank the entryway and the decorative arch I've had built for the bride and groom to stand with the minister."

"I love that idea," Ivy said.

Mitch put his arm around Shelly's shoulder. "You're amazing the way you can find discarded things and bring them back to life." He grinned. "Kind of like me."

"That's what I do," Shelly said, blushing a little.

Mitch tilted her chin and kissed her nose. "That's just one of the many reasons I love you. You breathe life into everything around you."

Ivy watched Shelly's face glow at Mitch's thoughtful words. These were the words of a man in love, and she couldn't be happier for Shelly. Ivy wondered what could be holding Mitch back—not that it was any of her business—but her sister's happiness was. Shelly didn't have much time left to start a family. Still, the foundation between a couple had to be strong before bringing children into the world. There would be challenges enough later in life.

"I just love designing with flowers," Shelly said. Happiness fairly shimmered on her face. "That's what drew me to creating designs for events in New York. Although it wasn't quite what I had studied in school, it made me happy. Even though there were the bridezillas and momzillas along the way, the best part was seeing the expressions on everyone's faces. People can't look at flowers and not be touched by their beauty. And if they aren't, then I know they're a big old grouch that I want to stay away from anyway."

Ivy laughed at that, but there was a lot of truth in what Shelly said. Ivy loved painting flowers, too. She finished wiping down the baluster and turned to Shelly. "I've decided to paint a new series based on your floral creations for this wedding. From the way you describe your plans, I know they're going to be spectacular."

"If Rachel only remembers one thing about her wedding, it's going to be the floral extravaganza." Shelly winked at her sister. "I'm really good at what I do."

A smile played on Mitch's lips, and Shelly swatted him on the arm. "Don't even say it."

Mitch's eyes widened with innocence. "Say what?"

Watching the banter between them, Ivy laughed. Surely they could find their way through the forest of doubt to the place where their souls could fully unite. Each one of them deserved happiness, and Ivy truly thought they were happier together.

She had never seen Shelly so much in love, and this time, it was a mature love. A love for the rest of her life. It disturbed Ivy to think this chance for happiness might slip away from them. What was it that Bennett had said to her on the drive home from the vineyard? *Let Mitch work it out by himself. He'll come around.*

It was all Ivy could do to keep her opinion to herself. She had to trust Bennett's judgment. If she said the wrong thing, it might drive Mitch even farther away. Ivy raked her teeth over her bottom lip. What, if anything, did Darla have to do with his hesitation?

As the week wore on, Shelly and Poppy tended to the decorations and supplies for Rachel's wedding. Ivy only wished that the excitement she saw in Shelly's eyes was for her wedding day instead of someone else's.

The time for their parents' departure was also drawing closer, and although Ivy was happy for them, she could hardly bear to say goodbye. Carlotta and Sterling were going to write regular posts on their voyage to keep everyone updated on their whereabouts and adventures. Ivy had invited all the siblings and their children to gather at the inn for a send-off party after the York wedding.

Ivy still wished that Shelly and Mitch could somehow get married before their parents left. But now it was too late to plan the wedding Shelly would have liked. They were all consumed with Rachel's wedding.

In the kitchen, Ivy removed two loaves of banana nut bread from the oven. This morning, she had devised a plan, although she hadn't told anyone about it. Banana nut bread was Darla's weakness, and Ivy meant to exploit that. Shelly would not be happy if she knew what Ivy was doing. Nor would Bennett.

Yet Ivy could no longer sit idly by and do nothing while Shelly might miss out on the wedding she'd dreamed of for so many years. If Ivy couldn't talk to Mitch, there was still something she could do about Darla. And maybe, just maybe, the two issues were somehow related.

While Ivy waited for the bread to cool, her phone rang.

"Hi, Eleanor," Ivy said, automatically pulling her Eleanor-to-do list from her pocket. "Yes, we have rooms reserved for family members. Here is who we have so far."

Ivy read off the names on the list. Most were checking in the morning of the wedding, which was being held on a Friday evening when the pastor they wanted to use would be available.

"I wish you had suites for everyone," Eleanor said, fretting over the phone. "Churchill's family is accustomed to fine accommodations. As you know, they're related to royalty."

This was Eleanor's familiar refrain. "The rooms are spacious, and I promise that we will shower them with attention to ensure their comfort. But I can't conjure suites out of thin air. We have what we have, Eleanor."

The woman sighed. "I suppose it's just for one night."

"They won't be languishing in the room for long. The wedding will be a magical affair. Shelly is outdoing herself with the floral arrangements, and the musicians have your musical request list." Ivy had asked Celia, who sponsored the music program at Summer Beach schools, to recommend musicians, which she had. "There will be delicious food, dancing, and revelry long into the night. We're doing everything we can to make it a wonderful, memorable weekend."

Eleanor was tightly wound today, but Ivy assumed that pre-wedding jitters were normal. Glancing at her list, she went over final arrangements for the cake, photography, menu, and other incidentals.

"One more thing," Eleanor said. "Where will people park?"

"We have plenty of street parking available." Yet even as Ivy said that she knew it was going to be a problem.

"We must have valet parking. After all, Churchill's family is—"

"I'll get right on it," Ivy said, knowing what was coming next. "That cost will be added to the budget." She was growing more accustomed to speaking about costs and asking for overages. As her mother said, *It's just business, honey.*

"That's fine, but please make sure they have good manners and uniforms. They must be respectful. Even though this wedding is much more modest than we had planned, I want everything to be perfect. For my Rachel, of course," she hastily added.

"Of course." Ivy made a few notes. She suspected Rachel would be relieved when the wedding was over.

"That's all I can think of now, but let's talk again. Twice a day until we arrive on Thursday to inspect everything."

Ivy signed off. She'd spoken to Rachel several times. The young woman was far more concerned about the baby than the wedding. Once, Rachel had called the whole affair a circus, and another time she said it was her mother's folly.

Ivy thought how nice it would be if the wedding brought mother and daughter together, but they seemed long past that. She wondered what it would take for Eleanor to honestly connect with her daughter.

The phone rang again. Ivy tapped to answer it.

"Mom, it's me."

Ivy smiled at the sound of Misty's voice. "And to what do I owe the pleasure of this call from my lovely daughter?"

"You won't believe it, but I slipped on ice last night outside of the theater and broke my arm."

"Oh, darling. What a bad break for you." Ivy winced as soon as the words were out of her mouth. Misty had been so excited about starting a new play.

"Actually, it was a pretty clean break," Misty said. "And I know you didn't mean the pun."

"I'm sorry, I was referring to the theater production you're in. What will that mean for you?"

"Well, I can't go on stage with the cast, but I have an understudy who can carry on. But here's the exciting part. Before I was cast in this play, I auditioned for a role in a television series. I didn't hear anything for the longest time, but I got a call back last week. My agent has been trying to figure out how I could take time off from the play to film. So this couldn't have come at a better time."

"That's wonderful, sweetheart. Will you film in New York?"

"That's the best part. It's in Los Angeles, so I'll be nearby. It begins filming in September. Until then, I have table reads for the script and costume fittings. My cast should be off before filming begins. My agent has also lined up voice-over work for me until then."

"My goodness," Ivy exclaimed, thrilled that Misty would be so close again. She could hear the excitement in her older daughter's voice.

"My roommates helped me pack my room, and I've booked a flight. I hope you have a room for me."

"You can share with Sunny or me. We're having a big wedding party here. And you'll be able to see your grandparents off, too. We're having a *bon voyage* party for them. Send your flight details, and one of us will pick you up at the airport."

"That's great. See you soon, Mom. Loves you."

"Loves you, too, sweetie." Ivy hung up, elated that Misty would be joining them.

After putting the phone down, Ivy glanced at the clock and checked her banana nut bread. "Perfect." She wrapped the bread in pretty new dishtowels she'd bought at Nailed It and arranged them in a basket with several of Shelly's fresh-cut roses.

Just then, the rear door to the kitchen slammed, startling Ivy.

"Sure smells good in here," Poppy said.

Ivy pressed a hand to her chest, relieved that it wasn't Shelly. "Oh, it's just you."

Poppy threw her a quizzical look.

"I didn't mean that the way it sounded," Ivy said quickly. "I mean, I thought you were Shelly. Excuse me, but I have to go somewhere. Don't tell Shelly where I've gone."

"Even if I knew, I wouldn't. Aunt Ivy, are you feeling okay?"

A spy she would never make. "I'm fine. Really. Just fine."

Ivy hurried to the front parlor and positioned herself by the window. Darla was a creature of habit. Lately, she had been going to another coffee shop in town, but one of the high points of her day was the daily post. As soon as the mail carrier deposited letters in Darla's metal mailbox and the lid clanked down, Darla eagerly emerged to collect it.

Ivy couldn't imagine what was so enchanting about bills and sales flyers, but she supposed it was a routine for the older woman.

The mail carrier was prompt. As soon as Ivy saw her walking toward her neighbor's house, she scooted out the front door with her basket. She had to be right behind the mail lady. She waited a moment on her property before scurrying behind the carrier.

"Don't mind me," Ivy said brightly. "Looks like we're going to the same place."

"That's surprising," the woman said with a grin.

Ivy sighed. Summer Beach was a very small town. "I thought I'd treat Darla to something special." She held a finger to her lips to indicate silence.

The postal carrier deposited the mail, and the lid made a resounding *clunk*. "Have a good day," she whispered, clearly amused.

Ivy pressed herself against the wall in case Darla looked through the peephole. She could hardly breathe from anticipation. She'd have to act fast.

Darla opened the door. In a flash, Ivy stepped to the door. "I just baked banana nut bread, and I have a couple of loaves left. I thought you might like them."

"That's a lie if I ever heard one," Darla said, moving to shut the door.

But Ivy had planned for this. She stuck the sturdy boot she'd put on—not exactly warm weather wear—into the door and wedged it open. "Sorry, Darla, but we have to talk. Now. I'm coming in." Ivy shut the door behind her.

She was in. Never having been in Darla's home, Ivy quickly glanced around. The living room opened into the kitchen beyond. Everything was circa the 1970s, from the harvest gold countertops to the avocado green refrigerator. Ivy quickly surmised that Darla didn't like change.

Darla's eyebrows shot up in shock. "I could call Chief Clarkson on you."

"For breaking and entering with hot baked goods? I don't think so. Besides, he's rather fond of this recipe, too."

Folding her arms, Darla narrowed her eyes. "What do you want?"

"I want to give you this," Ivy said, thrusting the basket toward her. "And I want you to stop this nonsense about Shelly."

"Ha." As if the basket were radioactive, Darla took a step back. "You're still upset about that day at Java Beach." She huffed. "That was nothing at all."

"Then why haven't you gone back? I've never known you to miss a day there."

"I needed a change."

Ivy lifted an edge of the flowered dishtowel. A mouthwatering aroma wafted toward Darla. "Just out of the oven."

Darla whipped around. "Oh, all right. I'm sorry. Now go." She tried to snatch the basket.

Ivy shifted it just out of reach and shook her head. "Not so fast. I need answers. Why are you doing this to poor Mitch? And Shelly? After I saved your life on the beach, I thought we'd become friends."

"For a while," Darla allowed. "I just don't want to see Mitch ruin his life."

Ivy held back. She'd expected this. "That's strange. Bennett told me he's never seen Mitch so happy or settled."

"Men don't always know what's best for them."

"Hmm. I think you're afraid that Mitch might forget about you after he marries."

Darla only shrugged.

"Did you know that Shelly looks upon you as Mitch's mother? She's hoping that after they have a baby, the child will call you Nana." Shelly hadn't exactly said that, but Ivy was grasping at anything to diffuse this situation.

Darla grew quiet, clearly considering this.

"I know Mitch is no replacement for your son, and I'm so sorry you lost him at such a young age. But sometimes, we get to choose the family we want. I know there's a lot of love between you and Mitch. He misses seeing you at Java Beach."

"He dropped off some croissants the other day."

"Did you two talk?"

"I didn't open the door." Darla hung her head.

"He's hurting, too," Ivy said softly.

"He is?"

Ivy nodded. "You see, he hopes that you and Shelly will get along. And I know you want to see him happy." She slid the basket onto the kitchen counter. "I can slice this for you right now."

"Well, okay." Darla brought out a cutting board in the shape of a pig and a bread knife. "While you do that, I'll get my mail." She returned with a stack of bills and flyers. On the top was a letter postmarked *Italy*.

Darla noticed Ivy glancing at it. "That's from the pen pal I've had since childhood," she said. "We've never met, but sometimes her letters are the only things I have to look forward to in a day. We began writing when we were kids, and her parents wanted her to have an English-speaking pen pal. "

Ivy was intrigued by this connection that Darla had. "Do you write often?"

"Every week now. Not so much when our children were young." Darla's voice faded away on that thought.

Ivy sliced off the end of the bread and gave Darla the next slice. Steam rose from it. "As for Mitch and Shelly, you can be an important part of their children's lives. I loved having my grandmother live nearby. She taught me so many things. In fact, this is her bread recipe. She taught me how to make it when I was about twelve years old."

"I could teach a child a thing or two. Good things," Darla added quickly. "Like fishing or skimming rocks."

"Things you did with your son, right?"

Darla glanced at a photo of a young boy on the wall and nodded. Tears rimmed her eyes. "I know Mitch loves Shelly. I suppose I hadn't thought too far ahead." A whisper of a smile crossed her face. "Imagine. Me, a grandmother. Hearing about my friends' grandchildren…" She stopped and shook her head.

"I'll bet that's hard," Ivy said softly. None of them—Shelly, Ivy, or Darla—were going anywhere other than Summer Beach. Ivy couldn't imagine selling the inn. So, they had to learn how to get along. "Soon, you'll have something to add to that conversation."

"I will, won't I?" Darla bit into the banana nut bread. "I think this is your best effort so far," she said with a mischievous glint in her eyes.

Ivy was relieved over Darla's change of heart. Yet she wasn't finished. "Now, about Charlie and this marriage wagering that he's been encouraging. What do you think it would take for him to call it off? That might be making Mitch nervous. What do you think?"

"Charlie likes to have fun and make a little bit on the side. I didn't think there was much harm in that. But I can see your point. You think that might cause Mitch to get cold feet?"

"I couldn't say." She hoped that Darla could connect the dots between that and the potential for grandchildren. "But it can't be helpful, especially right under Mitch's nose at Java Beach." She hesitated. "I don't suppose you'd have any influence over Charlie, would you?"

"Well, I should say I do. His wife Charity, rest her poor soul, was my best friend. If it weren't for me, she might've left him years ago. After Charity died, I cooked and cleaned for that man. Not that I wanted anything from him, mind you. Don't listen to what anyone else has to say about my motives.

They were pure, I tell you." She rolled her eyes. "Old gossip mongers."

Ivy rested her chin on her hand. "So, what shall we do about them and Charlie?"

"I'll take care of my friends. Now, about Charlie... I hardly think he'd do this except for the fact that he lost a little money at the horse races not long ago."

"Does Charlie do anything?"

"He has a small pension, that's all."

Ivy thought quickly. "I might have a way for him to make a little cash on the side—as long as he stops taking bets on our weddings. That's against the law, and I'd hate to see him suffer the consequences. Chief Clarkson can be mighty tough."

"You don't think the chief would arrest Charlie, do you?"

"I'm just saying it's a possibility, especially since he's taking bets on what the mayor is doing. Bennett is a city official, and well, it could be serious." Ivy held her breath and waited. She had no idea if that mattered, but she'd try anything.

"Oh, dear. I hadn't thought of it that way." Worry lines creased Darla's face. "I should call him right away and warn him. Still, I don't know how he'll respond."

"Ask him to come over. Maybe he'd like a loaf of bread." Ivy tapped the other loaf.

A smile grew on Darla's face, and she marched into the kitchen and plucked the receiver from the harvest gold wall phone. She dialed the number on the rotary dial—which seemed to take achingly forever. She cradled the phone between her ear and her shoulder and tapped her foot.

Ivy could hardly stand the wait.

Darla's eyes brightened when he answered. "Charlie, get over here," Darla said in a gruff voice. "I need to talk to you about something important." Switching to sweetness, she added, "And I have some warm banana nut bread right out of the oven for you."

Darla listened for a moment, then held up a finger to Ivy.

"Forget that. I need you to get here as fast as you can. It's an emergency."

Finally, Darla hung up the phone and nodded with satisfaction.

Ivy breathed out. She was determined to put an end to this mess. So far, she was halfway there.

15

*A*fter a day at City Hall, Bennett swung out of his SUV in the rear car court at the inn. Just before he'd left City Hall, Nan had been eager to share the latest Summer Beach happenings with him. His receptionist didn't have many details, but Bennett suspected Ivy might be behind it.

Not far away, Ivy was coming out of the kitchen, her purse on her arm and keys in her hand.

He shut the door and walked toward her, noticing how the sun glinted on her hair.

"Just who I wanted to see," he said, smiling.

She paused, shielding her eyes from the sun. "How was your day?"

"I just heard the most interesting news," Bennett began. "It seems old Charlie is leaving his life of crime to start a new event parking business. His first job is parking cars for the York wedding. You wouldn't know anything about that, would you?"

"Of course, I would," Ivy said. "I hired Charlie. Diego, the bank teller, is going to help out, too. Very industrious of them, don't you think?"

Bennett couldn't argue with that. "Here's where it gets

intriguing. Did you know Charlie gave everyone their money back for their bets? He said he doesn't need the money now that he's going to be working."

"Really?" Ivy seemed to feign surprise. "Well, that is a positive step for him."

Bennett narrowed his eyes. "Why do I have the feeling you had something to do with that?"

"Maybe Charlie had a moral reckoning," Ivy said, avoiding his question. "It's about time." She paused. "Come to think of it, he could have quite a little business going, what with all the restaurants and events going on in Summer Beach during the high season."

Grinning, Bennett folded his arms. "And you just happened to point that out to him?"

"I like to help my fellow entrepreneurs," Ivy said, but Bennett could tell she was trying to keep a straight face. Turning an innocent face up to him, she added, "Charlie came along at the perfect time."

Bennett was on to her. He swept her into his arms and lifted her from the ground. "You're a wonder. I don't know how you did it, but I'm impressed."

Her laughter bubbled up. "Women know how to get things done."

"Another reason why I love you, just in case I needed one more."

"I hope you're not upset," she said. "You warned me to keep out of it, but Shelly's my sister. I'd do anything for her."

Bennett remembered that. In this instance, he had under-estimated Ivy's creativity and determination.

"Actually, I appreciate it," he said. "All that team nonsense was getting to me. Probably to Mitch, too." He paused, thinking about the emotional turmoil Mitch was going through. "Did you know that Darla returned to Java Beach this afternoon? She set everyone straight in no uncertain terms." He grinned. "I don't think she'll say another word against those sassy, big-city girls."

"Why, Mr. Mayor. That sounds like gossip to me."

Bennett chuckled over that. "I'm just passing on the latest report from Nan."

Ivy only smiled. "Glad we got that out of the way."

She shifted her purse on her arm. "I was on my way to the grocery store. Shelly and Poppy are busy getting ready for the York wedding this weekend, and they drafted Sunny, Imani, and Jamir. I thought I'd make lasagna for everyone."

Ivy was always thinking of others. "You're busy, too. What do you need? I'll get it."

"I have everything but the lasagna noodles. We probably need more salad, too."

"Done. Be back in a minute. Call me if you think of anything else." Bennett climbed back into his SUV.

As he drove past Java Beach, he saw Mitch coming toward him, cruising on his skateboard on the sidewalk wearing his shades and sunhat. He often did quick errands to the bank or post office on his skateboard. Bennett grinned. Just another day at the office for Mitch. What a life he'd created for himself.

He lifted his hand to Mitch, who waved back as they passed each other.

Just then, a convertible full of beach-goers in front of Bennett did a sharp U-turn. He slowed to avoid them; then, he heard a scream. As he looked back, he saw Mitch's sun hat fly through the air.

With his heart in his throat, Bennett pulled over, flipped on his emergency flashers, and leapt from his SUV. Holding up his hand to stop traffic, he raced to the other side of the street, his pulse hammering.

Mitch was on the pavement, motionless.

With a prayer on his lips, Bennett ran toward him, yelling for someone to call for emergency help.

The driver of the convertible had turned too wide. Black tire marks arched over the sidewalk. In the car, the young woman driving was crying. "I'm so sorry. I didn't even see him."

Bennett reached Mitch first. He knelt beside his friend, gravel scraping his knees through the fabric of his slacks, but he didn't care. "Mitch, Mitch, can you hear me?"

Blood trickled from a cut above Mitch's eye.

No response.

He pressed his fingers against Mitch's neck, searching for a pulse in his carotid artery.

A second later, Bennett let out a breath. *He's alive. But how badly is he hurt?* Taking care not to aggravate possible injuries, he touched Mitch's arm.

"Mitch, can you hear me?"

No answer.

He shook his arm slightly. "Mitch, if you can hear me, you've been hurt, but I'm here with you. Help is on the way."

Bennett had also been trained in emergency response for the volunteer firefighting program, so he performed a cursory check. Mitch's breathing was regular, and his pulse was steady. He couldn't see any obviously broken limbs. Besides a cut above his eye, he also had bloodied knees and other abrasions. He didn't dare move him in case he was severely injured.

Gently, Bennett wiped blood dripping toward Mitch's eye. "Stay with me, Mitch. Open your eyes if you can. I'm right here with you, buddy."

He waited. After a few moments, Mitch's lashes fluttered. *Once. Twice.* Bennett leaned closer. Even though his heart was pounding, he tried to keep his voice steady and soothing. "If you can hear me, try to open your eyes."

Mitch's eyelids shifted again, and a moan escaped his lips.

Bennett's heart surged with hope. "That's it, come on. I know you can hear me. Stay still. Paramedics are on their way." Mitch seemed like he was struggling to form words. Bennett leaned over his friend, listening.

"Wha-at...happened?" Mitch managed to ask, though his voice was barely audible.

"A car made a U-turn, and the driver didn't see you."

Mitch lifted his hand to his face and touched his cut. Bringing his hand down, he saw the blood on his fingers. Closing his eyes, he struggled again to speak. "Tell Shelly...I love her."

Bennett forced back tears prickling his eyelids. "You'll tell her yourself. Hang in there, buddy. You're going to be okay, but don't try to move."

After what seemed like an hour but was probably only a couple of minutes, a Summer Beach emergency response vehicle pulled alongside them, and two paramedics rushed toward Mitch.

Bennett quickly told them what happened and reported on Mitch's pulse, breathing, and alertness.

"Thanks, Mayor. We'll take it from here."

Rocking back on his heels, Bennett made room for the first responders to work. Behind them, Chief Clark Clarkson and a partner arrived on the scene. The driver of the other car and her friends were huddled around the car, looking stricken.

While he kept one eye on Mitch, Bennett spoke to Clark and gave a brief statement. The other officer photographed the scene and Mitch's mangled skateboard. Bennett continued to stay with Mitch while the police chief moved on to speak with the young women.

Mitch opened his eyes a slit. "How's my board?"

One of the paramedics leaned over him. "A lot worse off than you are."

A guarded wave of relief swept through Bennett.

The paramedic went on to ask Mitch a few questions, and he gave coherent answers. The two paramedics continued to monitor him and dress his wounds. After a little while, they had Mitch sitting up.

Blinking, Mitch came out of his daze. "Man, that was wild." He ran a hand over the back of his neck.

Bennett peered at him. "Do you remember what happened?"

Mitch nodded slowly. "Out of the corner of my eye, I saw a car coming at a weird angle. I couldn't do much, so I jumped as high as I could out of the way. Unplanned like that, it was kind of awkward. I heard the board crunch before I came down. Guess my landing needs some work."

Bennett squatted down beside him and brushed dirt from Mitch's shoulders. "You got lucky that time." He turned to the paramedics. "Do you think he needs to go to the hospital?"

Mitch waved off the suggestion. "I don't need any hospital."

"Not so fast, buddy." Bennett discussed Mitch's condition with the paramedics. "It's better that you let a doctor check you. Come on. I'll go with you." Losing consciousness could indicate something more serious.

"Okay, if you say so," Mitch grumbled.

Bennett helped him to his feet. Local shopkeepers and onlookers had gathered around, and when Mitch stood, they broke out in applause.

Mitch gave them a thumbs-up and grinned. "First time I've ever had a standing ovation. Heck of a way to get it, though."

Bennett was glad to hear Mitch's sense of humor coming back. Still, he wanted to make sure his friend was okay. He remembered the noodles and salad. That would have to wait a little longer.

At the small local hospital, a doctor saw Mitch right away. After running tests and ordering an x-ray—all of which appeared normal—the physician released Mitch with a warning.

"I could take you home, but I don't want to leave you alone," Bennett said. "As the doctor said, we should continue to watch you for possible signs of a concussion. Why don't you come over to the inn? You can stay in my room, and Shelly can look after you."

"Sounds good," Mitch said as Bennett helped him into his SUV. "I need to see Shelly. Did you call her?"

"I wanted to make sure you were all right first. You can tell her what happened." Bennett started back to the inn. "That's a pretty impressive bandage above your eye. You're sure to get some sympathy for that."

Mitch nodded thoughtfully. "That happened so fast. One second I was cruising along, and in the next second, I was airborne. Life could have changed in an instant—and not in a good way."

"That can happen," Bennett said. "But it can change for the better, too. Think of the moment you first saw Shelly."

Mitch quirked a corner of his mouth. Touching the bandage above his eye, he added, "Just when you think you have forever ahead of you, maybe you don't."

16

*I*vy and Shelly were in the kitchen making supper when they heard the kitchen door slam.

"You sure took long enough," Ivy said, a little annoyed. Looking up, she saw blood on Bennett's white shirt. His face was drained of color. She cried out, "Oh, my goodness, what happened?"

He put up his hands. "Mitch is okay now, but—"

"Is he hurt?" Shelly dropped the cucumber she was slicing. "Where is he?" she demanded.

"I helped him up to my room," Bennett said. "He's resting on the couch, but he's pretty beat up. Nothing broken—except his skateboard. He checked out at the hospital, just to make sure. A car made a U-turn, and he had to leap out of the way. You might want to take some ice packs and pain medication if you have them. He's going to be sore tomorrow."

Ivy quickly pulled out ice packs from one of the refrigerators and shoved them into a grocery bag, along with dish towels. She handed the bag to Shelly. "Take these, and I'll bring some hot tea."

Shelly grabbed the bag and raced outside toward Bennett's apartment over the garage.

Watching her go, Ivy pressed a hand against her chest, thankful that Mitch wasn't badly injured. Shelly would have been devastated.

Ivy wrapped her arms around Bennett. "Thanks for bringing him back here. How did you find him?"

"I saw it happen. If that car had been going any faster, he wouldn't have had a chance." Bennett went on to tell her the whole story, and she put on a teapot as she listened.

When Bennett finished, Ivy asked, "Do you think he'll have to stay in bed for a while?"

"He's young, and nothing is broken. He'll probably ache tomorrow, but he should mend quickly."

"Thank goodness," Ivy said. "I'm so glad you were there."

"Me, too, though it was pretty tough to see."

When the tea was ready, Bennett carried the tray to Mitch while Ivy looked for pain relief medication in her bathroom. When she found some tablets, she hurried to join Bennett and Shelly, who were seated beside Mitch. Bennett had changed shirts, and Shelly was gently wiping Mitch's face and limbs with a damp washcloth.

Watching Shelly tend to Mitch touched Ivy's heart. He was in good hands with her. And Ivy knew that worked both ways. *They belong together*, she thought. Since the gossip in town had died down, maybe he'd gain the confidence he needed to move forward with their wedding.

She placed the pain medication on the coffee table. "I'm so glad you're okay, Mitch."

"I've got a great nurse here with me," he said, looking up at Shelly with love in his eyes.

"Watch him carefully," Bennett said, concern evident in his voice. "He could have a concussion." He went on to tell Shelly what changes to look for.

As Ivy watched them, Bennett put his arm around her. She could tell that he was worried about Mitch.

"We'll bring supper later," Ivy said softly.

As she and Bennett walked back to the main house, Ivy enjoyed the closeness of his arm around her. "That must have been scary to see," she said. "But I'm glad they have each other."

"It was," he agreed. "And it's good that Shelly is sticking by him. He'll get through this and everything else. I hope she can have just a little more patience."

"What do you mean by that?"

As if he'd slipped up and said something he shouldn't have, Bennett didn't answer right away. When he did, he simply said, "I meant his injuries."

Ivy sensed there was more, but Bennett seemed unwilling, or unable, to talk more this evening. He was shaken, too.

THE NEXT DAY, Ivy collected Amelia Erickson's wedding ensemble from the Laundry Basket. She hung the bridal gown, lace jacket, and lengths of lace in her closet. Lifting the breathable cotton cover Louise had placed over the vintage collection, she ran her hand over the supple fabric, admiring the artistry. After all these years, the garments were still beautiful.

When Ivy heard Sunny and Misty come into the room, she swept the clothes behind other items and hurried from the closet. Her eldest daughter was just arriving from Boston, and she'd been eager to see her.

"My darling," Ivy said, folding Misty into her arms. "How was your flight?"

"Fine, except for this." Misty lifted her forearm, which was encased in a cast. "At least my seatmate let me use the armrest."

Sunny had volunteered to pick up her sister at the San Diego airport, which wasn't too far from Sunny's university.

"Do you want to sleep in here with me?" Ivy asked.

"If it's okay, I'll stay with Sunny," Misty said. "We're going to hang out and sleep in the attic rooms. It's like having our own apartment up there."

Someday, Ivy planned to finish out those sparse rooms, but for now, it was a good place for the kids to bunk. "Did Sunny tell you about the wedding party that's here this weekend?"

"She did," Misty said. "If you need help, I'll pitch in as long as it doesn't involve much with my left forearm. Maybe I can direct."

"Just you being here is enough," Ivy said. "Let's see how Shelly is doing with the flowers and decorations."

Ivy made her way through the hall with Sunny and Misty. At once, Gilda's door opened, and she looked out. She held little Pixie in her arms.

"When Pixie heard Misty's voice, she went crazy," Gilda said. "Oh, I think I have something of yours that you left here at Christmas. Here, say hello to Pixie while I get it." She shoved the Chihuahua into Misty's arms.

Surprised, Misty laughed while Pixie sniffed her cast, yapped, and licked her face. "Did you nick something else, Pixie? I thought you left that thieving life behind."

Gilda returned with a tortoise-shell hair clip. "When I saw you wearing this, I thought it was so pretty. I guess Pixie did, too. I found it buried in her bed. But she's improved so much, haven't you, my precious little one?" Gilda took Pixie back. "She's been in therapy for her issue. See how remorseful she looks now?"

Ivy didn't see it, but she played along. Now, they all knew to look to Pixie whenever something went missing.

"Wow, I thought I'd lost that traveling," Misty said. She scratched Pixie's head. "You're a clever little pooch, aren't you?"

"I'd better finish my article before the festivities begin," Gilda said. "Do you think they'd mind if I watched from the stairway? I love weddings."

"I'll ask if you can sit in the back," Ivy replied. The guest list was quite small and restricted to family and a few close friends.

While Ivy understood that Eleanor was embarrassed that they moved the wedding date up, things like this happened. What was most important was that Rachel and Topper loved each other. They were looking forward to being parents and building their lives together. Ivy wondered when, or if, Eleanor would realize appearances weren't as important as family.

After saying goodbye to Gilda and Pixie, they passed another room. "That will be the bride's room," Ivy said. The bridesmaids were doubling up in the Sunset Suites, as were the groomsmen. Ivy had put Eleanor and her husband at the far end of the hallway, along with the groom's parents. The inn would be full this weekend.

Ivy continued downstairs to the long screened-in porch where Shelly taught yoga. Now, it was bursting with flowers, greenery, and decorations. Popular dance music was blasting from a set of speakers, and Shelly was in the flow swaying with the music.

After Mitch's accident yesterday, he had spent the night on Bennett's sofa, with Shelly sleeping on a guest cot beside him. He'd gone to sleep early and was up before sunrise with Shelly, who left early with Imani to buy flowers for the wedding. Although Mitch had skipped surfing, he'd gone to work at Java Beach, insisting he was only a little sore.

Shelly looked up from an arrangement she was working on. Petals clung to her messy topknot, but she looked happy. Nearby, Imani was trimming stems from roses.

"I brought reinforcements for you," Ivy said, gesturing to her daughters. "Although this new one is slightly wounded, she can certainly entertain you."

"Come to Auntie," Shelly said, holding her arms wide to Misty. "I'm thrilled to see you, but I'm so sorry you broke your arm. Those late spring snowfalls back east always took me by surprise, too."

"I went flying on a frozen puddle," Misty replied. "But now I've landed a part in a TV series." She lifted her cast. "You might say this is my lucky break."

Everyone laughed, and Ivy was glad they were all in good spirits after the trauma of Mitch's accident yesterday. That would help offset the stress that Eleanor brought on.

Shelly gestured to a workspace area. "You can be in charge of music and lists. And you have to fill us in with news from the East Coast."

"That I can do," Misty said.

Shelly motioned to Sunny. "You can help trim flowers, and you're also in charge of Sea Breeze cocktails." When Shelly saw the concern in Ivy's face, she quickly added, "Virgin only until after the ceremony. Then we'll have our own after-party."

"We're also having a *bon voyage* party this weekend after the wedding for your grandparents," Ivy said to Misty.

Shelly brought Sunny to a long table and showed her what to do. Before sunrise, Shelly and Imani had driven to the wholesale flower market in Los Angeles, where Shelly had bought enough flowers to fill the Jeep, as well as an enclosed crate she had strapped to the luggage rack on top. Ivy knew she was trying to pay Imani for her time, but so far, Imani had refused, insisting she was having fun.

Imani looked up, her smile as bright as the tie-dyed orange sundress she wore. "I'm so glad you girls are here. Shelly has incredible ideas, but not enough help to execute them."

"Is Jamir at Blossoms today?" Ivy asked.

"He is," Imani replied. "I don't know what I'll do when he graduates and starts a medical practice. But that's still years away."

Ivy gazed around the room. She had seldom seen Shelly prepare for an event of this magnitude. While Ivy lived in Boston and Shelly in New York, Ivy hadn't visited her sister in New York very often. Ivy was busy raising the girls, helping with homework, and making dinner, along with a thousand other little things she had to juggle to keep the family running. Shelly usually came to see them.

Ivy had seen photos of Shelly's arrangements, but she'd had little chance to see her sister execute a large job like this, besides tending to the arrangement in the foyer or working in the garden. Shelly had supplied the arrangements for Carol Reston's daughter's wedding last summer, but this job was several times that size. Watching Shelly work filled Ivy with fresh admiration for her sister's talents.

"The flowers are spectacular," Ivy said.

Shelly inclined her head and tapped her cheek. "These are all my favorites. If I had the money, this is what I would have at my wedding. So I'm living vicariously through all this."

Ivy slid her arm around Shelly's shoulder. "Someday, yours will be just as beautiful."

Shelly merely nodded and returned to building an arrangement on top of one of the vintage balusters. Deftly, she selected blossoms and tucked them in at just the right spots to create a cascading pattern of color. Roses, ranunculus, peonies, and anemones burst in shades of pink, coral, and red. Her training and confidence were on full display.

As Ivy watched, she caught Imani's gaze.

"Shelly is a true artist," Imani said, snipping stems. "You both are, only in different artistic mediums."

"She's amazing." Ivy continued watching. Shelly was in her creative zone now, humming to the music as she worked. She didn't notice Ivy taking photos.

Ivy looked at the images she was catching on her screen. An idea formed in her mind for a new watercolor series, not only of flowers but also of Shelly tending her arrangements. With Shelly's chestnut hair falling from her bun and petals in her hair as if strewn there by the breeze, the paintings would be beautiful romantic depictions.

Noticing the time, Ivy slipped away. Eleanor and Rachel

would be here soon, and Ivy wanted to inspect their rooms one last time before they arrived. She had added thoughtful touches in each room that she thought they might like. A selection of teas, fizzy water, and plain crackers in Rachel's room in case she felt queasy, and fruit baskets and wine in the parents' rooms.

Satisfied that the rooms were in order, Ivy checked her watch again. Charlie was reporting for work in five minutes. At Darla's, when Ivy heard Charlie mention that he had once driven a limo on weekends in Los Angeles and how much he enjoyed meeting people, a plan had clicked in her mind.

Charlie was bored in his retirement.

So she shared her thoughts with him. At first, he'd resisted, but as Ivy spoke, he grasped the idea that he could run a parking service for special events and maybe even a local car service.

Charlie arrived on the hour. He wore a white shirt, black slacks, a red bow-tie, and a dark jacket. He looked quite nice, and Ivy was relieved. She'd also checked her insurance to make sure she would be covered if someone banged up a BMW. Diego, the young bank teller and weekend surfer, hurried behind him. He also wore black slacks and a white shirt.

"How do we look?" Charlie asked, tucking his thumbs under his lapels.

"Fancy enough to serve royalty," Ivy said, thinking of Eleanor's claims. They walked outside, and she showed him where he could park cars.

Charlie lifted an eyebrow with skepticism. "If guests park on the street, it's not too far to walk."

"I know, but they'll be dressed up, and some might be frail or elderly. Above all, treat them as if they were cherished guests, which they are." Ivy hoped she hadn't made a mistake hiring Charlie, but it had seemed an opportune solution at the time.

"Right." Charlie tapped his temple. "I've got it all figured out. You can rest assured."

Just then, a late model European luxury car worth more than she'd made in years pulled to the curb. Eleanor and her husband, along with Rachel, were in the car.

Suddenly nervous, Ivy turned to Charlie and explained about Eleanor. "Would you help her with her door and the luggage?"

"Yes, ma'am," Charlie said. He snapped his fingers. "I'll get the doors, and Diego, you're in charge of luggage." To Ivy, he added, "Not a scratch, I promise." With a wink, Charlie set off for the car.

Ivy prayed Charlie could handle this role, but he seemed enthusiastic. In amazement, she watched him jog toward the car. Overnight, he seemed twenty years younger.

She smiled to herself. *That's what a purpose can do for you*, she thought.

17

*W*ith a pleasant smile, Ivy greeted the York family at the door.

Eleanor swept into the inn like a queen on the arm of her husband, who looked about twenty years older than his wife. With salt-and-pepper hair, a sweater vest, and horn-rimmed glasses, Churchill York had the appearance of old, comfortable money not trying to impress anyone. This was a stark contrast to photos Ivy had seen online of him wearing tuxedos at gala events with Eleanor.

Churchill's manner was as Rachel had described him. A warm smile and wonder filled his face as he gazed around the foyer. Ivy wouldn't have put Eleanor and Churchill together, though she assumed it might be a case of opposites attracting.

"Isn't this a charming place?" Eleanor cooed to her husband. Her arm was tucked through his, latched onto him as if she were afraid he might get away. She wore a peacock-blue designer knit suit with hose and heels and diamonds blazing at her ears, neck, fingers, and wrists.

"This reminds me of my family's old summer home in Santa Barbara," Churchill said as he took in parquet floors honeyed with age, chandeliers that had a few crystals missing, and the staircase with its hand-painted, cracked tile risers. "Comfortable and welcoming. I quite like it. Your sister came through for us again, my dear."

Eleanor's face froze, and she stood as motionless as a wax figure at Madame Tussauds.

Ivy contemplated a rivalry between the two sisters. While she couldn't help wondering why, it wasn't any of her business. She only wanted Rachel to have her beautiful wedding.

After Ivy brought out the room keys, Churchill gave her his credit card. "What an intriguing old house. I'm a professor of anthropology, so I'm always fascinated by the history of what survives over time."

Ivy told him about the architect, Julia Morgan, and her work on the house and Hearst Castle.

"I've heard about this home," he said, his eyes twinkling with interest.

While Ivy chatted with Churchill about the recent discoveries at the inn, Eleanor came to life. Ivy assumed that this was Eleanor's way of showing her disapproval, but Churchill ignored her and continued in his affable manner.

Outside, Rachel waited while another car pulled up with her bridesmaids. The four women who had stayed at the inn for the bachelorette party stood outside talking.

At last, another car arrived with a young man Ivy took to be Topper. Rachel threw her arms around his tall, lanky frame. His wavy dark hair fell across his eyes, and he seemed exuberant and outgoing. Several of his friends emerged from the car, laughing and slapping him on the back.

As the younger people made their way into the house, laughter rang out. They were all in high spirits. Ivy saw that Rachel was happy and relieved to be with Topper, who was sweetly attentive to her.

Ivy motioned to Poppy. "Would you help me show our guests to their rooms? Once they're settled, I'll take the Yorks on a tour of the preparations for tomorrow."

"I can check in the bridesmaids."

"Thanks," Ivy said. Poppy had pitched in to help, and Ivy didn't know how they could have accomplished everything without her. She'd stepped in when Shelly took time to care for Mitch.

In the last couple of days, Ivy had been watching Shelly and Mitch. They were so besotted with each other that Ivy almost cried with happiness. Her sister had finally met the one for her. Surely they could resolve whatever was troubling Mitch.

After the Yorks had freshened up after their trip, Ivy ushered them through the house to view the wedding preparations.

Churchill was quite pleased with the ballroom, while Rachel was mesmerized by Shelly's floral fantasies.

Rachel drank in the sweet floral aromas. "This is exactly what I wanted—I just didn't know how to express it."

Ivy watched as Rachel and Topper strolled around the property, deep in conversation. They walked on the beach by themselves while their friends lounged by the pool, laughing and swimming.

That evening, the rehearsal dinner was held in the dining room, and Ivy couldn't help but observe the family interactions. Rachel's favorite aunt, Lillian, arrived. Ivy chatted with her for a while and thanked her for referring Rachel and Eleanor.

Eleanor's minister, who would be officiating the ceremony, also arrived to conduct the simple rehearsal. Ivy was relieved that everything was on schedule, and Eleanor was calm.

Ivy was at the front desk when a man with longish, sandy-colored hair arrived. "May I help you?" she asked.

"I'm Rob Evans, father of the bride. My daughter Rachel is getting married tomorrow. I'm not checking in—I have friends I'm staying with—but I wouldn't miss my baby girl's big day." His voice dropped to a whisper. "Even if her mother disapproves."

Just then, Churchill was passing through to the ballroom, and the two men greeted each other warmly. "How's the music business treating you?" Churchill asked.

"Busier than ever," Rob replied. "Are you still teaching?"

"Not anymore. However, I'm working on a new book." Churchill glanced back into the ballroom. "I'm glad you received my message. I knew Rachel would be disappointed if you weren't here for the rehearsal."

"Where are they?" Rob asked.

"Eleanor is putting Rachel through her paces for the ceremony. She's a stern taskmaster."

"I remember," Rob said with a grin. "How you put up with that woman is beyond me. Does Rachel get along with Topper's parents?"

"Quite well," Churchill said. "She seems to have a good relationship with her future in-laws." He chuckled. "I married Eleanor precisely because my mother disapproved. That has made for amusing family gatherings over the years."

Ivy felt a little awkward overhearing these intimate family details, but she'd learned to fade into the background. She busied herself at the desk and acted as if she wasn't paying attention, although she stayed in case they needed anything. Still, she couldn't help being fascinated by the family dynamics at play.

"Daddy," Rachel cried out, racing toward her father with outstretched arms.

He wrapped her in a huge hug. "Did I make it in time for the rehearsal?"

"Perfect timing. Mom has been driving me crazy with her direction. She'll be so surprised to see you. She told me you had a late studio session today." She clasped his hand to lead him into the ballroom.

Rob threw a look at Churchill over his shoulder and waggled his eyebrows. "She might not be pleased to see me."

Rachel gave her father a sympathetic smile. "You can hang out with Topper and his parents. They're really cool, Dad. A lot like you."

Ivy could feel tension rising in the air like a heatwave. When she saw Shelly rush by, she pulled her aside. "I think Eleanor is about to blow up." She nodded toward the ballroom.

Shelly rolled her eyes. "Did you know she just asked me to bring in flowers and set them up in the front so they can take photos tonight? I pulled in Poppy and Sunny to help."

"What? That wasn't on the schedule." Ivy wondered what Eleanor was up to. She nodded toward the ballroom. "Rachel planned to have her father on one side and her stepfather on the other, honoring them both. I don't think Eleanor likes the idea."

Sure enough, voices from the ballroom began to rise.

"What's he doing here?" Eleanor screeched.

"Here we go," Shelly said, peeking around the corner. "This is going to be good. I'd better wait before bringing in the flowers. I don't want to get caught in the crossfire."

Ivy shushed her sister. "We don't talk about guests."

"It's not as if they can hear us over Eleanor," Shelly said, feigning a hoarse whisper. "Besides, you just did."

"I shouldn't have." Still, Ivy couldn't help leaning around Shelly for a glimpse of the action. "Thank goodness our family isn't like that."

"I didn't realize how lucky we were until I started working in the event business," Shelly whispered. "At least the food throwing and furniture smashing hasn't begun."

Worried, Ivy chewed on her lip. "You didn't need to share that with me."

Just then, a caravan of black SUVs arrived in front of the inn.

Shelly glanced out a front window. "Did someone call the FBI again?"

"Maybe it's Churchill's family," Ivy said, wondering if he actually was part of a royal family. She watched as Charlie and Diego swung into action, greeting the guests who spilled from the car.

Shelly frowned. "I hope they don't think they're staying here for the wedding. We're full."

Several tall, beautiful women emerged from the SUVs, along with equally handsome young men. Two black-clad young women brought out professional-looking cases and set up a clothing rack on wheels.

Ivy tore her attention from the melee in the ballroom. "Watch out for damage in there," she said to Shelly. "I'll tend to whoever this is."

"Looks like Central Casting has arrived," Shelly said, laughing.

Ivy recalled what Rachel had said about her mother wanting a dozen bridesmaids at the wedding. She pressed a hand to her mouth in horror. "I've got a terrible feeling you might be right."

An angular, authoritative-looking woman marched into the house. "I'm with West Coast Elite Models, and we're here for the York photo shoot." Her eyes flicked to the shouts emanating from the ballroom. "Where shall we set up?"

This was news to Ivy. "In the ballroom," Ivy began, gesturing the way. "But you might want to wait. They're having a…discussion."

The woman sniffed her displeasure. "We're on a schedule now, and overtime is often a problem with clients." She turned and motioned to her models and crew to follow her inside. On the clothing rack, Ivy saw what looked like bridesmaids' dresses—and they were identical to the one Rachel's cousin Carrie had brought in earlier. The models trooped after her.

As the woman marched inside the ballroom and called out

for Eleanor York, Shelly tugged on Ivy's sleeve. "We should be filming this. Or refereeing."

"Shh," Ivy said, growing flustered. "Don't do either. Unless they start damaging things."

Shelly arched an eyebrow. "Didn't I warn you against weddings?"

"Not now," Ivy said, desperately trying to stay calm.

Just then, Poppy, Sunny, and Misty came around the corner, their eyes wide. Gilda crept down the stairs holding Pixie, and Imani and Jamir were right behind her.

"What's all the racket?" Gilda asked. "Pixie is very upset." The little dog was shivering with fright.

"I'm sorry," Ivy said, holding up her hands. "I'll see to it." She had to regain order in the house.

But before she could go in, an artistic-looking man with long hair and tattoos stepped inside. "Where are we setting up for hair and makeup?"

As Ivy was thinking, one of the black-clad young women guiding the clothing rack asked, "Is there a room we can use for the models to dress?"

Ivy pressed a hand against her forehead. "Stay here, everyone. I'll handle this." Eleanor shouldn't disrupt other guests. She charged into the ballroom to speak to Eleanor.

She might as well have gotten in line.

Rachel and Rob were arguing with Eleanor, the woman with the models was demanding that the bride sit for hair and makeup, and Churchill—bless his mild-mannered heart—was trying to quiet everyone, but to no avail.

Ivy drew a breath. "Sorry to interrupt—"

"That's enough!" Topper took Rachel's arm and guided her away from the melee.

With tears in her eyes, Rachel looked up at him with a grateful expression. She whipped around. "Hear me on this, Mom. It's *our* wedding. Churchill, I'm sorry it has cost so much, but I'm not having any fake bridesmaids to impress Mom's friends."

"Darling, you specifically said you didn't want any at the wedding," Eleanor said. "A photo shoot will only take an hour or two. Think of it as part of the rehearsal. What's the harm in that?"

"Because it's not real, Mom. I don't care about my wedding appearing in your society magazines or giving you photos you can use to gloat over friends. Topper and I are drawing the line tonight. From here on, I'm calling the shots in my life."

With that, Rachel turned and left with Topper.

Ivy almost broke out in applause.

Churchill cleared his throat. "I think it's time we all retired for the evening."

The woman with the modeling company crossed her arms. "We're not leaving until we're fully compensated for the evening."

Holding up a hand, Churchill took out his wallet. As he was making arrangements with the modeling company, Rob hurried after his daughter.

Ivy returned to the front, where her daughters and other guests at the inn were buzzing at the excitement. Even Charlie was there, mining the latest gossip for Summer Beach.

Bennett was in the foyer, too. "I heard the commotion in my room. Do you need help with that in there?"

"No, it's just part of the wedding drama," Ivy replied. Turning, she said, "It's all over, everyone. Have a good night's rest."

Later, as she got ready for bed, Ivy thought about Rachel and Topper. She was glad the young woman had stood up to her mother and had her future husband's support. But she couldn't help wondering if the wedding would go forward tomorrow.

18

*I*vy lay awake, watching shadows from moonlit palm trees swaying across her walls. She slept with the window open to hear the ocean's lullaby, the ceaseless tide that usually put her to sleep and kept her in slumber.

But not tonight.

Something had woken her. Straining to listen, she detected the low idle of an engine. Someone was in the car court behind the house. Turning over, she blinked. The digital clock on the bedstand read 4:02 a.m. *How odd.* She rose and padded across the vintage wool rug onto the smooth wooden floor in front of the window.

Glancing out to the moonlit court below, she saw a car she didn't recognize. It was a convertible, but the headlights were off, and the top was up. At this time of year, nights were still chilly by the ocean. Her friends in Boston would have laughed at the mild weather, but she'd quickly acclimated.

A light in Bennett's apartment over the garage flicked on. He must have heard the car, too. And then, in the hallway, the old wooden floor creaked.

At once, Ivy knew what was happening. She grabbed a

cotton robe from a hook and wrapped it around her short nightgown.

As she opened her door, she saw the top of Rachel's head disappearing down the stairs. She hurried to the staircase. Rachel held her wedding dress folded over her arm, and she had a large bag slung over her shoulder.

"Did you get everything you need?" Ivy whispered.

Rachel looked back and nodded. The light in the stairway illuminated the young woman's radiant face.

As quietly as the old wooden floorboards would allow, the two women crept down the stairs to the foyer.

Ivy motioned for Rachel to follow her as she threaded her way through the house. The moonlight flooded through tall windows, and Ivy led her through the kitchen to the rear door. Lifting the knob slightly, she swung open the door.

"Do you think anyone else heard us?" Rachel whispered anxiously.

"I don't think so. Your parents' room was far enough away from yours."

Next to the late model Mustang convertible, Topper was in quiet conversation with Bennett, who looked like he'd just thrown on jeans and a wrinkled T-shirt. The two men turned as Ivy and Rachel came out.

The younger man's face was filled with such a pure expression of love that Ivy's heart swelled with happiness for them. She pressed a hand to her chest and sighed.

"Quickly," Topper said as he took Rachel's bag and dress. He draped the wedding gown carefully over their luggage.

Rachel turned to Ivy. "Thank you for listening to me. Without your advice, I don't know if I would have had the courage to do this." Her face bloomed with a dazzling smile. "My father knows of a beautiful spot in the mountains overlooking Lake Arrowhead where we can get married right away. We booked a room online, and he's going to meet us there. This will be my real dream wedding." She handed Ivy a folded note. "Will you give this to my cousin Carrie?"

"Of course," Ivy said. She glanced back at the darkened house. No one else was up. "Would you like to take the bouquet Shelly made for you?"

"Oh, yes." Rachel's eyes glittered. "If it's not too much trouble."

Ivy hurried through the kitchen and into the sunroom where Shelly had been working. Quickly, she wrapped the bridal bouquet. Clasping the fragrant flowers to her chest, she rushed back.

Topper placed the bouquet in the back seat. "It's going to smell great in there." He reached out to shake hands with Bennett. "Thanks for the directions, sir."

"That shortcut will help you avoid any morning traffic." Bennett put a hand on the younger man's shoulder. "You're doing the right thing, son. Safe travels."

With cheeks wet with tears of happiness and excitement, Rachel flung her arms around Ivy. "Thank you a thousand times." She cradled her slightly rounded abdomen. "For everything. We're so happy to be starting our new life exactly the way we want. Maybe we'll return on our anniversary."

"We'd like that," Ivy said, swiping a finger under her eyes, too. "We even have a crib we can put in your room."

Topper assisted Rachel into the car, and then he slid behind the wheel.

Bennett crossed to Ivy. They clasped hands and watched Rachel and Topper ease from the driveway. He flicked on the headlights, which illuminated frothy ocean waves ahead for a moment before they turned toward the village and the highway beyond.

They're free, Ivy thought happily. As the young couple disappeared into the night, she shivered. For the first time, she realized she was chilly in the cool night air.

Bennett wrapped his arms around her and pulled her

close. "Topper was a little worried about his parents, but he thought they'd understand. They're not fond of Eleanor, and if the rehearsal was any indication of the wedding, he didn't think they'd miss it much. His four older siblings have all married, so Topper figured they'd had enough of weddings anyway."

"They seem like reasonable people," Ivy said. "They'll probably be eager to leave Eleanor's orbit."

They stood for a few moments, watching the waves roll toward the shore. Ivy turned her face up to his. "Shall we go back to bed or enjoy the morning?"

"Let's have our coffee on the beach," he replied. "I have a blanket we can share. Then I'll help you prepare breakfast."

As they made their way into the kitchen, Ivy thought about Rachel. She was glad the young woman found the courage to do what she wanted, even though Ivy would have to deal with Eleanor. Rachel would have the wedding she wanted, and that was all that mattered to Ivy.

19

*B*ennett drew Ivy close beside him, huddling under his beach blanket on a flat rock on the beach, not far from the inn. All around them, the beach was coming to life, with shorebirds pecking at the sand and gulls swooping low across the water hunting for fish.

"I love the fresh ocean air in the early morning," Bennett said, breathing in.

Ivy did the same. "It's the time of the day that holds so much promise."

Bennett enjoyed the solitude of the beach with Ivy. Simply being together fulfilled him in a way he hadn't known for years.

As the sun slowly brightened the dusky sky with ribbons of rose, they sipped steaming coffee and talked about the surprising turn of events with Rachel and Topper. This was likely their only quiet moment of the day ahead. Behind them, nascent rays illuminated the ridgetop as the earth rotated, bringing the day closer.

"I enjoyed that," Ivy said, cradling her empty coffee cup. "But I suppose it's time to face morning at the inn."

"And all that it brings," Bennett said, thinking about the York's reaction once they discovered Rachel had eloped.

After they stood, Bennett shook sand from the blanket. As they strolled toward the inn, he felt such peace surrounding them. "This sure is a special way to start the morning."

"We should do this again," Ivy said, gazing up at him. "We could set our alarms for 4:00 a.m." Laughing softly, she added, "But not too often."

"I'd like that." Bennett smiled down at her. He could hardly wait to wake up with her, welcoming every day with the woman he loved.

Inside the kitchen, he tied on an apron that Nan had given him. The thick, yellow cotton was embroidered with blue waves and the slogan: *Life is Better in Summer Beach.* This morning it sure was.

Bennett opened a package of bacon and filled a cast iron skillet with slices. He liked cooking with Ivy. He'd missed puttering in the kitchen with Jackie, and he'd never been the sort of man who wanted a wife to wait on him. It was Ivy's strength and determination that had initially attracted him. That and her luminous green eyes blazing with curiosity, taking in the world around her.

"We'll keep the coffee in rotation in the dining room," Ivy said, starting another pot. "Especially today with so many guests."

"Minus two," Bennett said, grinning. At the smell of sizzling bacon, his stomach grumbled with hunger.

"Wait until Eleanor discovers that." Ivy shivered. "They will probably be up in an hour or so. We should nibble on something before Vesuvius erupts. Boom," she said, spreading her hands in the air.

Bennett laughed at that. "I'll be here to back you up. And we'll have crispy bacon in a few minutes."

"Don't you have to go into the office?"

"Fridays are usually quiet. I can work from here today."

Bennett glanced at the large kitchen table littered with stacks of napkins for the wedding, handwritten seating cards, and tiny bags of confetti. "Well, maybe not here, but on my balcony."

"Take your laptop computer to the library. That way, you'll hear the explosion when it happens."

Bennett turned the bacon. "I feel sorry for Churchill—he spent thousands on the wedding. What do you think they'll do with all this stuff?"

Ivy began to take condiments for breakfast from the refrigerator. "I've been thinking about that. We can take the flowers to nursing homes and hospitals in the area. I'm sure the food for the dinner has already been purchased and prepped. It's too late for the Yorks to ask for a refund. And to think of all the people I referred them to in Summer Beach. What a nightmare." Ivy pressed a hand against her forehead.

"It's not your fault, and the vendors have been paid. While it doesn't happen often, weddings do get called off at the last moment."

Ivy piled apples, oranges, and bananas in a large bamboo bowl. "You have a point, I suppose."

Suddenly inspired, Bennett stepped away from the stove and wrapped his arms around Ivy. "Have I told you I love you this morning?"

"Oh, once or twice," she said, laughing. She threw her arms around him and nuzzled his neck.

"One last hug before the household wakes up," Bennett said, smiling down at her.

While the bacon sizzled, he ran his hands over Ivy's tousled hair. He liked the way she looked in the morning, having just rolled out of bed. He had dated other women who were afraid to be seen without makeup, but that wasn't Ivy. She was confident in how she looked and who she was.

This past year, he'd marveled at her growth. She'd had a great deal to overcome, especially after having lived with an overbearing man like Jeremy for so long. It was as if Ivy was emerging from a cocoon, and he loved seeing her stretch her wings toward the light.

Soon the household would be awake, and this quiet time between them would slip away into the chaos of the morning. Bennett rubbed Ivy's back and kissed her forehead, enjoying the moment they had.

Finally, taking her hands, he said, "Why don't you go upstairs and get ready? I can handle everything down here, but you'll need to be ready for the onslaught. Since the wedding was scheduled for 1:00 p.m., our guests should start stirring soon."

"You're right," Ivy said, letting her hands linger in his. "It's been so nice spending the morning with you."

"Someday, it will be like this every day," he ventured, imagining the future that lay before them. "I'm not rushing you, though."

"And I appreciate that." She gazed up at him, seemingly in no hurry to leave.

Bennett liked that, and he could have taken all her time, but she needed to tend to her business. He pulled back. "I'll send you upstairs with a second cup of coffee."

"You're an angel."

"Why, yes, I am," he said with a wink. "Your angel, Ivy Bay."

She pressed her hands against his chest. "That makes me feel pretty safe."

A warm feeling filled him, and he tucked her hair behind her ears. "As long as I'm around, you are. I know you're perfectly capable of taking care of yourself and everyone else under this roof, but I like to watch out for you and lend a hand —when you'll let me."

"I like the idea of partners moving together through time. Sometimes we dance together, sometimes apart, but always together at the end of the dance."

Bennett twirled her around and swept her into his arms. "Like that?"

Ivy smiled. "Just like that."

Behind them, the coffee pot beeped. Bennett gave Ivy one last hug before pouring a large cup for her and pressing it into her hand.

"I'll be back soon," Ivy said, carrying her cup toward the door. "And don't let that bacon burn."

Bennett picked up his spatula and watched her go. He put on another batch of bacon and drained fresh coffee into a tall, insulated vacuum flask. They would need regular, decaffeinated, and the house specialty with vanilla and cinnamon.

The back door banged open. Bennett looked up; he made a mental note to fix that door. "Hey, Mitch."

"With the big party here, I thought I'd bring the pastries early." Mitch carried in two large pastry boxes.

"Not surfing today?"

"I'm still feeling a little beat up." Mitch glanced around. "You're on breakfast duty?"

"Ivy is getting ready, so I thought I'd pitch in."

Mitch slid the baked goods onto the long counter in the center of the room. Shifting from one foot to another, he touched his bandage. "That accident sure made me do some heavy thinking."

Bennett was grinding the next batch of coffee beans. When the noisy racket stopped, he prepared the next pot and tapped a button. "About what?" he asked, shifting back to the bacon.

Mitch ran a hand self-consciously over his spiky blond hair. "Life."

"That's a big little word."

"Yeah," Mitch said, snagging a slice of crisp bacon from a plate. "I've lived my life as a big kid for a long time."

"I don't know if I'd agree with that. You're running two businesses that you started. You had to grow up fast."

"That's not what I mean." Mitch eased onto a stool. "I've been letting fear keep me from having honest, adult relationships. What happened to me as a kid isn't who I am."

Bennett listened. "Coffee?" he asked.

"Sure. I'll have another."

Bennett poured a cup for Mitch and sat across from him. "Sounds like you've been doing a lot of work with your therapist."

"He's a good guy with a lot of insights," Mitch said. "Seems what I've been feeling isn't uncommon for people like me who were knocked around as kids. He also said I'm very resilient."

"I would agree with that," Bennett said.

"When I came to after almost being hit, I had some troubling thoughts." Mitch touched the bandage over his eye again. "I realized I don't want to die without living life. I don't want to miss out because I'm afraid of being hurt—or hurting someone else."

"Being aware of that potential is a huge step."

Mitch nodded. "I also wanted to be honest with Shelly about how my folks treated me. We talked about my fear that I could fall into the intergenerational abuse trap." He quirked his mouth to one side. "I know, big words from me, right?"

"You're smarter than you give yourself credit for." Bennett had tried to imagine what it might have been like to have grown up as Mitch did. Besides the physical abuse, never hearing encouragement or reinforcement and being inundated with hateful, debilitating messages must have been devastating for him. Seeing how far Mitch had come made Bennett admire him even more. "So you're planning on telling Shelly?"

"I already did," Mitch said with a small smile. "That was one of the scariest things I've ever done. It was that night I spent on your sofa with Shelly looking after me. I told her that

I wanted to have a family with her, but that I have this deep fear that I might mess up like my pop did."

"How did she take it?"

"Pretty good. She understood and was glad I told her. I plan to continue seeing this therapist, so I wanted her to know why I'm going. She's cool with it. And I told her that I'm cool with having kids." He grinned and looked up. "I think I might even make a pretty good dad."

"I have complete confidence in you," Bennett said.

Mitch seemed relieved that he'd unburdened himself to Shelly. Taking these first steps was a major accomplishment, and Bennett was happy for him.

Bennett and Mitch carried the pastries, bacon, fruit, and coffee into the dining room to set up for breakfast. They had to rearrange the table and chairs after last night's rehearsal dinner, but Bennett knew how to set up for breakfast. After he'd decided to lease out his home on the ridgetop, he'd been feeling more at home here and pitching in like one of the family when he could.

Bennett was putting out napkins when Eleanor appeared in the doorway, her face masked with concern.

"Have you seen Rachel this morning? She's not in her room, and Topper isn't answering his phone." She peered uneasily out the window. "I don't see them on the beach."

"No one else has been up," Mitch said.

Bennett hadn't had the chance to tell Mitch about the elopement. He ran a hand across the back of his neck. He hardly knew this woman, yet someone had to tell her that Rachel and Topper had left.

To Bennett's relief, Churchill meandered in for breakfast. "The kids will turn up, Eleanor. They're probably out on the beach where we can't see them."

Just then, Ivy walked in, dressed in a floral sundress and sandals. She gave Bennett a brisk nod and joined Eleanor and Churchill.

"May we have a word with you?" Ivy began.

Bennett didn't envy her this task, but he wouldn't leave her side. Mitch busied himself arranging the muffins and croissants.

The Yorks sat down, and Ivy joined them, folding her hands in front of her. "This isn't easy to say, but Rachel and Topper left very early this morning."

Eleanor's eyes flew open. "They're gone? Where?"

"I don't know, but I'm sure they'll be in touch with you," Ivy said.

Rising, Eleanor jabbed a finger at Ivy. "And how do you know this? Did you see them leave?"

"I heard a car and went to investigate."

"And you didn't think to try to stop her or call me? For what I'm paying, you should have done that."

"Please calm down, dear," Churchill said. "Rachel is an adult, after all."

Eleanor narrowed her eyes. "Are they coming back, or did they say the wedding is off?"

As Ivy shook her head, Bennett stepped in. "Mr. and Mrs. York, I understand you're distressed. I saw them, too. They both seemed fine and determined to leave, and they didn't want to wake anyone else."

Eleanor threw her hands up. "After all that I have spent in this city, I would have thought the mayor would have the decency to put a stop to their escape and wake their parents."

"They *are* adults," Bennett said, turning to Churchill, who nodded wearily.

"Perhaps you'd like to take breakfast in your room," Ivy said.

"That's an excellent idea," Churchill said.

While Eleanor continued her rant, Churchill stood abruptly and took her arm. "We'll talk about this in the room, Eleanor." He nodded to Ivy and Bennett before ushering Eleanor from the dining room. Churchill guided her to the second floor, yet her shrill voice carried through the house.

Upstairs, Bennett could hear Pixie furiously yapping as Eleanor continued screaming about how ungrateful Rachel was and how this was Lillian's fault for being a bad influence. Finally, the door to their room slammed, muffling her voice.

"Wow," Mitch said, turning around. "The wedding is off?"

Ivy pressed a hand to her chest. "Rachel and Topper eloped this morning. Bennett and I saw them off."

"Good for them," Mitch said. "So what happens with all the flowers and everything?"

"Whatever the Yorks decide. I'll offer to take the arrangements to nursing homes and hospitals."

Bennett heard rapid footsteps descending the stairs. Moments later, Shelly flew into the dining room. "What the heck is going on? That woman woke the entire household."

Ivy told her what happened.

Shelly dissolved with laughter. "Good for you, Rachel," she said, thrusting a fist into the air. "Woo-hoo!"

"I've got to take breakfast trays up to them," Ivy said. "Better prepare one for Topper's parents, too."

"I'll give you a hand," Bennett said, leaving Mitch and Shelly in the dining room.

Soon, news of the elopement ricocheted throughout the inn, with exclamations emitted from various rooms. The bridesmaids and groomsmen gathered in the dining room gossiping and comparing texts they'd received. Bennett heard snippets of conversations between calls to the office until Nan finally suggested he take the rest of the day off.

Topper must have contacted his parents because they were the first to pack and leave, announcing that they were happy for the young couple. Rachel's friends avoided Eleanor but managed to enjoy the morning at the pool, especially when Topper's buddies joined them. Soon they packed their bags and continued the party at the beach. Bennett was glad someone was enjoying the sunshine and having a good time.

Bennett was in the library when he heard Eleanor and Churchill checking out. He sauntered out to be near Ivy. Just in case.

"I wish we'd met under better circumstances," Churchill said as he signed the final bill.

Eleanor was sitting nearby looking pale and deflated, her fiery anger doused with cold reality. Bennett felt sorry for her, even though she had brought most of this upon herself.

Ivy sat next to her and gave her a box of mementos. "I'm sorry the wedding didn't turn out the way you'd hoped, but Rachel and Topper seem happy. Soon you'll be welcoming a new baby into the family. That will be such a joy for you and Rachel."

Dabbing her eyes, Eleanor turned to her. "I only wanted Rachel to have a day she could look back on to remember all of her life. Was that so terrible of me?"

Ivy rested her hand on the other woman's. "I have two daughters about Rachel's age. I have to remind myself to listen to what they're trying to tell me."

Eleanor looked surprised. "Churchill told me the same thing." She thanked Ivy and apologized for how she'd acted.

Ivy glanced around. "Is there anything you want to take with you?"

Eleanor shook her head. "Can you dispose of everything? I don't want the reminders. Maybe you can give the flowers away."

"Of course," Ivy said.

At that moment, Bennett joined them. Watching Ivy deal with Eleanor spoke volumes to him of her character and compassion. Every day he fell a little bit more in love with her.

After the Yorks and Eleanor's sister Lillian had departed, Bennett followed Ivy to the sunroom where Shelly and Mitch were talking, surrounded by mounds of flowers.

"It's over," Ivy said, sinking into a chair. Bennett sat beside her, marveling at the work Shelly had put into the flowers.

"And all this?" Shelly asked, gesturing around the room.

"To do with as we like," Ivy replied.

With a look that lit his face with joy, Mitch waggled his eyebrows. Bennett stared at him until it dawned on him what Mitch had in mind.

And he thought it was perfect.

Gingerly, Mitch eased himself to the floor on one knee and took Shelly's hand. "Shelly Bay," he began. "You're the moon to my tides. I love you more than the infinite grains of sand. Will you marry me on the beach tonight, surrounded by all these sweet flowers and those we love?"

Shelly broke into a smile, and she cried out, "Oh, yes! Yes, I will."

"Now you're going to have to help me up," Mitch said, gritting his teeth through his joyful smile. "I mean it. I banged up both knees in that accident, and I can't move."

Through tears of happiness, Shelly helped him up.

All at once, there were hugs all around. Ivy embraced her sister, Bennett hugged Mitch and Ivy, and Shelly threw her arms around everyone.

"Woo-hoo," Shelly called out. "We're going to have a wedding!"

Bennett had never seen Ivy so happy for Shelly. As they went out to phone Carlotta and Sterling, Bennett clasped Ivy's hand. "I wish the same for us someday soon."

"So do I," Ivy said, drawing his hand to her heart. "We'll need that marriage license first." She sighed. "I have so much paperwork to straighten out that I hardly know where to start."

Bennett chuckled. "It's okay. Do what you have to do. I'm not going anywhere." Whether they were married or not, his heart belonged to Ivy.

20

*I*vy was thrilled that Shelly and Mitch were getting married today. She couldn't think of a better ending to the disaster that Eleanor had perpetrated. In the flower-filled sunroom that overlooked the pool, Ivy sat at a round table making a list of everything they needed to arrange for Shelly. Poppy, Sunny, and Misty were also there and eager to pitch in.

Carlotta was at home contacting local family members to invite them. She and Sterling were planning to set sail for the coast of Mexico within a few days, but they were dropping everything to celebrate with Shelly and Mitch.

"Shelly has already done enough here," Ivy said, taking in the flowers that surrounded them. "Except that she'll have to make another bridal bouquet. I gave the one Shelly made to Rachel to take with them. The rest of today should be as relaxing as we can make it for Shelly."

"How about sending her to the spa in the village?" Sunny suggested. "They can do her hair and makeup, too."

Ivy pressed her lips together, considering this. "Shelly might love a massage. Maybe someone can pin up her hair, so it's not always falling from her messy bun."

"But then she wouldn't be Aunt Shelly," Poppy said. Everyone laughed.

Poppy crossed off a line on her list. "We won't need those stuffy nameplates Eleanor ordered on the dinner table."

"Shelly wants everything outside," Ivy said. "At the moment, the weather looks fairly good today for the ceremony and the dinner afterward. Let's keep our fingers crossed."

Anything could happen at the beach, from gusty winds to storms that rolled in from the ocean, sweeping across the coastline. Not today, Ivy hoped.

She went on. "Marina from the Coral Cafe is contracted to cater the dinner, so I'll call her to see if she'd like to do that for us. Her sister Kai and Shelly are friends."

Poppy jotted a note. "I'll have my brothers come early to move the tables outside. Rocky and Reed can do it in no time, and I'll oversee the table linens and place settings. We can put out the flowers, too. Aunt Shelly created a placement plan that I can use."

Sunny raised her hand. "Count me in on the tables and flowers."

"How about a minister?" Misty asked.

"Bennett said Mitch is taking care of that," Ivy said, checking that off her list. "We should be on the lookout for someone named Brother Rip."

Misty tilted her head. "What kind of a name is that for a pastor?"

"Bennett says he's a surfer-turned-minister," Ivy said. "Rip is short for riptide. Something about an old surfer nickname." She made a note on her tablet. "And the photographer is a friend of Shelly's from New York. Mom and Dad are going to pay her for Shelly and Mitch instead."

Misty tapped her cast. "I can't do much, but I can shadow the photographer and make sure she gets the right shots of family and friends."

"Perfect," Ivy said. "You're down for that."

"What about the rings?" Sunny asked.

They all looked at each other. "That's up to Mitch and Shelly," Ivy said. "I don't know if they've made any arrangements, but they don't need them to get married. They can choose rings later if they want."

Ivy drew a finger down her list. "About parking...I'll have to tell Charlie that the York wedding is off. We won't need them." As soon as she said that, she remembered something else. "We have to tell Darla. Mitch will want her there, but he's so busy. I don't want us to forget her, especially since we just reached a peaceful co-existence."

The room fell quiet, and no one volunteered.

"I suppose that's my place," Ivy said, putting a star by Darla's name. "I'll find out if the guys have invited her. Bennett is helping Mitch figure out what to wear right now."

Misty frowned. "What is Aunt Shelly going to wear?"

"That's going to be a surprise." Ivy could hardly wait to show Shelly what she had in mind. Her sister could still wear the white swimsuit and beach wrap she'd teased about, but Ivy hoped she'd at least think about what Louise at the Laundry Basket had created.

With only a few hours to spare, everyone went to work. Ivy thought about how fortunate they were that Churchill had paid them in full and didn't care what they did with everything left over. She wondered how many other times he had paid for Eleanor's misdeeds. After her initial outbreak, the woman seemed repentant. Ivy hoped so, for Rachel's sake.

When her mother arrived, Ivy hurried downstairs to meet her.

"Where is our bride?" Carlotta asked.

"I'm so glad you're here. Shelly has been on the phone, and I think she's trying to decide what to wear right now. Remember the wedding gown I told you about?"

"Could that work?" Carlotta asked, raising her brow. "It might be musty and dank."

"I had it cleaned, and I added something to it, just in case Shelly wanted to wear it. She doesn't know it yet, and I wanted to wait until you arrived to show her."

"I'd love to see it."

Ivy led her mother upstairs and brought out the wedding dress. "Shelly loved it, but she thought it was too short for her. As for me, it's too slim of a fit."

"The workmanship is exquisite," Carlotta said, turning over the rich silk.

"It's lasted a hundred years," Ivy said. "I think Amelia Erickson would have wanted Shelly to wear it. We saved her home and found the treasures she'd kept safe for future generations." Ivy lifted a length of lace. "This was probably meant for a veil, but I asked Louise if she could fashion a skirt to go under the dress and have an expanse of lace peeking out at the bottom of the dress."

"Shelly would look lovely in this," Carlotta said. "Let's bring her in right away."

They hurried to Shelly's room. She was in her closet, digging through shoes. "Mom, I'm so glad you're here." Shelly emerged, holding a pair of silver sandals, and flung her arms around her mother.

"You're radiant, *mija*," Carlotta said, hugging her youngest child. "I'm so happy for you."

Shelly's hair was even wilder than usual, with multiple strands tumbling out of her topknot. "I have no idea which dress to wear, but I have these sandals. What do you think?" Shelly asked, gesturing toward several dresses on the bed. "I don't have time to find that white coverup, and I'm not really crazy about any of these for a wedding, but who cares? I'm getting married—that's all that matters."

"Come with us," Carlotta said. "Your sister has a surprise."

When they returned to Ivy's room, Ivy led Shelly into the

closet and dressing room. "I had the vintage wedding gown cleaned for you."

"That was so sweet of you," Shelly said, her eyes widening. "I suppose it doesn't have to be long." A wistful smile crossed her face.

"I disagree," Carlotta said. "Because your sister had a special underskirt made. See?" She took a hanger from the rod and revealed a new silk slip. Designed to fit slim around the waist and hips, it flared from mid-thigh with a trumpet-shaped skirt made of the stunning vintage lace.

"Why, that's perfect." Shelly's eyes glittered with gratitude. "May I try it on?"

"Of course," Ivy said, laughing. She and her mother helped Shelly change into the dress. When her sister stepped onto the round, raised fitting platform in front of the three-way mirror, Ivy caught her breath. Shelly was breathtaking.

"It's the most beautiful dress I've ever seen," Shelly said, running her hands over the silk. "I can hardly believe how fresh it looks now."

Carlotta pressed her hands together. "It looks like it was made for you."

"The bottom half was," Shelly said, laughing. "And with my little silver kitten heels I just found, it will be the perfect length. How did you know?"

"I went into your closet and measured your clothes," Ivy said. "You came in and caught me, so I had to act like I was looking for one of Mom's dresses she'd given us." Ivy held up Shelly's sandals. "Try these on."

"I thought that was odd because it didn't fit you," Shelly said as she slipped on her little heels. "This is the most beautiful dress I've ever worn. It even feels good on the inside."

Carlotta smiled as she fastened the tiny buttons in the back. "That's the silk lining and finished seams. Beautifully made. Couture, I would say." She paused and studied a label sewn into the garment. "*Callot Soeurs*. I don't recognize that, but this gown is quite old."

Ivy and Carlotta stepped back to admire the dress on Shelly. Ivy thought her sister was the most unique bride she'd ever seen, although all brides were beautiful.

Carlotta picked up her purse. "I think it's missing an important element." She reached inside. "I visited my safety deposit box at the bank on the way."

As Carlotta unrolled a satin jewelry bag, Shelly's lips curved up. "I might not be a pearls-every-day kind of girl, but I'm feeling it very much today. Thanks, Mom. This means a lot to me."

"This is your day, Shelly," Carlotta said, fastening the strand on Shelly's neck. "You should wear whatever you want." She brought out pearl earrings to go with the necklace.

Ivy stood back, appraising the outfit. "Mom, do you have that brooch that Dad gave you on your wedding day?"

"Of course." Carlotta brought out a delicate round leaf design studded with dainty pearls and tiny blue sapphires.

Their father didn't have much money then, but what he'd chosen was exquisite. Ivy and Shelly had always admired it.

"I have an idea for the skirt." She knelt at the platform and brought up a length of the silk hem. "We can drape the fabric like so and secure it at your hip with the brooch." She rocked back on her heels to take in the new look.

"Oh, I like that," Shelly said. "It looks like a rippling waterfall and exposes more of the lace underneath."

As Carlotta clapped her hands, her silver bracelets clinked. "The bride is ready. We'll keep everything here for when you're ready to dress. Until then, would you like to go into the village and have a massage at the spa? I've reserved appointments for you and Mitch if you'd like to go while we organize everything here."

"I'd love that," Shelly said. "Mitch is still pretty achy from the accident. And I think I need to get myself centered and breathe." She shook her hands. "I want to make my bouquet, and I'm starting to get a little nervous. But I don't know about Mitch." Shelly paused and bit her lip. "What if he panics again? What if—"

"Don't even think about that," Ivy said quickly. That was unimaginable. Both of them needed a respite this afternoon. "Bennett is with him, and he just texted to say that Mitch is up for massages, too."

"That's settled," Carlotta said. She glanced at her watch. "Will you have enough time to make your bouquet?"

"Plenty," Shelly said. "Now help me get out of this fabulous dress."

As Ivy unfastened the row of buttons down the back, she could feel Shelly fairly quivering with excitement. A massage would be calming for Shelly and give Ivy a chance to make sure everything was ready for her and Mitch to say their vows.

Ivy was so happy for her sister. Today was her dream come true. Still, Ivy prayed that nothing else would come between Shelly and Mitch.

AFTER SHELLY LEFT, the front bell rang, and Ivy hurried to the foyer to see who it might be.

"Megan, what a surprise," Ivy said, greeting her friend. "Please come in."

"I just received the translation of the swatch book, and I hoped I'd catch you." Clutching a folder, the young documentary filmmaker stepped inside.

"Let's go outside on the terrace," Ivy said. "This is a crazy day." She told Megan that Shelly and Mitch were getting married tonight and asked if she and Josh would like to attend.

"We'd love to, but we're driving to Los Angeles to fly out to a film festival," Megan said. "That's why I wanted to drop this off today. I only have ten or fifteen minutes, but this is exciting."

Ivy led Megan outside, and they sat at a table covered by an orange beach umbrella. When Megan received a phone call, Ivy excused herself to the kitchen, returning with a tall glass of sparkling water with lime.

Megan completed her call. "That was Josh, worried about our flight. I can't stay long, but I'm so thrilled with what my friend translated." She opened the folder, which had clips on each side at the top. "I have the copies on one side and the translation on the other, so you can look at them side by side. This has added to my research on Amelia Erickson. I didn't know she had been married before."

"Were you able to find anything about her first husband?" Ivy asked.

"Assuming the Josef in the photo you found was her first husband, that is. I'll need more time to research that."

"She was a fascinating woman," Ivy said. "With every discovery we make, another layer is revealed. I hope you're not in a hurry to produce this documentary."

"This one is a labor of love," Megan said. "We're working on another film that will be completed first, but this one is close to my heart. I want to give this remarkable woman her full due for the work she did—mostly uncredited. Amelia Erickson seemed fearless, from rescuing art and artifacts to forgotten lives, But I don't think we know her full back story yet."

"I'm glad you're thorough—and patient."

"Here's what I've found so far in my research." Megan opened the folder. "As you surmised, this book contains swatches and sketches of Amelia's clothes. Back then, women's clothing was handmade. Based on the quality of the fabric, the designs, and the notes she made, it seems that Amelia's family was quite well-to-do. Women in that social strata had their favorite dressmakers, many of whom we recognize as early couturiers. In the 1800s, Englishman Charles Frederick Worth establish the House of Worth in Paris, and just after the turn of the century, others followed him."

"Could these be House of Worth designs?"

"Possibly, but I saw a notation, and my guess is that some might be from Callot Soeurs. The four Callot sisters opened their atelier in 1895 in Paris. They exhibited at the World's Fair in 1900 and developed an international clientele. Besides France, they also had showrooms in London and Buenos Aires. Shortly thereafter in the early 1900s came Madeleine Vionnet, who had been the head of the workroom for the Callot sisters, along with Jeanne Lanvin, Paul Poiret, and Coco Chanel with their ateliers."

A flutter of recognition filled Ivy. "As Shelly was trying on the dress today, my mother saw a label in the wedding gown. I'll have to check again, but I believe she said it read Callot Soeurs. We didn't recognize that name."

"That's interesting." Megan flipped a couple of pages. "The wedding gown has a notation of Callot. Another dress is marked Vionnet. Other notes are descriptions of the style and where she wore the garment. It's quite interesting. Many fashionable women in Europe shopped in Paris, so it's possible that her family did, too."

"Then Shelly will be wearing an authentic couture gown," Ivy said. Her sister would like that.

"If you saw a label, then it's probably the real deal. On other pages, those couturiers might have been referenced because the garments were copies of those designs. Without the clothing, we just don't know. I'll consult a fashion historian to see what I can learn. And if I were you, I'd poke around more. Maybe you can find other clothing."

"We sure will." Ivy was glad she hadn't altered the gown. "Shelly is going to wear it for her ceremony."

"That will be very special." Megan turned to the last page.

"Sadly, the black dress was part of a mourning outfit for her husband. Presumably Josef."

"Oh, that poor woman," Ivy said. "Twice widowed." And then, her gaze fell on a translated line from the last page of Amelia's book. *Life is a risk worth taking.*

Megan closed the folder. "You can read the rest of this at your leisure."

"Thank you for doing this," Ivy said. Amelia's last line stayed in her mind. She walked Megan to the front door and wished her a wonderful trip. They promised each other they would meet for lunch again when Megan returned.

Ivy could hardly wait to share the history of the dress and the swatch book with Shelly. But first, she had to visit Darla. As she started across the connecting lawn to her neighbor's home, she hoped she would find her in good spirits. With Darla, she never knew.

21

*J*vy knocked on Darla's door and called out. "Darla, are you in? I have good news." She needed to deliver this invitation in person.

The door swung open, and Darla flung her arms around Ivy. "Have you heard the news? Well, of course you have. That's why you're here, isn't it? My baby's getting married."

Ivy had to laugh. She wondered if Mitch knew Darla called him that.

The other woman's cheeks colored. "He's not my actual baby, of course, but I like to think of him that way. This is so exciting," she said, clasping her hands. "It feels like my son is getting married."

"I'm glad he called," Ivy said. "I wanted to make sure you weren't forgotten. We'll seat you at the front as family."

A look of awe and appreciation filled Darla's face, and her eyes glazed with happy tears. "You'd do that for me?"

"Of course," Ivy said, putting a hand over Darla's. In the unlikeliest of pairings, Mitch and Darla were the family member the other one lacked.

"Would you help me pick out a dress?" Darla's bright eyes glanced toward the hallway to the bedrooms. "I know I've never told you, but you always look nice, even if you are a bit pudgy around the middle. So if you can manage to look good, then maybe you can help me, too."

That was the strangest compliment—if it was one, that is —Ivy had ever heard. But today was Shelly's wedding day, and Ivy couldn't be bothered to take issue with an awkward comment. She put her arm around Darla's shoulders. "I'd be honored. Let's do this."

Darla leaned into Ivy. "You're a good egg after all."

Ivy laughed, and the two women made their way to Darla's closet.

After Ivy had helped Darla choose just the right dress to complement her blue eyes and hair, she walked back to the inn. Everyone was buzzing around, getting ready for the wedding. Ivy climbed the stairs and started toward her room.

As she passed Gilda's room, the door swung open. "I heard your footsteps," Gilda said. "Pixie always knows it's you, too. Could I ask for your advice on what to wear to the wedding?"

"Sure," Ivy said, stepping inside the room.

Gilda brought out three miniature dog outfits. "The pink lace, the purple glitter, or the white organza?"

Ivy chuckled. "I think the organza is lovely for a wedding."

"But only the bride is supposed to wear white. The pink lace must be altered to fit Pixie's svelte torso, and the purple is a little loud, don't you think?"

"Definitely. I'm sure my sister won't mind if Pixie is in white." While Shelly and Pixie had gotten off to a challenging beginning, their relationship had improved.

"The organza it is, then," Gilda said, ruffling her hot pink hair. "A good choice for a spring wedding. She picked it out, but she's never worn it." Gilda opened a drawer full of dog sweaters and outfits and tucked in the other two dresses.

Ivy was amused. "Did you say Pixie chose it?"

Gilda placed the frilly doggie-dress on the dresser. "I get

catalogs in the mail, and Pixie taps on outfits she likes. Don't you, my little sweetikums?" She rubbed her nose against Pixie's. "She'll look fabulous."

"As long as she's not wearing any hot gemstones. Pixie can be a little rascal," Ivy added, scratching the Chihuahua behind the ears.

Gilda's eyes brightened. "Why, that gives me an idea…"

"I'll see you at the ceremony." Ivy didn't have time to hear the rest. However, after leaving Gilda's room, she immediately returned to her bedroom and tucked away her mother's jewelry—just in case Pixie sneaked out and managed to wedge her way through the door.

Now, after having served as stylist to Darla and Pixie, Ivy made her way to the terrace, where her nephews were arranging tables. Poppy and Sunny followed behind them, draping tablecloths and anchoring the fabric with clips and Shelly's collection of weathered beach accents, including seashells and driftwood. They placed ivory candles in vintage hurricane glass holders and scattered rose and turquoise beach glass tumbled smooth by waves.

"We'll drape the flower runners that Shelly created down the center of the tables," Poppy said, showing Ivy what they'd accomplished. "Imani is going to help us with the flowers, too. With the candles lit, it's going to be gorgeous. I'm so glad we have a professional photographer coming."

Misty stepped outside beside Ivy. "I'll make sure she takes photos you can use to market the inn as a venue for weddings, Mom."

"I hope not all the weddings turn out like the York's," Ivy said. "I can take only so many Eleanors of the world." She glanced at her watch. "Brother Rip will be here in about three hours. We'll want to get ready before Shelly returns so we can help her with her dress and hair."

"Nana said the rest of the family will be arriving soon," Misty said. "Even Elena is driving in from Los Angeles. She has an employee she trusts to watch the jewelry boutique now. Will Mitch's family be able to come?"

Ivy realized Misty didn't know about Mitch's family. "He doesn't have any family, honey. That's why we need to welcome him into the Bay family with open arms."

As Ivy and Misty talked about the outdoor seating arrangements taking shape, a voice rang out.

"Hello, I'm here with the cake." A woman wearing a pink T-shirt emblazoned with *That Takes the Cake*, waved.

"Oh my gosh, I forgot about the wedding cake," Ivy said. She and Misty went to meet the woman. Ivy told her about the change of wedding plans.

"Not the first time," the woman said, glancing at the order slip she held in her hand. "I'll assemble it here and put on the finishing touches. You were going to decorate it with flowers, right?"

"Sure, we can do that," Ivy said, wondering what Shelly had planned. "Maybe not as well as Shelly, but she's having a massage right now. The last thing she needs to spend her precious time doing today is decorating her cake."

"I would stay and help, but I have another delivery," the woman said.

Ivy checked her watch again and turned to Misty. "Could you find Imani? Maybe she could give us some pointers."

"I think I saw her on the front lawn talking to someone." Misty took off.

Just then, Ivy heard a familiar voice. Marina Moore from the Coral Cottage was making her way toward her. Her brownish red hair was pulled back, and her clear hazel eyes took in everything around her. Though petite, she was poised and exuded confidence, likely from her years working as a news anchor in San Francisco before moving here.

Ivy had been so pleased that Marina insisted on fulfilling Eleanor's contract for dinner and brunch the next day.

"Everything is coming together beautifully," Marina said, looking at the tables and decorations.

"I'm so glad you're here for this," Ivy said. "Do you want to set up in the kitchen?"

"That's a fabulous kitchen for catering," Marina said. "I brought Kai along, too. Our other sister is watching the cafe along with a part-timer we hired, so we're all yours tonight. What luck this is for Shelly, right?"

"We could never have done all this for her," Ivy said. "So far, everything has worked out so well for Shelly. The finest flowers, a couture gown, and a catered affair. And most of all, the perfect partner for her."

"She's a lucky bride," Marina said.

Ivy hoped their luck would hold out. She glanced up, frowning. A few clouds were gathering in the sky now. If it began raining, they could simply sweep everything back inside. By then, their brothers Flint and Forrest would be here, too. They would have plenty of hands to help. No matter what, they were going to have a wonderful wedding.

"We'll prep in the kitchen and set up a buffet as you suggested earlier," Marina said. "It's more casual than table service, which is what Eleanor wanted."

"I haven't stopped to count how many guests we have," Ivy said. "Poppy is trying to create a list, but I have no idea how many people might show up outside of the family. I think we're skating on the edge of chaos right now."

Marina laughed. "We'll manage. I know that spot well."

Ivy had been prepared to oversee this process for Eleanor, but now that they'd made changes, she hadn't factored in time for dressing Shelly or inviting others. Still, Ivy was confident everything would somehow come together.

As Ivy turned, she saw Carlotta walking toward her.

"Darling, I'd like to introduce you to the pastor," Carlotta said, gesturing toward a tall man crowned with an intricate pattern of braids that brushed his shoulders. "This is Brother Rip, the pastor who'll be performing the ceremony."

"Hello, it's nice to meet the sister of the bride," Brother Rip said in a soft Jamaican accent. He put his palms together and nodded. A sense of serenity surrounded him.

Brother Rip's deep voice and gentle, melodic speech was enchanting. "I understand you and Mitch are old friends," Ivy said. Bennett had told her that Brother Rip was a regular on the beaches in Southern California, claiming surfers in his flock and holding sunrise ceremonies before riding the waves.

"From way back," he said. "Before we each found our paths. Mitch and I have come through the riptides together. I still carry the nickname," he added, smiling. "I'm so honored he asked me here today."

They chatted for a few minutes while Brother Rip told her how he'd met Mitch on the beach. Ivy thought this gentle giant was ideal for performing the marriage ceremony for Mitch and Shelly.

After excusing herself, Ivy ping-ponged between family members who were beginning to arrive. Her father, brothers, nieces, and nephews, as well as vendors, including musicians, and Marina and Kai. Although Ivy's head was spinning with details, she was enjoying every moment.

Ivy barely had time to freshen up and slip into a silky, blush-pink dress her mother had given her before Shelly returned from the spa looking blissful. Her sister had her hair styled in a curly updo at the salon.

"You're going to look stunning," Ivy said as she helped Shelly into the gown. She couldn't help checking the label again. When she did, she gave a tiny gasp. *Callot Soeurs*.

"What's wrong?" Shelly asked.

As Ivy secured the tiny buttons, she told her. "Megan came by while you were having your massage. I'll share the whole story later, but I want you to know you're getting married in an authentic couture gown from Paris. Only the best for my sister."

Shelly sucked in a breath. "I knew it was special from the moment I saw it. Thank you so much for what you did so I could wear it."

Once Shelly was buttoned into the dress, Carlotta pinned fresh white roses in her daughter's chestnut hair and fastened the pearls she'd worn on her wedding day around her neck.

"I've dreamed of this day for you, *mija*," Carlotta said, kissing Shelly's cheek. "You're a lovely vision."

Exercising care, Ivy and her mother hugged Shelly and blinked back tears of happiness. It was almost time for the wedding to begin.

"Is the bride ready?" Brother Rip asked, his deep, rich voice drawing everyone into the moment. Behind him, the sun dipped toward the horizon, bathing the scene with a golden glow.

"She is," Ivy said, nodding at Mitch, who stood to one side looking relaxed after his massage. Ivy scanned the crowd that had gathered. "And everyone is here."

As family and friends gathered on the terrace, Ivy had taken her place to one side of the pastor. Across from her stood Bennett, acting as Mitch's best man. A group of musicians played against the sounds of the surf in the background, with crashing waves punctuating the sweet strains.

Ivy breathed in the sweet scent of flowers, mingling with sea breezes. Arching above the pastor was a cascade of roses, fragrant lilies, and voluptuous peonies, among a riot of other flowers.

Imani had finished decorating the arch that Poppy and Sunny had positioned on the wide terrace, draping it with the flowers that Shelly had enmeshed with an ombré technique, bursting from vivid coral and seashell pink that faded dramatically into sunset shades of mauve and dusky red. The arch framed turquoise waves and a blue sky shot with golden beams —the vision was spectacular.

And not a raincloud was in sight.

Ivy held a bouquet of blush-pink roses and peonies that matched her dress. She was so eager for the ceremony to begin.

The Bay family brothers, Flint and Forrest, sat at the front with their wives and children, including Poppy. Their eldest sister Honey and her husband were in Sydney, but their daughter Elena had joined them from Los Angeles.

Elena had brought a tablet and called her mom on it so that Honey could see her sister get married. Elena lifted the tablet, and the Bay family waved at Honey and her husband, Gabe.

Also seated in the front was Darla, her royal-blue hair dazzling against a rhinestone-studded visor and a sky-blue dress that Ivy had helped her select. Darla was as nervous and happy as any natural parent would be, and Ivy was relieved that she and Shelly had managed to resolve their differences with Darla.

Ivy looked out across the crowd of impromptu well-wishers. To balance Shelly's extensive Bay family clan, they'd also invited a few people in town that Mitch knew particularly well.

Beside Darla sat Ginger Delavie from the Coral Cottage— and grandmother to Marina and Kai, who were catering the wedding. When Mitch opened Java Beach, Ginger taught him how to make her favorite recipes for muffins, croissants, and scones.

Seated near Darla were Jen and George from Nailed It, the hardware store next to Java Beach. Behind them was the Summer Beach Police Chief, Clark Clarkson, with Imani, wearing a gorgeous flowing dress painted with watercolor-like florals. Clark and Mitch had bonded over an earlier situation in which Mitch had been mistakenly accused of jewelry theft.

Nan from City Hall and her husband Arthur, who owned Antique Times and was a regular at Java Beach, were also seated in the small group of well-wishers.

As Ivy glanced around, she realized that while Mitch didn't have family in the traditional sense, he had become a son of Summer Beach and an integral part of the village family.

Before the ceremony, Bennett had told Ivy that he'd dressed up Mitch fairly well on short notice. Mitch didn't want to wear a suit or tuxedo, so they'd raided Bennett's closet, opting for marine-blue slacks and a white shirt with leather slip-ons. Around Mitch's neck was a puka shell necklace and a traditional Hawaiian wedding lei of ti leaves and white orchids, gifts from Leilani and her husband, owners of the Hidden Garden nursery where Mitch and Shelly often shopped for plants. Leilani and Roy were also there; they'd brought traditional leis for Carlotta, Sterling, and Darla, too.

With his sun-bleached hair and eyes the color of the sea he loved, Mitch stepped into place beside Bennett, giving the mayor and Brother Rip fist bumps. Mitch's grin was infectious as he turned toward the crowd and whistled, surprising everyone. He motioned to Gilda, who knelt at the other end of the center aisle.

At his command, Gilda released Pixie. The diminutive Chihuahua looked proud to wear her new white organza doggie dress. With her head and tail held high, she pranced down the aisle.

Laughter rippled across the crowd.

Halfway down the aisle, Pixie paused. Craning her neck, she latched onto a white satin ribbon looped around her neck with her teeth. Ivy laughed. This must have been what Gilda had in mind.

Suddenly, Pixie ducked between chairs and legs and shot toward the beach as fast as her little legs would go. Her eyes were wild, and she growled at anyone who dared try to stop her.

Ivy gasped. "Catch her!" A few people scrambled toward her, but they were immediately repelled with a fury of barks and nips.

"Hey, Pixie," Mitch called. He whistled again. Behind him, Brother Rip let out deep, bellowing laughter that filled the air with a joyful sound.

At that, Pixie stopped. She eyed Mitch and the pastor warily.

Mitch knelt and held out his open hand.

Shivering from the thrill of running free, Pixie lifted her nose to the air. Catching a whiff of the treat in Mitch's hand, she turned and raced back, her tiny legs pumping.

Everyone let out a sigh of relief.

Wriggling with excitement, Pixie leapt up and snatched the dog biscuit from Mitch's hand. In a flash, she turned to flee with her treasure.

"Hang on, Pixie," Mitch said. Before Pixie could escape, he lifted her into his arms—her little legs still churning—and held her up for all to see. As the small gathering cheered and applauded, Mitch removed the white ribbon looped over her head, despite Pixie's snarling complaints. Chuckling, he said, "Hold still, Pixie. This is critical."

When he put her down, Pixie clenched the biscuit between her teeth and tore back down the aisle toward Gilda. She scooped up the little dog and sat down, sweetly scolding her. "You knew what to do, didn't you? You were just teasing all of us."

Ivy saw the photographer, Shelly's friend from New York, snapping and filming with glee. Ivy was glad this highlight of Pixie as a ring bearer had been captured.

Laughing, Mitch passed the slightly soggy treasure to Bennett.

As the music rose, Shelly stepped into the aisle, flanked by her mother and father. Tears formed in the corner of Ivy's eyes as she watched her sister. Shelly's vintage gown gleamed under the rays of the setting sun. She wore her mother's pearls and a white orchid lei around her neck, also courtesy of Leilani. In her hands, she held a voluptuous, stunning bouquet made of blush rose, ranunculus, and peony with silvery eucalyptus and trailing ivy vines.

On either side of Shelly, Carlotta and Sterling beamed with pride. After delivering the bride to Mitch, her parents took their seats.

When Shelly handed her bouquet to Ivy, the two sisters exchanged a look of sheer happiness. "It's really happening," Shelly whispered gleefully.

As the bride and groom joined hands, Brother Rip began. "We're gathered here to celebrate a story of love between Shelly and Mitch, and to join this happy couple together."

Ivy saw Shelly blinking through tears of joy while Mitch wore the most loving expression. Despite the nervousness he'd shown for months, he was now calm and serene, clasping Shelly's hands with assurance and love.

"My wish for this couple is that their bond will grow stronger with each sunrise," Brother Rip said, his deep voice resonating against the hypnotic sound of ocean waves. "I wish for them a lifetime of love and happy moments that they can cherish in the fullness of their years. Today, you will sail into the sunrise of your lives together."

Ivy smiled, remembering Shelly's heartfelt wish.

Just before Mitch said his vows, he turned to Bennett, who handed him the white ribbon from Pixie. Untying the bow, he slipped a ring from the ribbon.

Shelly gasped, and a smile wreathed her face. Ivy knew this was a surprise to her—to all of them. She could hardly wait to see the ring.

"With this ring," Mitch began. "I promise to love and

cherish you forever—through the high tides and low tides and everything in between."

As Ivy gazed at the happy couple, she saw Bennett looking past them at her. In his eyes, she saw the possibility of their future together. She held his gaze, feeling the fullness of his love for her—and returning her love to him.

When Shelly and Mitch kissed, the gathering erupted in cheers. The ecstatic couple turned toward their family and friends, and Poppy gave a cue. The entire group—even Brother Rip and little Pixie, aided by Gilda—shot their hands in the air and shouted together, "Woo-hoo!"

Shelly and Mitch laughed and joined them. Soon, the champagne was flowing, people were lining up for the buffet, and the photographer was capturing sweet moments.

Unable to contain her curiosity, Ivy made her way to Shelly and Mitch. "I've got to see this surprise ring."

"Wasn't that sweet?" Shelly held up her hand, revealing a platinum band designed of old-fashioned filigree studded with glowing sapphires. "I once said I loved sapphires because they're the color of the ocean. Elena knew what I liked, so this is exactly what I wanted. I can wear it all the time, and it won't snag inside my gardening gloves."

Ivy smiled at her sister's practicality. Turning to Mitch, she asked, "How did you manage to pull this off?"

As Mitch waggled his eyebrows, their niece Elena turned around. "Surprise," she said, laughing. A tiny, rare blue diamond sparkled on the side of her nose. "Mitch came to me with his idea, and we've been working on the ring for a while. Fortunately, I'd finished it just last week, but he hadn't seen it yet."

"And it's a perfect fit," Shelly said, her eyes glowing.

Mitch hugged her. "This is my real treasure," he said before they were whisked away by other well-wishers.

As the sun set over the happy gathering, the lights that Poppy and Sunny had strung up outside began to glow in the balmy evening air. Ivy watched her family and new Summer Beach friends reveling with the newlyweds. She pressed a hand against her heart, still marveling at the miracle of the past twenty-four hours.

And the weekend was still young.

22

As other wedding guests lined up at the buffet, Ivy looked around for Bennett. She spotted him strolling toward her carrying two vintage crystal champagne coupes.

"Would you like to join me by the firepit before dinner?" he asked. "Looks like we have a few minutes before the buffet line clears out."

"I'd like that," she said, tucking her hand through the crook in his elbow. Shelly and Mitch were at the head of the line, and all the nieces and nephews and friends were queued up behind them. They had time to slip away.

Ivy slipped out of her sandals and lifted the blush-pink silk above her ankles. The sand was cool between her toes.

They strolled across the beach toward the firepit and eased onto one of the curved benches that flanked it. Flames danced in the sea breeze, spewing forth tiny orange embers like miniature fireworks that quickly burned out. Ivy leaned toward the fire, enjoying the scent and warmth on her face.

Bennett handed her a glass of champagne. "To your unwavering support of Shelly and the amazing effort you put forth today. Who knew this day would end with such a happy crescendo?"

"Sometimes things fall into place just as they're meant," Ivy said, recalling their 4:00 a.m. wake-up with eloping guests. As she touched her crystal glass to his, a sweet tone rang in the air as if heralding a new beginning. "To Shelly and Mitch, and Rachel and Topper. What a day for weddings." She sipped her champagne, enjoying the chilly bubbles against the warmth of her face.

"I have faith that fate will soon orchestrate something special for us, too," Bennett said, putting his arm around her.

She leaned her head against his. "Maybe so."

Bennett laced his fingers with hers. "I won't push you anymore. We'll know when the time is right."

"I have to see to my paperwork," Ivy said, her voice trailing off.

"Perhaps we could have it expedited."

"I suppose so."

"That didn't sound very strong."

Ivy sipped her champagne, considering her words. "It's not that I'm not looking forward to marrying you."

"Ouch," Bennett said with a soft chuckle. "I'm not sure that was positive."

Ivy kissed his cheek. "It's just that I was married for two decades. I was a wife and a mother, but I'd forgotten what Ivy Bay had once wanted."

Bennett nodded slowly. "You'll have to tell me what that means."

Ivy hadn't thought about having this conversation tonight. Yet whether it was the champagne or the early wake-up call they'd had, she felt ready now.

She drew a breath. "I love you very much, my darling. But I need more time. You've had ten years to discover yourself and arrange your life as you like. I haven't had that."

"I hope it won't be ten years," Bennett said, his smile dimming.

"I don't think it will be." Ivy squeezed his hand, unsure

how to proceed. She had so much to say, so many feelings she needed to share. *Was this the right time?*

Bennett brought her hand to his lips. "I sense there's more. I'm listening."

Ivy gazed into Bennett's calm eyes. Right now, at this moment, Ivy needed to speak her truth. She blinked and began. "In the past, I've had many responsibilities to other people. I'm not saying that was inconvenient or bad—I'm proud of raising two fairly well-adjusted young women. And I was proud of the home that I made for my husband and the relationship we enjoyed for a long time. I know it's difficult to believe, but there were many good times before our relationship soured."

"I understand. It wasn't your fault, Ivy. I knew him, too."

She grew quiet. In truth, she had often wondered if she could have prevented Jeremy's infidelity, but she knew in her heart that was a fruitless exercise. Still, she wondered when Jeremy had fallen out of love with her. He might not have been the man she would choose for a partner today, but she had loved the good man beneath the one who had spiraled out of control. *Highly intelligent, spontaneous, romantic.* And dedicated to his daughters.

A thought struck her. Perhaps Jeremy had never been loyal to her, or only in stretches of time. She would never know, and moreover, she didn't want to know now.

Ivy knew enough.

She glanced back at the grand old house. On the other hand, she had Jeremy to thank for this home. Perhaps in a karmic manner, his deceitful actions had brought on his demise. Was there only so much duplicity a person could live with?

Ivy took Bennett's hand. "I know it's been two years, but I'm still recovering from Jeremy's death and the shocks he left in his wake." She didn't want to lose Bennett, but she had to be honest. "I don't know how long that will take or when I'll be ready." As she said those words, the light in Bennett's eyes dimmed.

Still, Bennett held her gaze. "It's not what I wanted to hear, but it's what I needed to know." He stroked the back of her hand as he spoke. "I've had years to recover from the death of my wife. I was lonely for a long time, but after some grief counseling, I began to step back into the world and discover a different life."

"That's exactly what I mean."

Bennett sipped his champagne. "I've been thinking a lot, too. When you and I first met—all those years ago—I was a guitar-playing surf bum, but I grew into someone who wanted more out of life. In Jackie, I found a partner who cheered me on as much as I supported her efforts."

"That's what I want for us," Ivy said, pleased that he seemed to feel the need to talk, too.

"After Jackie died, I put myself out there," Bennett said. "I learned how to connect people in the community, then I learned how to be a leader, and yes, I'm even taking up surfing again." He paused. "I guess you need that chance, too."

"I do." A flicker of hope brightened Ivy's heart. Yet, while Bennett might understand, disappointment still edged his voice.

Bennett squeezed her hand. "Then that's what I want for you."

Ivy had spoken the truth from deep within her soul, from a place she had hardly known existed. For years, she'd been so busy trying to be Ivy Marin, perfect wife and mother, that she had not asked what Ivy Bay desired in a long, long time.

She thought about how, years ago, when she met Jeremy, she had first put her dreams on hold to start their family, and then tucked them far beneath his. Yet her reward had been two beautiful daughters that she loved fiercely.

The question of marriage still hung in the air between her and Bennett. "There's more, too. For now, my children still need me, especially Sunny. She's grieved and acted out of pain. I don't want her to feel like I've abandoned her or that you've taken precedence in my heart and in our lives. This is a critical time for our family. And I include you in that, too. You're becoming part of our family." Ivy paused, blinking back emotions.

"I feel the same way." Bennett gazed into the flickering fire as he spoke. "When I think back over the period after Jackie died, the first two years were a seismic transition. At the end of that time, I certainly wasn't ready for another relationship. I don't know how it is for others who've been widowed, but I needed more time." He let out a slow, deep breath. "So I can't fault you."

"I know you're disappointed," Ivy said. "And I wouldn't blame you if you decided that you can't wait for me. But when I'm ready, I promise that I will come to you with my identity firmly in place. Not depending on you or looking to you for anything but love. I will bring the best version of myself to our relationship so that we can be full partners in love and marriage. Is it enough for me to love you right now without that legal commitment of marriage?"

Bennett took her hand. "I'm committed to you, Ivy. I'm not looking for anyone else, and I'm certainly not looking for a wife to make my dinner and bring my slippers."

She smiled at that. "If I'd been looking for the words to sway my decision today, those might have been the ones."

Bennett laughed and clinked her glass.

After finishing their champagne, they strolled back to the wedding dinner. Bennett drew his arm around her. "I have new respect for you," he said. "You've always had that, but tonight you raised my admiration to a new level. It takes guts for people to listen to their inner compass and stick to it. Getting to know each other better can't hurt us. There's always next summer—or whenever."

Ivy looked up at Bennett with happiness. Love was one

element of a good marriage; respect was another. "Thanks for the good talk," she said.

He kissed her forehead. "Anytime."

After going through the buffet and eating at the long tables draped with flowers, one of Mitch's surfing friends brought in a turntable to kick up the party a notch. Shelly and Mitch led everyone onto an area on the terrace that had been cleared for dancing. All the younger cousins joined them—Poppy, Elena, Coral, Rocky, Reed, and the rest. It didn't take much coaxing for Carlotta and Sterling to join in, too. Even Brother Rip was drafted onto the dance floor.

Bennett jerked his thumb toward the younger cousins, who were intent on bringing everyone to the dance floor. "They're not going to let us sit this one out," he said, his eyes twinkling in the light of tiki torches that dotted the patio.

"Let's beat them to it," Ivy said, taking Bennett's hand.

As the music pumped under the stars, Ivy and Bennett danced across the patio to Shelly and Mitch. Linking hands, they laughed and danced, spinning under the stars, celebrating the life they had and the life ahead of them—without pressure.

Ivy thought this had been the perfect wedding and send-off weekend for their parents, too. She was so happy how events had worked out for everyone, from Shelly and Mitch to Rachel and Topper. Maybe the only one disappointed would be Eleanor, but Ivy imagined a beautiful grandchild would soon bring her joy.

Everyone had lessons to learn and different paths to traverse in life. In many ways, Ivy was entering a new phase, too. She wanted the chance to learn and grow and enjoy every minute. Later, when the time was right, she and Bennett would sail into a sunrise of their own.

23

The following morning, Ivy woke with the sun, stretching in bed. She was thankful that Poppy had taken charge of clean-up last night and pressed or shamed her cousins into service. With youthful energy and enthusiasm, they turned on music and made quick work of the task. Ivy had heard them upstairs in the attic rooms talking and laughing until the wee hours, but she didn't mind the sounds of happiness. Everyone seemed to be having a wonderful time this weekend.

Her family's dynamics were shifting and changing, from the younger nieces and nephews growing older and becoming independent to Shelly's marriage and their parents' pending departure. With her parents leasing out their home, having this house to serve as a gathering place for her extended family meant even more to Ivy.

Through the open window, Ivy heard a door shut and peered outside. Across the car court, she saw Bennett heading toward the beach for his morning run. She smiled as she watched him stretch before his run. Soon, they would meet for breakfast downstairs as they often did. She'd grown accustomed to the pleasant routine, yet after their talk last night, she wondered if her hesitation might someday hinder their relationship. Still, she had to follow her instincts. For now, Bennett respected that.

One day at a time, she told herself, turning from the window. First, she had to tend to the inn and her livelihood to ensure her financial stability.

Ivy's stomach rumbled, and she had a slight headache from the revelry last night. But soon, nourishment would be arriving. Since Eleanor had paid for a catered brunch, Marina and Kai were bringing the food she had ordered. As they had done last night, they planned to set up a buffet outside on the terrace. Ivy pulled on yoga pants and a sweatshirt and padded downstairs.

With the York party gone, guest rooms had become available, so Ivy's parents and several of the cousins stayed over. Ivy didn't want anyone to drive home after indulging in too much champagne.

Carlotta joined her in the hallway. Her mother's eyes brimmed with happiness. "Good morning, *mija*. How about a walk on the beach with me?"

"I'd like that," Ivy said.

Stepping outside, the two women headed toward the shore. In the fresh morning air, a few other people were strolling or walking dogs. Ivy tucked her hands into the pockets of her sweatshirt.

"Let's go the other way," Carlotta said. "Fewer people."

Turning away from the community beach, they walked toward the more deserted, rugged side.

"What a beautiful wedding that was," Carlotta said. "I don't suppose you've heard from Shelly."

"Not a peep, but I wouldn't expect to, even though Mitch is an early riser."

Last night, Shelly and Mitch had changed into casual clothes and left, saying they were going to the marina to spend their wedding night on Mitch's boat under the stars.

Ivy thought that sounded so romantic—and perfect for them.

"I'm so glad that we could see Shelly get married before we left," Carlotta said. "It will be up to you and your brothers to make sure Mitch is welcomed into the family."

"We will," Ivy said. "Forrest and Flint are already planning a fishing trip with him."

Carlotta laughed. "That should be interesting. Mitch will be like a younger brother to them. And if Shelly has her way, we might be welcoming a little one into the family soon. It's been a long time since we've had a baby among us."

A baby. "You'll miss the big event," Ivy said with a twinge of sadness.

"We're already planning to fly home for that," Carlotta said. "Your father is just as excited as I am."

As the sun streamed across the morning sky, Ivy and her mother strolled along the sand, laughing about highlights from the wedding and planning for the future. It struck Ivy that this was a bittersweet day; Shelly would no longer be living at the inn, and her parents were leaving tomorrow. They were off on happy new adventures.

Ivy put her arm around her mother. "I'm going to miss you and Dad, even though I'm happy that you're taking this trip. I know how much it means to you."

"We've always wanted to be free to take our time sailing around the world. And now, with this new Jeanneau sailboat we've saved for, our dream is finally here."

"When is the new family moving into the house?" Ivy asked.

"Soon. They have been delayed a little due to work. While we're gone, Forrest will manage the house. His construction crew can handle any needed repairs."

Ivy listened, realizing that the time for her parents' departure was almost here. The thought hit her like a cold splash of water. She shivered involuntarily. "Maybe I could meet you in port somewhere."

"How about Sydney?" Carlotta asked, brightening. "Honey wants us to stop there. You could see your sister and Gabe at the same time. Or maybe you could travel with Elena. She's planning on flying back then, too." Carlotta paused. "Wasn't that a beautiful ring Elena designed for Shelly?"

"That was so thoughtful of Mitch." Ivy would never forget the sheer delight in Shelly's face at the sight of the sapphire band.

As they walked, Ivy felt her mother's observant gaze. She seldom missed anything where her daughters were concerned.

"What about you, *mija*? Have you and Bennett decided on a wedding date now?"

"He would in a heartbeat, Mom. But I want to take some time before we get married. I'm not quite ready." Ivy went on to tell her mother how she felt. Here in the quiet of the morning, her words flowed with ease. She would miss these talks with her mother.

Carlotta peered at Ivy. "If you're in love with Bennett and committed to him, what is holding you back? You're both old enough to know what you want in a partner."

"I want to be confident in my abilities—and myself. I want to know that I can manage this house and the inn business. That I can mold myself into who I want to be first—without molding myself to a husband's idea of who I should be."

"I understand, and that sounds like a wise plan," her mother said, nodding. "I know Jeremy was exciting in the beginning, but he became overbearing—and then almost nonexistent in your marriage."

"Sometimes it was hard to see that from inside the relationship," Ivy said. Her mother had summed up her marriage pretty well.

"Of course it is," Carlotta said. "After a certain age, many women emerge from marriages—either through divorce or widowhood—feeling freer than ever, shedding the constraints of social dictates. As many of my friends matured, they experienced a metamorphosis."

Ivy hadn't considered that, but she could feel those shifts occurring in her, too. She kicked up a little sand as she walked.

Carlotta clasped Ivy's hand. "Over this past year, you've certainly shown a talent for reinvention. I'm proud of you for all you've come through and accomplished in such a short period."

"Thanks, Mom. But I still feel like I'm just getting started on this new phase. What happened to the last two years?"

"Time slips away from us, my dear. Be aware of that." A contemplative look filled Carlotta's face. "To decide on one course means to cut off another. If you delay your marriage to Bennett, think about what could be lost in the interim. I don't mean to rush you—and marriage isn't necessarily right for some couples—but when you become certain about a future with him, don't waste precious days you could be spending together. We haven't as many as we would like on this earth."

Ivy squeezed her hand. "Which is why you're committed to this voyage, right?"

"That's part of it," Carlotta said, smiling. "Your father and I worked together as equal partners for many years. Now that our work is finished and our children are grown, we want to enjoy being together. We want to recapture the wonder and magic of discovery that first brought us together. At the heart of it all, we're best friends and lovers of life." A small smile curved her lips. "And never lose the romance, my dear."

Ivy liked to hear this. If she needed role models for a good marriage, she didn't have far to look.

A moment later, her mother's smile faded. "However, you must also consider the potential for loss that a delay might have."

"I'm not sure what you mean."

"Bennett is attractive, dynamic, and kind—that's a rare combination to find in a man, especially at our ages. Frankly, I'd be surprised if he hasn't had opportunities with other women before you. Would he consider a delay a denial? Ultimately, you should ask yourself this: Would you be willing to lose him to find yourself?"

"This isn't a competition, and he says he'll wait for me." Ivy lifted her chin. "If our connection is that tenuous, then I shouldn't mourn the loss if another woman could step in so swiftly."

"That's nice to think, but you would be heartbroken, wouldn't you?"

Ivy sighed. Her mother could always cut through to her deepest feelings.

"Weigh the alternatives and be sure about your decision," Carlotta said. "Keep the communication with him open." She stooped to pick up an interesting shell. "How does Bennett feel about this plan?"

"I'm fairly sure he understands. I told him I'm committed to him in my heart." Ivy paused, thinking about their last conversation. She realized the risk her mother had brought up. "When I decide the time is right to get married again, I'd like for you and Dad to be there for our wedding. Maybe when you return."

"When *you* decide? Don't assume he'll be patiently waiting to act on your desires, regardless of what he says." Carlotta shook her head. "And don't wait so long that he loses interest, darling. Ideally, you want to feel like your husband is your best friend, but it's a fine line. He's your husband, your partner, *and* your lover. Be careful that he doesn't start treating you too much like a friend before the marriage."

"Mom," Ivy protested. "I'm sorry, but that's an old-fashioned attitude." Irritated, she bent over, snagged a piece of driftwood, and flung it out to the ocean.

Carlotta tossed the shell into the surf. "Maybe, but I've

seen it happen. Another woman swoops in and offers the excitement a man is craving. I don't think men have changed that much, *mija*. However you do it, be sure he knows you love him every day. Complacency can destroy even the best relationships."

WHEN IVY and her mother returned to the inn, Ivy glanced up at Bennett's apartment across the car court. He was pounding up the steps after his run. She paused. Even after a run, he looked good. When she saw her mother watching her, she glanced away, recalling their conversation.

"He is easy on the eyes, *mija*," Carlotta said with a knowing smile.

Just then, Marina and Kai arrived, their car loaded with supplies.

"Breakfast has arrived," Marina said as she opened the car door.

"Come in," Ivy said, opening the rear door to the kitchen. This time, it swung open easily. "Bennett must have realigned the door," Ivy said.

Carlotta raised an eyebrow. "And he's handy, too."

"Mom, please." *That's not helping,* Ivy thought. Still, an odd feeling gathered on her neck.

Kai hefted a carton of muffins through the door and placed them on the counter. "Ginger and Marina made these. Blueberry, apple, and cranberry orange. They're fabulous."

Marina laughed. "Let the customer decide that. We have more in the car, and I'll set up a table to make custom omelets for everyone, too."

Carlotta followed them in. Hugging Ivy, she said, "I always have your best interests in mind. I'll dress and see you on the terrace in a little while."

"Thanks, Mom," Ivy said, holding her mother a moment longer. Too soon, she would have to let her go.

Turning back to Marina and Kai, Ivy said, "We'll set up just as you did last night." As they walked into the kitchen, she told them how much everyone had enjoyed the dinner they'd provided. "I think you're going to do well with the new Coral Cafe."

"With the summer ahead, this will be a critical time," Marina said. "We have to turn a profit as soon as we can. I really want to stay in Summer Beach."

"I'm always happy to refer guests to you." Ivy and Marina had bonded again over their start-up stories.

As Kai arranged muffins and croissants, she chatted about the wedding. With her strawberry blond hair, expressive eyes, and lean, athletic frame, Kai looked and moved like the musical theater actress she was. She often attended Shelly's yoga class.

"Shelly wore the most gorgeous wedding gown," Kai said. "She'd told me last week that she had no idea what to wear. But that gown looked vintage. Was it your mother's wedding dress?"

"We found the dress here in the house," Ivy replied. "It belonged to the owner, Amelia Erickson, and she wore it for her first wedding." Ivy remembered the rest of the old clothing they'd found upstairs. "I understand you're working with Axe on the new outdoor theater. We found a lot of early twentieth-century clothing that's beautifully made and preserved. If you're building a costume wardrobe, we'd be happy to donate some of the garments we found."

Kai's face lit. "Axe will be excited to hear that. It would be great to have costumes available for period performances."

"I'll bring it all down before you leave today," Ivy said, glad she'd found a home for the beautifully constructed clothing.

As the cousins began filtering into the dining room, Ivy greeted her father. "We have made-to-order omelets along with muffins, croissants, lox, and bagels." Fruit, yogurt, and oatmeal rounded out the brunch offerings.

"Sure was nice to see Bennett last night," Sterling said, putting his arm around her. "Your mother and I can depart knowing that you have a good man in your life."

"He is, Dad." Ivy smiled. The three of them had a long talk last night about the pending voyage and the ports of call her parents had planned. Still, what her mother had said about Bennett loomed in her mind.

Ivy checked on other family members, who were lining up for omelets. Imani, Jamir, and Gilda joined them, too. Since they had so much food, Ivy had also asked Bennett to invite his sister and her husband and their young son, Logan. She was fond of Kendra and Dave.

Bennett strolled in, looking relaxed in a white shirt and casual trousers. Ivy noticed how warmly her family greeted him. Bennett and her father spoke for a while.

"If you two keep jabbering, you'll miss all the food," Ivy said, chiding them.

Carlotta brought her husband a plate. "When Sterling gets started on boat talk, he could starve."

Ivy's father laughed. "Join us at our end of the table," he said.

"Would you like for me to get a plate for you?" Bennett asked Ivy.

"No, but thank you. I'll be there in a moment. I want to check on Kai in the kitchen and see if she needs anything."

Bennett got in line behind Flint, and they began chatting.

"What a glorious morning," a deep voice boomed over the gathering crowd.

Ivy turned to see Brother Rip, who had stayed in a guest room last night on Ivy's insistence. "Good morning. Did you sleep well?"

"Excellent," he said, his smooth face serene. "I can't remember the last time I danced like that. The good Lord sure had me moving in mysterious ways last night." He laughed heartily at his joke. "And look at this feast. What a blessing to start a day like this."

"I hope you're staying with us a little longer," Ivy said. "Do you perform many weddings?"

"A few every month," Brother Rip replied. "I also perform renewal of vows, commitment ceremonies, funerals, and blessings of all descriptions. Would you like to attend one of our sunrise celebrations? The surfing afterward is optional," he added.

"I'd like that," Ivy said, imagining what a sight it must be on the beach. She hesitated. Something he'd said intrigued her. "What exactly is a commitment ceremony?"

"That depends on the parties," he replied. "It's a wedding or union bound by spirit rather than law. Some couples simply want to mark and express their deep commitment to each other. It might be as simple as a few words on the beach. People have different, personal reasons for such unions."

His explanation touched a nerve deep within Ivy. "I see," she managed to say, a thought forming in her mind. "That sounds like a lovely gesture."

Brother Rip placed his hand gently over hers. As though looking into her soul, he added, "You might be more ready than you imagine."

The warm strength of Brother Rip's hand on hers was like nothing she had ever felt—as if he had a divine touch. "I'll let you know," she replied solemnly.

"Yes, I believe you will." His face broke into a broad grin. "Now, let's partake of this marvelous bounty."

When he removed his hand, Ivy glanced down at hers. Her skin was so warm, and a pink imprint of his hand was visible. Feeling a little light-headed, she ran her fingers over the mark and looked up.

Bennett was staring at her. His gaze was direct, but there

was something more in it. It was a feeling, a connection, so deep she couldn't look away.

He started toward her. "Are you all right? Brother Rip is known for his powerful observations."

Ivy swept a hand across her face. "On second thought, I think maybe I need something to eat right now. Did you hear what he said?"

"I did," he said quietly, his eyes never leaving hers.

Feeling slightly unsettled, Ivy glanced at the family table behind her. "I should check Shelly's garden after we eat. I promised I'd watch the tomatoes. Will you join me?"

"You don't have to ask." He handed her the plate he was holding. "Here, I ordered your favorite omelet. Muenster cheese, bacon, avocado, and sliced green onions sprinkled on the top. Go sit with your parents, and I'll be right there."

"That was thoughtful." She hadn't realized he'd ever noticed what she'd ordered the few times they'd gone out for brunch. Two, maybe three times? She couldn't recall.

"I know you want to spend as much time as you can with them today."

Ivy pressed her cheek to his. "Thank you. I'll save you a seat."

She sat with her parents, watching how they finished each other's sentences and observing the small things they did for each other—so seamlessly that Ivy had never noticed before. Her father scooped salsa onto her mother's plate unbidden; her mother passed the pepper to him; her father picked up a napkin Carlotta dropped and gave her a fresh one; her mother refilled Sterling's water glass. None of these actions were requested. Rather, this was a perfectly choreographed suite of intuitive movements known only to them.

As they ate, her parents spoke animatedly about their pending departure, which would be tomorrow morning from the marina near their home.

"Here's what we've decided to do," Sterling said. "After we

reach Panama, we'll sail to French Polynesia. The next stretch is to Fiji, and then to Sydney. From Australia, it's on to South Africa. Then we have a long crossing to the Caribbean, and finally, we'll pass through the Panama canal and return home. Of course, we'll stop at other ports along the way, but at any of those major junctures, we can store the boat, fly home, and return later."

"In case we have to return for special family events," Carlotta said, her eyes twinkling. "Such as a new baby or another wedding." She glanced around the table. "And extra crew is always welcome."

Family members smiled around the table, even some of the nieces and nephews. Ivy wondered if any of them had serious relationships yet. She knew they dated, but none of them were engaged. Perhaps Elena was the closest; she was the eldest of the cousins and had been dating a man for some time.

After the wedding, Mitch had told Ivy that he and Shelly had decided they would try to start their family soon. He said that with each passing year, a first pregnancy would become riskier for Shelly, who was already considered high risk at her age. Ivy was impressed. Mitch was certainly thinking ahead—and thinking about Shelly.

Sterling glanced at Ivy. "Or any other special event we wouldn't want to miss."

Ivy knew what her father meant. She glanced at Bennett, who caught that, too. He grinned at her.

Frowning, Ivy pressed her lips together. "Mom and Dad, you will be careful, won't you?"

"Of course, darling," Carlotta said, resting her hand on Ivy's. "Oh, dear. Are you worried about us?"

"We all are," Ivy said, as her brothers joined in the conversation, voicing their concerns, too.

"Well, I'll be," Sterling said, slapping the edge of the table. "I never thought I'd see the day when the kids would be worried about us." He chuckled. "You all know we're cautious, safety-first sailors. Please don't be concerned."

Ivy relaxed a little. She had to trust in her parents' expertise and experience.

"We'll be back for every special occasion that rolls around," Carlotta said. "Just give us enough time to reach a port." Pausing, she gazed around the table at each of her children and grandchildren and extended family. "I want each of you to remember that if you don't take risks, you'll never really live. Rising to meet a worthy challenge is one of the finest feelings you can have."

Ivy thought about that. What her mother said reminded her of what Amelia had written after the death of her husband. *Regardless, life is a risk worth taking.* She'd had no regrets.

From launching the Seabreeze Inn to forming a relationship with Bennett, Ivy had certainly taken risks and risen to challenges this past year.

Her mother was right. Today, Ivy had no regrets, and she was pleased with how her life had turned out. She cast another glance at Bennett. Yet, could she be playing it too safe?

*a*fter brunch, Ivy and Bennett excused themselves to check on Shelly's vegetable garden. Against the smell of fresh tomatoes, basil, and oregano and the lulling sound of the ocean, Ivy picked up the conversation where they had left off yesterday. Only now, she had another idea.

Bennett listened while he plucked ripe tomatoes and nestled them in a basket.

When Ivy finished explaining her thoughts, she paused, turned to him, and took his hands. "What do you think?" she asked, holding her breath. "Is it a crazy idea?"

"I'm in total agreement," he replied solemnly. "The same thought was in my mind, too."

Ivy smiled. "I saw it in your eyes." She wrapped her arms around his neck, and he lifted her until her toes were dangling. "Let's go now," she said happily. "But give me a few minutes to freshen up."

Bennett whirled her around. "I'll make arrangements and meet you on the beach."

When they returned to the house, Ivy went straight upstairs. In her large dressing area, she quickly shed her clothes and stepped into a delicate, mint-green silk dress that her mother had left with her. With thin straps, it skimmed her waist and fell to her calves. But it needed something else. She spun around and reached for the vintage lace coat.

After trying it on, she turned to the mirror and caught her breath. This was everything she could have wanted. Around her neck she fastened Bennett's gift, the emerald cabochon necklace on its platinum chain. She selected a pair of her mother's simple diamond stud earrings and clipped up her hair up. With a swipe of lip gloss and a light spritz of the airy floral *eau de parfum* Bennett loved on her, she was ready.

But a piece of her heart was missing.

She blinked at her image in the mirror. *If only Shelly could be here, too.*

Ivy went downstairs. Outside, she paused at the edge of the terrace before joining her family gathered on the beach. Everyone she loved was there: Her parents, her daughters, her brothers and their families—all the younger cousins. Bennett's sister and her family stood with him. Marina and Kai had joined them, too. Even their Seabreeze Inn family was present: Imani, Jamir, and Gilda with Pixie in her arms.

Suddenly, Shelly and Mitch appeared, racing across the beach in T-shirts and jeans they'd probably just thrown on to join them. Shelly waved, and Ivy broke into a broad smile.

Her sister was here for her after all.

Ivy pressed a hand to her mouth, blinking back tears of happiness. Bennett must have called them. She continued toward the gathering, drawn by Bennett's earnest gaze.

Everyone looked surprised at the sight of Ivy, and Carlotta clasped her hands against her chest.

"You look so lovely, *mija*," her mother said, her eyes wide with questions. "Bennett asked us to come out here to see something special."

"And you will," she said, kissing her mother's cheek. Ivy's heart was racing, yet she felt calm. She and Bennett had made the right decision for them—together.

"Is this what I think it is?" Carlotta asked, her face shimmering with joy. "But I didn't think you had a marriage license."

Ivy smiled. "Just wait."

Sunny and Misty stood beside her mother, wearing expressions of awe and excitement. Ivy could see the happiness in their eyes as they giggled with each other. They both liked Bennett, and someday, when the time was right, they would all become a family.

Ivy wrapped her arms around her daughters and hugged them. "I'm glad you're pleased."

"Of course I am, Mom," Misty said.

"I'm in, too," Sunny added. "Bennett's pretty cool."

Ivy kissed them on their cheeks, relieved at their acceptance. She hadn't meant to spring this on them, but she thought they would understand once they realized what their mother had decided.

Bennett stepped forward, extending his hand toward her. "My love."

She slipped her hand into his, and it felt so natural and right. Beside Bennett stood Brother Rip with a joyful expression on his tranquil face. He swept his braids over his shoulder and placed his hands over theirs, enveloping them with his powerful touch.

As waves rolled toward the shore and fresh breezes ruffled their hair, Brother Rip brought the family closer together. "We are gathered here to witness the joy of two people committing their hearts to one another. Not yet in marriage, but as a first step toward devoting their lives to each other."

The energy coursing through their joined hands was beyond anything Ivy had ever known. The power of love and commitment was almost overwhelming, and she blinked back tears of joy that sprang to her eyes.

When Brother Rip was through speaking, he held their joined hands aloft, and her family broke out in cheers.

"This is our beginning," she whispered to Bennett.

"The beginning of our forever," he added, touching his lips to hers.

In her heart, Ivy knew this to be true. Today was their first step, yet Bennett had also promised her the time she needed.

With outstretched arms, Ivy and Bennett delivered hugs all around, and especially to Carlotta and Sterling. Ivy was so happy that they could witness this before they left. Tomorrow they would see them off on their grand voyage, but today the celebration would continue.

"What a perfect weekend," Carlotta said, taking Ivy's and Shelly's hands. "Seeing two of my girls stepping into the sunshine of their lives just before we sail. I'm so happy for both of you, and I'm proud of your decisions."

Laughing, Shelly flung her arms around Ivy. "This will teach people to bet against us."

Flint and Forrest clapped Bennett on the back and called him their new brother, while Sterling and Carlotta welcomed him into the family.

"Not so fast," Ivy said, teasing Bennett. "We're still in the trial period."

Bennett laughed and kissed her hand. "I'll be on my toes forever with you—and I wouldn't have it any other way."

THE REST of the day was devoted to eating, laughing, and sharing time as a large, extended family. While some of the younger cousins rigged up a volleyball net on the beach and had a rousing game, others played in the surf. Some of the Bay family siblings swam in the pool while other family and friends played cards and chatted under umbrellas on the terrace.

After a day of pleasure, they watched a brilliant golden sunset while Bennett and Mitch fired up the grill for a cook-out. "Shrimp and burgers on the barbie," Bennett called out.

"And grilled bean burgers and portobellos for the vegans," Mitch added, brandishing a long-handled spatula.

"It's our turn to serve you," Ivy told Marina and Kai, insisting that they stay. She even invited Darla, who was delighted to be included and beamed to see Mitch and Shelly together.

The family had a lot to celebrate. They were also honoring Carlotta and Sterling, who would be casting off tomorrow.

Later that evening after they ate, Ivy gathered with her family and friends, relaxing with a glass of wine. She cuddled next to Bennett on a wide chaise lounge.

"I never imagined the week would end like this," she said.

Bennett touched her glass with his. "Here's to embracing the unexpected—something I've learned to expect around here."

Ivy smiled. "Not knowing what lies ahead of life's curves can be fun."

"Especially with you," Bennett said, tapping her nose.

With their arms around each other and surrounded by those they loved, Ivy and Bennett watched the waves, enjoying the last hours of a day they would never forget.

THE NEXT MORNING, Carlotta and Sterling left early, eager to prepare their sailing craft for departure. After preparing breakfast and cleaning the kitchen, Ivy's siblings and their children joined them at the marina where the new yacht was docked. Ivy sent everyone ahead while she chatted with Imani and Gilda, who promised to look after the inn while she and the family were gone. No guests were expected, but Ivy wanted to be sure guests could reach her if needed.

When Ivy and Bennett arrived at the marina, it looked like a party was going on by her parents' new yacht, *Bay Dreams*. Fortunately, the sky was clear and the ocean calm. It was a good day for Carlotta and Sterling to embark on their journey.

"They'll be missed," Ivy said as they approached the gathering. She drew in her lip. Even though the time was here, it was still difficult to see her parents leave.

"Just think of the fun they'll have," Bennett said, rubbing her shoulders. "Try not to worry too much. They're vital, healthy, and experienced." He put his arm around her. "You can still communicate with them during their voyage."

That was true; her parents had given them an itinerary and promised to call them in port. They could also keep in touch via a satellite phone.

Ivy leaned into Bennett, grateful for his support. "Life is all about enjoying the moments we can." After all she'd been through the last two years, she'd learned that life was ever changing.

"Every day," Bennett said. "Some periods are rough, but that only makes the good days sweeter."

Sterling waved to them. "Come aboard," he called out, motioning to them. He and Carlotta wore their favorite deck shoes and windbreakers, ready for their voyage.

Ivy and Bennett stepped onto the gleaming vessel. The family was gathered on the spacious deck, seated around a table, lounging on cushioned seating, or inspecting the craft.

"Isn't she a beauty?" Pride was evident in Sterling's voice.

"A true work of art," Bennett said, looking around.

"She's a Jeanneau Sun Odyssey 54DS," Sterling said. "She has a deep-draft keel, an in-mast furling mainsail, and a full battened main. We've worked hard to get just what we wanted," he added, nodding toward Carlotta, who looked happy and excited.

"You've both earned it, Dad." Ivy smiled up at her father. His eyes glittered, and his white hair ruffled in the breeze. She couldn't recall when she'd seen him so full of life and excitement.

This is what they needed, Ivy realized. They'd been active explorers all their lives. Just as they'd let her go when she moved to Boston, she had to let them go, too.

Ivy glanced at Shelly, Flint, Forrest, and their families. Mixed emotions filled their faces, too. Most seemed happy that Carlotta and Sterling were healthy and vital enough to pursue their dream.

She would celebrate this voyage for her parents, too. Ivy hugged her father. "This is so exciting. Show me around and tell me all your plans, Dad."

"Sure will, peanut," Sterling said, using Ivy's childhood nickname and kissing the top of her head. "We have a great time planned. This vessel is specifically designed to withstand the rigors of circumnavigation—with plenty of luxury and space to satisfy your mother."

"That was your idea," Carlotta said, laughing.

"We've earned that, too," Sterling said. "We needed extra room in case we take on crew or have visitors." He nodded toward the younger cousins. "We're trying to talk Reed and Rocky and Coral into joining us. They're young, strong sailors. You and Bennett are welcome—if you can break away from the inn and City Hall."

Ivy and Bennett looked at each other and grinned. "You never know, Dad." That would be quite the adventure. Unexpected, but then, Ivy was getting used to that, too.

They followed her father onto a lower deck. Ivy glanced around. From polished wood interiors to a spacious galley and cabins that could sleep six, the boat was perfect for her parents.

After looking around and then rejoining the rest of the family, they visited for a while. Finally, Ivy realized the time for her parents' departure was drawing near. Carlotta was pouring Sea Breezes and champagne and passing them around.

Ivy swallowed hard, willing herself to be strong. Her

daughters were also blinking back tears. She clasped hands with Sunny and Misty. "Your grandparents will have the time of their lives. They'll be fine."

"A final toast," Sterling said, raising his glass with everyone. "May you be fearless in exploring uncharted waters. Here's to sailing through life with a smile on your face and joy in your heart—even when the seas are rough. Remember, there are always blue skies ahead."

"Hear, hear," Ivy said amidst the clinking of glasses.

After other toasts and well wishes, Ivy and her family took turns hugging Carlotta and Sterling.

It was time to let them go.

Her eyes shimmering with love, Carlotta framed Ivy's face with her hands. "I love you, *mija*. Try not to worry—your parents are going to have a grand old time."

"I'm so happy for you, knowing that you're living your dream," Ivy said, wrapping her arms tightly around her mother and blinking back tears. "I love you for showing us what it means to live—and love."

Finally, Ivy stepped from the yacht, joining the rest of the family to watch the departure. Bennett put his arms around her, and she rested her head on his shoulder. "Someday, that could be us."

"We have a lot of adventures ahead of us," he said, smoothing her hair as strands lifted in the breeze.

As her parents eased the boat from the marina, they turned and waved. Ivy and the rest of her family called out, cheering them on.

Watching her parents sail away, Ivy heaved a sigh.

"Are you okay?" Bennett asked, touching her cheek.

"I am," she said, shielding the sun from her eyes as the *Bay Dreams* took to the open water. "I've learned a lot this past year."

Bennett clasped her hand, and they turned to leave, following the rest of the family. "And what might that be?" he asked.

As they strolled along the weathered planks, Ivy thought about that question. She realized she had made great strides in coming to terms with her past, her parents' voyage, and her life ahead with Bennett. While she still had a few things to work out, there was time for that. She felt an even deeper connection with Bennett than before their ceremony.

Ivy paused and turned to him. Smiling, she said, "I've learned that life is a risk worth taking."

The End

AUTHOR'S NOTE:

Thank you for reading *Seabreeze Wedding*, and I hope you enjoyed the wedding events at the Seabreeze Inn. Be sure to read the next story in the series, *Seabreeze Book Club*. Find out what happens when Ivy starts a book club at the inn to help Pages Bookshop in the village.

If you've read the Coral Cottage at Summer Beach series, join Marina and Kai and the rest of the Delavie-Moore family as the cafe expands and the performing arts center debuts in *Coral Holiday*.

Keep up with my new releases on my website at JanMoran.com. Please join my Reader's Club there to receive news about special deals and other goodies.

MORE TO ENJOY

If this is your first book in the Seabreeze Inn at Summer Beach series, I invite you to revisit Ivy and Shelly as they renovate a historic beach house in *Seabreeze Inn*, the first book in the original Summer Beach series. In the Coral Cottage series, you'll meet Ivy's friend Marina in *Coral Cottage*.

If you'd like more sunshine and international travel, meet

a group of friends in the *Love California* series, beginning with *Flawless* and an exciting trip to Paris.

Finally, I invite you to read my standalone family sagas, including *Hepburn's Necklace* and *The Chocolatier*, 1950s novels set in gorgeous Italy.

Most of my books are available in ebook, paperback or hardcover, audiobooks, and large print. And as always, I wish you happy reading!

ABOUT THE AUTHOR

JAN MORAN is a *USA Today* bestselling author of romantic women's fiction. A few of her favorite things include a fine cup of coffee, dark chocolate, fresh flowers, laughter, and music that touches her soul. She loves to travel, and her favorite places for inspiration are those rich with history and mystery and set against snowy mountains, palm-treed beaches, or sparkly city lights. Jan is originally from Austin, Texas, and a trace of a drawl still survives, although she has lived in Southern California near the beach for years.

Most of her books are available as audiobooks, and her historical fiction is translated into German, Italian, Polish, Dutch, Turkish, Russian, Bulgarian, Portuguese, and Lithuanian, and other languages.

Visit Jan at JanMoran.com. If you enjoyed this book, please consider leaving a brief review online for your fellow readers where you purchased this book or on Goodreads or Bookbub.

Made in the USA
Middletown, DE
30 May 2024

55087821R00149